WHEREVER YOU WILL GO

Fran Clark

Book Cover by Rima Salloum

Print design by Karen Hamiltion-Bannis
@AK-Wilde
Classidel Tropical Palms

ISBN: 978-0-9933381-7-5

Wherever You Will Go

The Hope Series Book 1

To Those Who Came In Search of a Better Life

Chapter 1

Essie

Dominica 1948

Ginnie sticks out her little pink tongue when she catches me smiling at her through the tall mirror leaning against the wall. Only, her little pink tongue isn't pink. It's bright red, and so are her fingers. She'd better not come over, put her arms around me and congratulate me the way everyone else has this morning. Mama would skin her alive if she ruined my wedding dress. Or, at least, Mama would threaten to, but Ginnie would be out past the gate before Mama could swing an arm in her direction.

'Ginnie, why you just sitting there like that?' Mama asks. She looks up at our mother with big round eyes, then slides off the bed and runs out of the bedroom. Mama shakes her head and shakes out my veil. Again.

'There. Perfect. You look beautiful, Essie. Just beautiful.'

She takes my hand and leads me into the living room where Daddy sits forward in his armchair, his round tummy hanging between his thighs as he scoots even closer to get a better look. One day soon I'll be too far away for him to look at me at all. He stares as if he's trying to capture my image forever, and I see tears collect into the rims of his eyes. I want to cry for him. He looks as though he's already missing me. He blinks, and a salty stream flows easily down his

1

cheeks. He wipes it away before Mama can scold him for being 'too soff'.

'We have to go.' My mother ushers me towards the front door, fluffing the skirt of my dress and spreading out my netted veil.

I sniff my tears away and leave the house. Mama and Daddy are on either side of me as we cross the narrow road to the car. Mr Carpenter was only invited to the wedding because he's the only one between here and town with a car and it is important to Mama that I ride to the church in a car, even though the man I'm marrying 'don't have more than a few damn shillings to his name'. But I love LeJeune Francis more than money. More than Ginnie, and more than Mama and Daddy. So I don't care. Marrying him was all I ever wanted since the day I met him. He proposed one month after our first kiss, and I've been planning a wedding ever since.

Ginnie jumps into the passenger seat. She tucks her skinny legs under her bottom and swivels round so that she can watch as I get into the back seat. Mama and Daddy slide in on either side of me.

'Ginnie, you don't see is your Daddy who have to sit in the front?' Mama's voice scolding Ginnie about this, that or something else is a sound I can live without after I'm married. In fact, I won't hear Mama's voice at all once LeJeune sends for me to live with him in England. He's been there before. In the war, when he was a soldier. He said it was the best place for us. We'd have a future there. But I don't mind where I live as long as it's with him. I haven't even considered what it would be like to live in England. London to be precise. I don't know what I'll do with myself all day if I'm not bandaging Ginnie's knee or helping Mama prepare food. And there is always so much food to prepare where Mama is concerned. Food can heal everything from hunger to sickness, and Mama feeds everyone. Her soup is famous in our village. She makes a pot and takes some to whichever friend or relative she happened to be visiting that day. To the sick man at the foot of the lane who can't feed himself; to the mother of six who is about to have her seventh child and doesn't have the energy to cook.

Ginnie stares at me with large eyes, the whites so bright it's like the sun is shining in the car. She pokes her tongue out at me again and I do it back. She giggles. Covering her missing front teeth with her little hand, she stares at me for the whole trip to the church.

I'll miss her when I go to England. And she'll miss me. That's why she won't stop staring at me. I want to cry because I'll never watch her grow up, but she has told me, more than once, that she'll be in England in no time. She doesn't think I can look after myself. I haven't admitted to her how scared I am about leaving home, boarding a ship on my own and going all the way across an ocean to a place I'd known nothing about until LeJeune talked of paved streets, houses all in a row, buses and tall buildings, people who speak English the proper way.

He'd been stationed in England during the war. He'd spent a lot of time in London. He told me I would love it. That Dominica isn't the place for young people and that we could make a good life over there. Ginnie is only eight, but she would have had a few questions to ask about this great and wonderful country he knew so much about. But I didn't doubt him. Not once.

As we get closer to the church, a dancing feeling begins in my stomach. At age nineteen, I shouldn't be this nervous.

But travelling across an ocean on my own is more real now that the wedding ceremony is minutes away. Will everything be as wonderful as LeJeune says? For the rest of my life, I will be apart from my family. Away from everyone and everything I know.

Mr Carpenter stops the car. Mama's solid frame has prevented what little breeze has blown in through the window from cooling me down, and all of a sudden I'm too hot for this dress, too hot for this veil, too hot for this cloudless morning and too hot for the way Ginnie keeps looking at me as if I'm a *femme fol*. A mad woman. I tell myself again that I'm lucky, that I'm happy and that I love LeJeune with all my heart. That much I know is true. So I grin at Ginnie and shuffle out after Mama, whose skirt is creased and sticking to the backs of her thighs.

'Here we are.' Daddy always announces things we already know. He slams the door shut, and there's the church with its open doors and there's the wooden cross above the door, and there are the people standing outside to wave me inside and out of the blaze of the sun. I don't recognise a single face, I'm that nervous. My heart pounds boldly. I can see lips moving, including Mama's, but I can't tell what they're saying. At the church doors, Ginnie holds my bouquet. She had the sense to grab it from the back shelf of Mr Carpenter's Ford and presses it in my direction.

'What would Cousin Delima say if you walked in without it?'

Mama covers my face with the veil, and in my trembling grip is the bouquet. I begin to walk down the aisle. There is music. Daddy is beside me, trying to cover up his limp the way Mama told him to, but I can sense he's shaking, too. Then I see LeJeune, standing by the altar in his new suit. His back is to me at first, his hair cut so short I can see the tiny patch of pale skin where he has a scar and the hair around it never grew back. Then he turns and grins at me. He looks so young today. Like a teenager, because he's clean-shaven, his strong jaw smooth as a rose petal. Though I'm sure he'd sniff at being compared to a flower because he is such a strong man, both physically and mentally. He's ten years older than me. He will take good care of me. I am safe. I am happy. And now I can breathe.

*

Before the afternoon is even finished and before the last piece of wedding cake has been eaten, Mama takes me out of the reception and tells me that I won't be sleeping at Le-Jeune's house tonight.

'If in case he don't send for you when he get to England and leave you here with a big belly.'

'What do you mean?'

'Essie, you know how they making babies. Don't tell me I have to explain all that now.'

'I mean, it's my wedding night. LeJeune will expect I–'

'It doesn't matter what he expect. He going on a ship to England tomorrow. Sailing across the sea. What if something happen and you don't see him again?'

'And why is that you find to say? You trying to give me bad luck?'

'No, of course not. I happy you marry and you going and live in England but…'

'But what?'

'But I don't know much about LeJeune. He have no family.'

'He have family. He have his mother.'

'And she like to keep herself to herself.'

'There is nothing wrong with being quiet. I'm quiet.'

'I know. And it's I who must speak up for you. Essie, just trust me. LeJeune have so many years more than you. He been away fighting in a war and he seen many things. You are practically a child and I don't want to see a child carrying a child until they ready for all that. Especially if is only you alone carrying the burden.'

'Mama, you have just cursed me.'

'Don't say that. I'm looking out for you. He have things to arrange. We will wave him goodbye at the port and you will wait until he send for you, and when it's your time to leave, the only thing you will be carrying is your grip.'

I've never been able to do battle with Mama. She has a lot to say and I, as always, don't know how to speak up for myself. The tears warming my eyes and face are all I can speak with, and all Mama does is soak them up with the palms of her rough hands and say, 'There, there.' How do I tell my mother that she has just taken away the enormous part of married life that I've so been looking forward to?

'Come, darling. You have people waiting to congratulate you and give you presents. Talk to LeJeune, he will understand. Now, come.'

Mama takes my hand as if I'm a little girl. I am, I suppose, because I can't match her, married woman for married woman. When LeJeune spots me coming back into the room, led by Mama, he screws his eyebrows. I only hope that my eyes aren't pink with tears and that he doesn't change his mind about me.

*

Just one other person is boarding the boat with LeJeune, a skinny man with a bad cold who coughs and coughs as if he's trying to draw the insides out of his body through his throat. He has no one to see him off, but LeJeune has me and Mama and Daddy, and Ginnie, of course, who is kicking a flattened can into the sea. Not even LeJeune's mother has come to bid her son goodbye. He won't be coming back, and I wonder why that in itself didn't encourage Mrs Francis to see her son off.

'Well, Esperanza, the next time I see you will be at a port in England. I already miss you.'

I love that LeJeune uses my full name. It makes me feel important. More mature.

'I already miss you, too.' I really have to stretch my neck upwards to look into LeJeune's eyes. Grey and clear. His skin so bright. It's like looking into a whole bed of yellow bells. 'How long before you send for me?'

'Like I said, I hope it won't be long. I have the job, and as soon as I find a nice little place to live, I'll buy your ticket. This is forever, you and me. This is going to be my greatest adventure.'

'And mine.'

'Of course.'

'What will I do when I get there?'

'Do?'

'Yes, for work. I was thinking that maybe I could train as a teacher.'

'Esperanza, that's a wonderful idea. You know my intention was always to provide for you and I stand by that. But it's your new life, too, and all I want is for us to be happy. Always you and me.'

'Always.'

When LeJeune walks along the gangplank to the boat, I feel as if someone is pulling the guts out of my body by a string through my navel. I can't stand upright. I can't fall forward. I can't stop tears, streaming down my face, and when Ginnie looks up at me with those large eyes, I can't stop the sound peeling from my very stomach and out of my mouth. LeJeune hears my cry because he turns around and he waves. He doesn't stop waving, and I'm sure he is trying to calm me, soothe me. He has the words to do that. Kind and thoughtful. Good and strong. I feel weak without him, and I don't know if I can stand a second without him here, with me on this island, our island, not the one that's so far away.

As if Mama can tell I'm about to go jumping off the pier and swimming out to the small passenger boat to Jamaica, she pulls me by my shoulders and half drags me back to the wagon where Daddy is all ready for us to set off home. I'm not ready. Why doesn't anyone understand? Then Ginnie is in front of me again. Her eyes round like saucers of milk with a black stone in the middle.

'You are not alone, Essie. As long as you're here. There's me. I'm not ready for you to leave me.' Her voice is the softest I've ever heard it.

I pull her to my body and hug her with all my might. For now, until LeJeune sends for me, I'll try to be as strong as Ginnie and pray every day that my family will be waving me off soon.

Chapter 2

Essie

Dominica 1948

The word 'soon' is used so often. It will rain soon, better get those clothes in from the line. Don't eat that, dinner will be ready soon and you'll cut your appetite. Soon, soon, soon and I'm no closer to being in London, with LeJeune. He wrote, only once, a letter with no return address that arrived two weeks after I saw him last. 'I've arrived' was practically all he said. Apart from signing it 'Love LeJeune', there had been no talk of love, his new job or where exactly he was living. Nothing. That was three months ago.

I have been trying to avoid seeing my friends, which isn't easy. I've grown weary of them asking when I am going to England and have I heard anything from that husband of mine. I'm quite sure they are tired of asking. I have run out of excuses and reasons why he's been unable to write. I've asked Mrs Cartwright at the sorting office in town to search every conceivable corner of the post room for a letter from England. I bleated to this mountain of a woman, begging for her to make sure a letter hadn't fallen behind a shelf or been kicked under a loose floor tile. I'd questioned her for a whole hour about the likelihood of someone else having picked up my letter by mistake, and then for a further hour I'd asked if anyone had returned a letter that hadn't belonged

9

to them. Mrs Cartwright's fortitude had melted into kindness and understanding. She'd searched and searched, her head tilting in my direction every once in a while to check I was happy with her investigation. She had humoured me every time I'd been in looking for a lost or overlooked letter from England. Now she walks straight up to me from behind her desk with open palms, saying, '*La pa ni ayen.*' There's nothing here for you.

She calls, 'I'm sorry,' from the counter as I leave and walk into the hot Wednesday morning where the people in town are busy going about their business and can't see me leaving the post office in tears again. I'm too ashamed to go to the bus station while I'm like this. I walk for a long while until I'm outside town. On my way, I pass an old woman with a full sack of food on her head, walking with bowed legs towards town. I turn from her so that I don't have to greet her, sniffing as I do and hoping she won't greet me.

By the time I arrive home, I have made up my mind that I'll go to England myself and find LeJeune. Something has to have happened to him. I've listed countless reasons in my head about why he has only sent one letter in all of this time. Not once did I assume that he'd changed his mind about me. He couldn't. He loves me more than anything. He'd said it a million times. He must be hurt. Sick. His job hasn't worked out and he's short of money. He is a very proud man. He might be ashamed to say he's too broke to send for me quite yet. He doesn't want me to feel let down.

'Essie, come for your supper.'

Mama stands at the open doorway to my bedroom. She smells of spices from the kitchen and she's perspiring. She hasn't called me to help with dinner for weeks, too afraid to say anything that might upset me. Even Ginnie has been on her best behaviour and there has been little to no noise in the house. No scolding, laughter or chatter. Nothing for anyone to say except call me for dinner.

'I'm going and look for him.' Before I put a morsel of food in my mouth, I sit up and declare this, looking around at them all to see how they will react.

'Going where and look for who?' Mama asks.

'You know I mean LeJeune. Something terrible has happened.'

'If something terrible happen, then you would get word.' Mama starts to eat and won't look at me.

'But maybe no one knows who to write to if something has gone wrong,' I say. 'I don't know who LeJeune knows in London and if he has friends who know to send word to me.'

'You mean his people there don't know he married?' Ginnie looks across the table at me. She always knows the right thing to ask. The grown-up, sensible thing. The things I don't even question or consider.

'I don't know who he has.' I look down at my plate.

'Like a woman?' Mama asks.

'Of course there isn't a woman.' My words choke in my throat and I need to blink quickly. I will not entertain the idea that LeJeune could have done something wrong. Something wrong might have happened to *him* and I need to find out what. I know he needs me, and all this time he must wonder why I haven't found my way to him.

'I'm going,' I say again.

'And with which money you going?' Mama asks, letting her fork drop on the table.

'I'll find it.'

'You don't even have job. How you will find money to pay your passage?'

'I will find a job.'

'Doing what?'

'I don't know.'

Our conversation bounces off the walls of the living room. I'm deafened by it and know that we could keep going like this until my throat dries up. Mama will never relent. How many times has she hinted that I should give up hope of ever seeing him again? Men can be like that sometimes. But not LeJeune. Not my husband. I should be with him.

'You really make up your mind?' Daddy speaks for the first time and I look towards him. I nod my head as if I'm four and he's asked me if I want the water from the coconut he's cut.

'I have to go,' I say. 'That's all I can do. If something happened, I have to know. I need to know.'

'I will give you the money.' His voice is calm. Direct.

'What?' All eyes are on Mama now. She looks hot. Her eyes change from staring Daddy down to squinting at him as if she can't believe she's heard right. 'You serious?'

'Of course I'm serious. Look at Essie. Look how skinny she is. This girl is worried and so am I. I will not see my girl come skinny, skinny like that any more. Is best she just go and see what is going on. Then she will know. Then we will all know.'

I can't stop smiling at Daddy. I dare not turn my head to look at Mama who stands now, edging the chair back to make way for her to leave the room. She goes outside. I can see her throw her hands up, and I know she would like to curse but she can't even manage that. She comes back to the table and sits, her fingers gripping the course-grained wood.

'And where you getting the money?' Her eyes open wide at Daddy, who looks down. 'No, Abel. You cannot take all we have and send this girl all the way to England with it.'

'I don't know what else I can do,' Daddy says. 'I really don't.' He covers my hand with a sweaty one and gives mine a shake. I spring up from my seat, wrap my arms around his damp collar and kiss him until my tears mingle with the heat of his neck. When I open my eyes, I see Mama shaking her head and I see Ginnie's large eyes looking questioningly at me.

I can't explain this decision. I only know it's the right one, and I only know that somewhere across that ocean is a man who needs me and I no longer want to imagine to what extent.

Chapter 3

1943

They were lined up outside the front window of The Dock-man's Arms. Five West Indian soldiers, sharp and handsome in their uniforms. They stood, chatting loudly, laughing louder still, so animated their pints of beer sloshed and splashed in their hands. LeJeune had put his to rest on the thick windowsill as he took out his handkerchief to sneeze and blow his nose.

'You still not used to the climate?' A Jamaican soldier cackled loudly, patting LeJeune's shoulder. 'With your light skin, I did take you for a white man and wondered why you always sneezing and coughing so.'

LeJeune didn't answer. He was sick and tired of people commenting on how light his skin was. He was a Black man, just like them. Bought his own way over to England in a trade ship from Jamaica because there wasn't a recruitment office in Dominica. It had cost him fifteen pounds for the passage to England. He hadn't had the money at first but sold off all of his goats and the smallholding near his mother's house to fund it. He wanted to answer the call from the motherland to her colonies to join the war effort. He wanted to make a difference. It was all he'd wanted, no matter how much his mother protested. He understood she didn't want to be left alone, but there was Cousin Blanc who wasn't too far from his mother's house. He was old, but he would carry down food for her and keep her company. It wouldn't be long before the war was over and then he'd be back. He'd found himself at the RAF offices in London where he was laughed at by the guards at the gate when he'd said he'd come all the way from the West Indies to sign up for the cause.

'Look here,' a voice had said over the din the young recruits were making. 'I've read about your part of the colonies, and I'd love to go and visit West Africa one day.'

The officer had guided LeJeune by the shoulder and led him to a Jeep.

'But I don't think the RAF is for you. Ground soldier. That's where I see you fitting in. Hop on. I'm going home by way of the recruitment offices. Let's see if we can't get you enlisted properly. Never mind those chaps.'

A hazy light coloured the built-up streets of London. Summer in London, and LeJeune's fingertips were icy. He'd sailed across the ocean in nothing more than a short-sleeved shirt, a thin jacket and an old pair of work overalls. He smelt of travel and sleeping outdoors. He'd barely eaten and had no money in his pockets. Only a flat cap that bulged from the front pocket of his grey overalls. The truck bumped along and the officer whistled. He asked LeJeune all about home and who he'd left behind. Question after question. Age: *twenty-three*. Skills: *farming*. Heritage: *I don't understand*. Social standing: *I'm an honest working man*. Had he done anything of note: LeJeune had fallen silent. *Not yet*.

'What do they call you, then? What's your name?'

'My name is Francis. LeJeune Francis.'

'Jen? Your Christian name is *Jen*? Sounds a bit too feminine for the army. Tell them it's John. That's a good name. One an Englishman can say.' He began laughing, and LeJeune stared at the officer's reddening cheeks, the row of creases by his eyes and the way he tapped the ash of his cigarette out of the window and tossed it into the street when he'd finished smoking. He had lines on the sleeve of his uniform, but LeJeune couldn't tell his rank. Just knew it was high and that this man was important. He'd made assumptions about LeJeune's country of origin. *Not West Africa*, he kept saying in his mind. *West Indies*. But he thought correcting the officer would be disrespectful. And though he had dreamt of becoming a member of the RAF, the army would do just fine. And so would his new name.

He was unused to the line of questions the officer posed and wished he could have spoken up for himself. Though he'd done quite well at school, he hoped there wasn't going to be a written test to join the army. He'd come this far. He refused to go back without fulfilling his mission to serve.

LeJeune and his friends were on leave. They hadn't felt comfortable inside the pub. The drinkers, mostly older Englishmen, too old to have enlisted, and the small groups of young women who sat with the white British soldiers, did nothing but glare at the Black men as they tried to order drinks.

LeJeune sipped his Guinness. He was about to wipe the froth from his lip when he spotted a blonde girl walking hurriedly in the direction of the pub followed by three white GIs who wolf-whistled and asked her if she wanted to come in for a drink. One pulled her elbow, and she shook him off.

'Would you just leave me be?' She turned to them just as she came in line with LeJeune and his colleagues.

'Would you just give me a kiss?' All three GIs began laughing, and one stood to block the young woman's way. LeJeune stared at her yellow hair and the way it shone like silky ribbons, curls soft around her neck and onto the collar of her bright blue jacket. He stared at her pink lipstick and the light blue of her eyes when she flashed LeJeune a look of exasperation.

'I think you should leave her alone.' The words flew from his lips like wind across the ocean. Uncontrolled and forceful. He felt his drinking buddies seep into the pub's brickwork. He felt his heart come to a standstill, and he lacked any moisture in his mouth as he swallowed. One of the GIs stepped up to him. LeJeune looked into the soldier's dark eyes, the slight twitch under the left one and the flaring of his narrow nostrils.

'You didn't just say that did you, boy?'

'You heard me,' said LeJeune, squaring his broad shoulders.

'You coloured Limeys need to learn your place. Our black boys know better than to even look at one of us.'

'I'm not your "black boy". I'm not anybody's, and your Jim Crow laws don't apply over here or to me.' LeJeune clenched his fist around his pint glass, loathe to turn and put it back on the window ledge in case the GI took it as an opportunity to push his head through the window. His colleagues shuffled forward, and the two other GIs shuffled back.

'Come on, Jack. We only came for a drink. We don't need this.'

'I only wanted to ask you for a drink,' the American soldier said to the blonde girl.

'I can get me own,' she replied.

She stood with the West Indian soldiers as they watched the Americans saunter inside The Dockman's Arms.

'Oh blow,' the girl said. 'They would have to go in there.'

'You meeting someone inside?' asked LeJeune.

She turned full on to face him. Her cheeks were pink, like her lipstick. She looked young. Maybe a teenager with more make-up on her face than she actually needed. She was already beautiful.

'I work in there.'

'You old enough to work?' LeJeune spluttered but slapped his hand to his mouth and shook his head in apology. She laughed.

'Give over. I'm twenty-two. Old enough I'll have you know.'

'I'm sorry. I didn't mean...'

''S all right,' she said, tapping his arm. 'You weren't to know. Your next one's on me.'

Turning on her brown leather heels and smiling broadly at LeJeune, she clacked her way to the door. LeJeune sipped slowly from his glass, watching the bounce of her curls as the door closed after her.

'Oh, John boy!' one of his colleagues exclaimed. 'Look like you find your first girlfriend, and look like she very white. You think she don't mistake you for one of them?'

'Quiet Eugene. You just drink your drink and we'll get back to the barracks.'

'But the night is young, man.'

'Those GIs looking for trouble, and I didn't come all this way to fight in a war only to get killed by someone on the same side as me.'

Chapter 4

Essie

London 1948

I have Myrtle Young's address squashed into the corner of my pocket. I've recited it over and over so I know it off by heart. I just don't know how to find it. I've never known such a loud and busy place, and I've never seen so many white people in my life before. For the most part, they can't seem to understand me and they are very good at ignoring me, too. I want to curl into a ball and cry, but I know I can't do that. I'm twenty years old now, a married woman and I have a responsibility to my husband. Before I got on the boat to Jamaica, I had gone to see LeJeune's mother to tell her I was going to England and to ask if she had a message for her son.

I stopped at her house most weeks after coming back from the post office in town, just to let her know that I still hadn't any news and to ask had she heard from LeJeune. The first time I'd gone to her house was three weeks after he'd sent the one and only letter he'd written. I took it to her because I'd wanted to see if there was anything in it that might suggest his whereabouts. Something that would help me begin my search. Maybe something in his language might hint at anything he feared or planned to do. I needed to understand his silence, and the letter was the only form of evidence that

20

a man called LeJeune Francis who had married me several weeks ago had ever existed. I know she must have thought I sounded desperate, deranged even. I'd asked if he'd written to her, but she shook her head and said she never got a letter.

'Aren't you worried?' I'd asked her.

'You know he is a grown man with his own mind. When he went the first time, went in that war, I had beg for him not to go. He was so angry with me for saying so. Told me I don't understand that he has a duty. A duty to die? But he leave the country without a word. Three years I don't see him. Not even a few words on a scrap of paper he send me during the war. So why he would write to me now?'

'I'm sorry,' I had said. Given this, I'd hoped that LeJeune was just not the type to write. If he hadn't written to his own mother in three years, then surely he might do the same with his wife. But how could I wait three years? How could I wait any longer? With a heavy heart and hesitant feet, I had continued visiting Mrs Francis, just to be sure. But when I went the last time, to say I was leaving for England, she barely looked up from her cup of tea.

'I'll make sure he writes you this time,' I'd said. 'No. *I* will send a letter to you and tell you everything is fine. But I wonder, Mrs Francis, if there is any chance you might know where in London LeJeune might go? Anywhere he might be?'

'Stepney,' she had said and continued sipping her tea.

'Stepney? Is that a place or the name of the factory his job is at?' I felt foolish for asking because though I knew his job was in a factory, I just didn't know the name of it. I should know these things. I should have been like Ginnie and asked the right questions. Now LeJeune is lost on the other side of the planet and I have no idea where to start looking.

'Stepney is the last place in London where he was living.'
Mrs Francis had put down her cup. 'Anything else, I don't
know.'

When I'd left her house and gone to tell Mama, she'd gone
straight to the small drawer in the dresser and found Myrtle's
address to give to me. My mother's cousin has been living in
London since long before the war. She is a trained nurse and
Mama said she knows all about London.

On the ship over, I had befriended a woman called Wilma.
She and her family, her husband and small son, were on their
way to London, too, because the husband had a job at the
post office lined up. I imagined Wilma's husband at the sorting office desk like the one in town, back home, where Le-
Jeune's letters didn't show up and where my heart broke just
that bit more every time I went there in hope. Hope eventually became frustration. But from what I understood from
Wilma, her husband would be riding a bicycle and delivering
letters to people's houses. It was hard to imagine having a
letter arrive at your door. An image of Catherine from the
sorting office back home came to mind. This enormous woman riding straight past the front gate every day, puffing and
sweating. No letter for me.

It was Wilma and her husband who helped me negotiate
my way to the city from the port. I rode in a long bus all the
way to a train station and got on a noisy, rattling train into
the heart of London where my excitement at seeing LeJeune
transformed into fear. Firstly, the fear of being on my own
when the family I'd travelled with would be parting ways
with me, and secondly, that finding my husband would be an
impossibility with nothing but the place name, Stepney, to
go by.

When Wilma says goodbye outside Victoria Station, I'm standing on a busy street where railings separate the pedestrians from the road but the cars look mean enough to drive straight through the metal bars.

'You think you'll find this husband today?' Wilma asks, holding my hand as if she wants to take me with her.

'First I must find Cousin Myrtle. She has a bed for me, and maybe I can start to look for him tomorrow.'

'Well,' says Wilma giving a sidewards glance to her husband who looks irritated by the two large grips he has been hauling from Tilbury Dock to Victoria. It seems as if we've been on our feet for a day and a half, but it's just hours since we docked. 'Goodbye and good luck, I suppose.' Wilma touches a soft hand to my cheek. Her son says he urgently needs to relieve himself, and her husband begins to walk away with the cases, her son hopping agitatedly at her side, pulling her hand in an attempt to catch up with his father.

'You should go,' I say in a small voice. 'I will be all right.'

My cousin Myrtle's address is not far from Paddington Station. As I ask the fifth person I've had the courage to speak to, a woman with white hair and teeth too large for her small mouth, she points me in the direction of the station I've just emerged from.

'Best if you catch a train. It's not like you can walk there from here.'

'Oh. Silly,' I say. 'I just followed the family I came with and they were going to catch a bus.'

'You'd be best off taking a taxi by the looks of you. You look worn out.'

'I do feel tired. And hungry.' My voice is fading fast as I remember the cup of tea I had on the ship not long before disembarking. They had laid out biscuits, but by the time I got to the top of the queue, there were none left. My stomach is hollow. I hadn't been able to keep much down for the whole of the journey.

The woman edges around me to get on her way.

'Just ask someone in there to put you on the right train. They'll know.'

It's becoming dark as I exit Paddington Station. I decide to turn right to find Myrtle's address even though I have no idea which way to go and how long it will take me to get there. There had been hints of sun in the sky when I arrived, but those hints only provided light and not warmth. I'm shivering now in the jacket I wear. I should really have something heavier, warmer, though no one else notices the cold. I try to push my discomfort aside and focus on what awaits. Firstly, a warm welcome from my cousin, and secondly, I'll be on my way to finding LeJeune.

I decide to cross a wide road and turn to look at the oncoming traffic. Turning back, I am jostled by a tall man in a hat and a brown suit.

'Careful, love,' he says in a voice that seems friendly and as if he knows me.

'I'm sorry. I was a bit…'

'Bit what?' He stops. He looks serious, and I wonder if he is someone important in his suit, neatly cut hair and smelling of sweet fragrance, a nice aftershave that has traces of a forest and a freshwater fountain. 'Lost?' he asks.

I nod my head and look down. Slowly, I pull the address out of my pocket. Still holding onto my case, I try to unfold the note which looks as though it has been in my pocket for a whole year and the jacket had fallen into a river with the note still in it. He is patient. He takes a deep breath and looks over my shoulder to read the address.

'Craven Road?' A sidewards grin appears on his face. 'Yes, I know it.' I'm so relieved, but he keeps sniffing a sort of laugh to himself.

'Is it close?'

'Actually, it isn't that far from my house.' He rubs his chin, grabs for my suitcase and takes it off me.

'Oh,' I say and feel as if my arm can float upwards after carrying a tightly packed case all this way.

'I can carry this for you if you'd like. It's a bit on the heavy side.'

'No, no. I can manage. I just need some directions.'

'Like I say, it's just around the corner from me so I can show you. Personally.'

I can't swallow properly. A prickling sensation creeps its way up my spine. I reach for my case.

'It's fine. Just tell me where it is and I'll go there when my friend gets here.'

He puts the case down.

'Sorry,' he says. 'I didn't mean to impose, I just thought I was helping.' He stands and stares at me as if he's making calculations about my age, where I'm from and what business I have in Craven Road. He shifts his weight, clears his throat. 'So you walk all the way to the end of this road. It's a bit of a walk if I'm honest.' He looks down at my flat shoes to my thin jacket and up to the headscarf tied under my chin. 'Then cross that road. Keep going and take the first left turn, and Craven Road is one of the ones on your right. You can't miss it.'

He pauses and looks at the case by my feet. I don't pick it up because I want him to walk on. Then I remember my manners.

'Thank you.' I nod and pick up my case.

'How long is your friend going to be?' he asks. His brow is screwed up as if he doesn't believe I'm waiting for anyone. I shrug my shoulders, so he pulls his lips into a smile, nods and carries on along the road.

When I can't see him, I follow his footsteps. I feel as if the soles of my feet will rub away. They are so sore and I want to put them up, maybe soak them first. I'm cold and I'm hungry and I want to be at Cousin Myrtle's before it's dark.

On the last stretch of my journey, when the sunlight has finally gone and the houses look like shadowy hills that are moving closer and closer to me from either side, I hear footsteps. I turn but there is no one there. I cross the road to look at the street names that approach me on the right so that I can look out for Craven Road, just like the man in the suit told me, and I can hear the footsteps crossing the road, too. I turn quickly and can't see anyone but hear a person cough.

'That's it, you're on the right track,' a voice says.

From out of the shadows, the man in the brown suit appears right beside me. He doesn't smell of the forest now. Just cigarettes, and the smoke of one drifts around his hand as he draws the cigarette to his mouth and blows smoke into my face. This time it's me who coughs. I turn quickly to continue on, aware that he has not left my side and that each of his footsteps matches mine exactly. I don't know if I should slow down or speed up or if I should turn into one of these dark streets, knock on a random door and cry for help. A foolish notion. There are so many, which would I choose, anyway? If only Wilma and her husband could have helped me the rest of the way. Myrtle had offered to meet me at the port but I'd refused. I hadn't wanted to be a bother because she'd have to take time off work. But now ... now that I am afraid to even breathe, I wish for her to be beside me. If it were Ginnie, she would have had something to say to the man in the brown suit. Demand to know what the hell he thinks he's doing, walking right beside her like they were friends. She'd be able to think straight and do something sensible, like keep an eye on the street names instead of her feet or downright tell this man to leave her alone.

'That's it,' he says and my heart stops in my chest. I stop dead.

'What?' I manage to utter.

'Craven Road. You need to go down there.' He points with his cigarette.

I can hardly turn my head to look, I'm shaking so much I will collapse if I move.

'You are a silly thing,' he says and puffs at his cigarette. 'I'll just stand here until you find it. The right door.'

My hand is so damp the handle of the suitcase feels slippery. I grip it and turn into Craven Road without even checking for myself that I have the right street and he's laughing.

'At least I know where to find you.' His voice trails into the distance. I can't smell his cigarette or the forest. I can't really feel what my body is doing, but I'm out of breath and my chest feels tight. I hear the pad, pad, pad of my soles on the paving stones. I'm running, checking door numbers. I'm close. I look over my shoulder and he's still there. He's a dark outline with a flame-red dot beside it.

'Essie?'

I stop and look back across the road. Someone has called my name for the first time in days.

'It is you, isn't it?' My eyes scan for the red dot and move quickly back to the tall, thin woman in a dressing gown who ran across to greet me. I nod my head at her.

'What happened? Why you running?'

'I'm sorry.'

'What you sorry for?' She holds me tightly by the arms. 'I was waiting at the living room window, I heard running, saw a girl and came out. I knew I should have come for you. I'm Cousin Myrtle.'

'I'm so glad I found you. I'm Essie.' I release my arms so that I can put down my case.

She chuckles. 'If you didn't tell me, I would have guessed. Even in this light you resemble your mother too much. Come inside.' She picks up my case, and I follow her across the road with my eyes on the street corner where the man turns and walks away. I hate myself for trusting him with my cousin's address. I have to do better than this. I have to be more like Ginnie. She trusts no one. I need her strength. All of mine is drained.

Myrtle leads me to the sofa in her living room. A small, cluttered square that also houses a side cabinet, an impossibly low coffee table and one easy chair where a fat cat is curled up, sleeping. Like a rag doll, I collapse against a colourful nest of cushions. I'm breathless and try to soften my audible attempts to draw breath.

'But you did good,' Myrtle is saying. 'Finding your way here. How did you manage? Your mother said you were clever and you are. That's good.' She stands from crouching in front of me. 'Stay there. Let me bring you a cup of tea to warm you up. Winter is still months away, but I can feel it in my bones already.'

Her voice trails down the corridor and the cat, whom I didn't suspect would ever wake, suddenly leaps from the chair and follows Myrtle out of the cramped, square room. I hear Myrtle talking to the cat, telling it that there is nothing else for it to eat tonight. But by the time she returns with a steaming cup of tea for me, I know she has relented and poured her cat a saucer of milk.

'There,' she says, handing me the cup. The handle is thin and so is the porcelain body. When I grasp it, my fingers sting from the heat. Myrtle eases herself into the cat's chair and stares at me. 'Yes, I heard running, and when I looked out, I could swear it was my cousin I could see. You really resemble Ida.'

'People always say that.'

'And it's true.' She chuckles and shakes her head from side to side, appraising both me and the flimsy cup of weak tea that balances on my knee, burning it in the process so that I have to move it from one knee to the other. 'So, Essie, Cousin Ida tells me you got married?'

It seems like half a lifetime ago that I walked down the aisle and returned from it as Mrs LeJeune Francis. But it has been four months. Four months of agony and worry. I don't feel married at all. Just lost.

'And that's why I came. Did Mama tell you about him? My husband?' I hesitate over this word because I really don't know what it's like to have a husband and if I feel like a wife. I'm not sure how it's supposed to feel. 'It's just that I've heard nothing from him since his letter saying he arrived.'

'And you came to look for him.' Her eyes do not hide the fact that it is her belief I should not have come. That I've wasted my time. Like everyone back home, she thinks that LeJeune has had a change of heart, that he doesn't love me anymore and he has abandoned me. I sit up, straighten my slouching shoulders to demonstrate my determination to prove everyone wrong. I really wish there was someone on my side because it is a lonely place otherwise. I know Daddy just pitied me when he gave me the money to come. But like Mama and Ginnie, and the rest of them, he doesn't believe for a moment that I have any chance of finding LeJeune, let alone the reason why he has left no way of tracing him.

'It's strange, don't you think?' I say. 'That he could disappear. He is not the type of man who would do anything so lightly. If he didn't love me, then why marry me? Why make me such promises?'

Myrtle considers this for a long time. The cat slinks back into the room from the kitchen. It turns its nose up at me and trots over to Myrtle's feet, covering them with the long, brown fur of its tummy. Rolling onto its side, it waits just a second before Myrtle leans forward to tickle its fat stomach.

'He told you he loves you?' Myrtle looks up at me now. The cat rolls off its side and squints pale eyes at me.

'Yes.' I nod. 'Several times. And I know he means it.'

'I believe he does.' But she still looks grave. 'And when were you supposed to join him?'

'When he had the money.'

'Maybe he couldn't find a job and he feels ashamed.'

'He had a job ready and waiting. It was in a factory or something. But the job was certain.'

'Nothing is certain in this world, Essie. And where did you say the job is?'

'I didn't. And neither did he tell me.' I hold the cup to my lips but don't drink. I feel like a fool again. Chasing a shadow as Mama says. 'But his mother says that when Le-Jeune was in London, he stayed in Stepney.'

Myrtle brightens.

'Stepney, you say? Well, we are far from Stepney but the hospital I work at isn't far from there. I used to live around that way for years, but I had to move during the war because my room got bombed when I was at the hospital.' She shakes her head, exhales with a light whistle and forms the sign of the cross.

'That must have been terrible, Cousin.'

'Oh, it's a story all right. But you, your husband. We'll have to think of some way of… Oh, but my upstairs neighbour is from Stepney. Mrs Rogers. I've known her from way back before the war and she is the one who told me about this flat after me and my husband lost everything. I'll ask if she remembers any factories in Stepney.'

I'm too ashamed to say that LeJeune's factory might not be there exactly, but it is the only place I can associate him with. Though Myrtle is only trying to help, I begin to wish that I had asked for more information about my husband's new job. I lower the cup of tea.

'It's a start, Ess.' Myrtle smiles.

'I know, but a rather poor one. And … well, as you said, what if the job did fall through?'

'Then I'm sure he has been trying to find another one.'

'But why couldn't he have written to let me know?'

'That is the real mystery. Why he didn't write.' She reaches down to scratch the cat's head as though it can impart some wisdom. She suddenly claps her hands to her cheeks, and I think she's come up with something that will help me find LeJeune. 'Silly of me. I have a plate of dinner in the oven on a low heat.' She eases out of her chair, and the cat trots out of the living room ahead of her.

'Come.' I follow her along the little passageway to the kitchen, disappointed that we're not discussing LeJeune now. Myrtle holds my plate of dinner between her fingers, protecting them from the warmth of it with a tea towel. She removes the top plate covering the food. 'Mind you don't burn your tongue. It's hot. I'll get you a spoon.'

'Thank you.'

She has made a reddish-brown stew which has seeped into a small mound of mashed potato. Both of which look crisp on top. It has an unusual taste, but it will warm me up at least. Just one mouthful reminds me of how I miss home, my family and Mama's food. The aromas from her kitchen and the way she taught me her recipes. I allow myself to forget my mission as I reminisce. The cat winds around my feet, purring deliberately now that I have my cousin's attention.

'You don't mind Moorhouse, do you?' Cousin Myrtle asks.

'Moorhouse?'

'The cat. He can be a bit nosy but he's good company.'

'No, I don't mind him at all.'

Moorhouse's fur is soft and warm, and he settles the weight of his body onto my toes. I still have on my jacket because as tiny as this ground floor flat is, it doesn't seem to hold warmth and my bones are chilled through from a day spent outdoors. My body is worn out, but my mind has eased since the danger I might have been in from the man in the brown suit. Who was he and would he be hanging around here now that he knows the address? Should I tell Myrtle? Should I be afraid? As I spoon down the stew and chew slowly, I think about what a day it's been. I've been cold and nervous for most of it. I think about LeJeune arriving in the summer and wonder if arriving here on a sunny day was a happy and exciting time for him. He was returning to a country he'd said he'd grown to love and had a new job to look forward to. He'd told me once that he'd thought about re-enlisting. What if he has joined the army again instead of starting the new job and has been shipped out somewhere at short notice? Even so, he still would have found the time to write and tell me. Stop me worrying. I just want to find him and know the truth. However ugly it is. I just want to know.

Chapter 5

1943

LeJeune's regiment had been in France for several months, though to him it had felt like years. When he returned to England and his ship berthed at the port, the exhausted and bewildered soldiers fell heavily into the army truck. As it trundled its way back from the coast and along country paths, he felt a sense of coming home. He found himself smiling at the familiarity of the big city. He couldn't understand why London felt like home and Dominica a place so foreign. So far away. Everything about London, the cold that dampened his bones, the dark mornings, and food that tasted of air and never filled his belly, said 'home' to him. When this war was over, he'd stay. Learn to live like an Englishman. Discover what the city was like in peacetime. He looked forward to that day.

It was summer now, and though the days were not filled with the kaleidoscope of colours like his faraway island, the sun bathed the rows of brick houses and narrow streets. It was not nearly as hot as Dominica. In fact, the wind laid a sheet of cool over his skin, penetrating the stale uniform that he couldn't wait to take off. He'd be assigned his usual duties now that he was back. Vehicle maintenance. He'd learnt a lot about motor mechanics. Skills he could use when he settled here. If he managed to stay alive until the end, he'd be qualified as a mechanic, a job that would enable him to find a room in London and who knows what could happen from there? He grinned as he jumped off the truck, his kitbag hoisted over his shoulder. Before he could head for the barracks, Eugene hugged an arm around him.

'We make it!' Eugene exclaimed loudly into his ear. He led him across the drive to the makeshift building that served as army barracks, a training camp and mechanical workshop. The Ministry Of Defence had requisitioned the site and buildings which used to be a glue factory on the outskirts of Stepney. It wasn't the first time Eugene had cheered and rejoiced that they'd survived their mission. It was his third time across enemy lines. Eugene had taken a bullet, a scrape across his upper thigh as they were running for cover. It hadn't bled for long, but the sight of it had frightened both men. Eugene was still shaking after he'd received medical aid, and LeJeune had had the same nightmare for several nights of being unable to run fast enough and catching more than one bullet, the last being fatal. His own yell had blasted him awake, his shirt soaked through. Immediately after Eugene's narrow escape, LeJeune had been called to help fix a hole in the fuel tank, though all attempts had been in vain. The truck would never make it back out of enemy territory. LeJeune, or John as they called him, had been sent to fetch another vehicle to help get the men back to camp.

'Johnny the hero,' Eugene said as they crashed onto their bunks. 'Imagine if you never get that vehicle in time. We would all be dead.' He made a circle with his finger to signify the fatigued soldiers, some sprawled on their bunks, looking fast asleep already, some lighting cigarettes, hands shaking as they would in the bunkers.

'I was just doing my job,' said LeJeune, pulling off his boots and shaking them empty. He had to peel his socks from his feet: they had stuck to the blisters and raw skin. His boots had never fitted right, but he hadn't complained. Not about anything. Not even about the way Eugene never stopped talking. The man even spoke in his sleep.

He'd told LeJeune that in the months before LeJeune had enlisted, he'd slept with at least three white women. On the journey back to Stepney, he'd encouraged LeJeune to do the same.

'A little recreation never do no one no harm. And we fighting for them, so it make sense we should sleep with them, too.'

'There are Black women in the service, you know?' LeJeune reminded him.

'Johnny, Johnny, Johnny. It's not the same. You don't have to marry the white ones, and the black ones will insist you do.'

'So what's wrong with that? Marrying a white woman?'

'Don't talk crazy, man. We are just an experiment to these women. While their men away. After this…' He raised both hands. 'Everything changes. There will be no war to fight, and they will ship us all back to where we belong. Besides. Know your place. Marrying a white woman. That would never be allowed.'

*

The following evening, LeJeune followed a few of the men to The Dockman's Arms. It wasn't far from the barracks. He secretly hoped to see the girl he'd spoken to and defended several months ago when she was being harassed by GIs. He hadn't seen her since then. He'd been too put off by the look in the American soldiers' faces when they thought he'd been speaking to them out of turn. He knew the Black American soldiers were segregated, even whilst away from the United States, and that certain white GIs were taking the law into their own hands when it came to the treatment of their black and brown counterparts. No matter how light-skinned Le-Jeune was, he was a Black man, and he'd seen an American soldier with skin far lighter than his be kicked in the head as sport for one of these GIs because he dared to dance with a white woman, even though she'd been the one to ask the soldier to dance.

Luckily she was there, the girl with the yellow hair. She was staring straight at him as he took a corner seat and waited for Eugene to buy the first round of drinks. She smiled, so he smiled back. She laughed at something Eugene said, and both Eugene and the girl looked over at him. Le-Jeune shook his head. What nonsense was that Jamaican getting him into now?

Eugene carried two tumblers sloshing with froth and beer to the wobbly table in the corner and slammed them down as if he'd already had five pints previous to these. But LeJeune noticed that it didn't take much to have Eugene talking and acting as if he were drunk. So full of merriment all the time, even after he'd been shot. Joking about how he'd go back home and tell them he was a war hero. LeJeune knew a return to home or anywhere else was not guaranteed. He'd seen death come to him in complicated dreams that had made no sense at all. He'd had them years ago, when the war had broken out. Once, a voice in the dream had beckoned him to sign up. To fly. To be where the action was happening. He was excited in the dream, he remembered that, but in

all of his dreams, his life was cut short, though how it ended
was never clear. Perhaps the plane he flew blew up; perhaps
the day he was led by the nose to sign up for the army instead of the RAF meant he'd be spared. Seeing Eugene rubbing his wound, he wondered if his dreams were borne of
fear. Everyone was afraid, even if they didn't admit it: even
Eugene was scared.

'I think you have an admirer, Johnny my boy.' Eugene
loved to mimic English voices. Sometimes, LeJeune would
have to do a double take to check whether a white man had
entered the room without him knowing.

'How come?'

'Now come on, you small island boy.' His accent was
broad Jamaican again. 'The young gyal dere so. She like
you. Maybe it's the grey eyes and the light skin because she
didn't even look at me. Looked at you the whole time she
was asking your name, rank and number. Everything but
your inside leg measurement. You can give her that yourself.'

LeJeune shook his head as if he were exasperated by Eugene, but a quick side look at the bar told him the girl was
still glancing into his corner.

The bar began to fill up, grow hot. So much so that Le-
Jeune had to loosen his tie and undo his top button. They had
arrived in their shirt sleeves, with the permission of their
commanding officer, under a strict reminder that they served
the Crown and, as such, should not let this relaxing of the
dress code make them unruly. There was an unwritten rule
that the soldiers should not drink to excess as they never
knew when they might be called away. German aircraft had
already begun attacks, dropping bombs over London. Le-

Jeune had noticed the number of shelters that had been constructed and knew that evacuation of children was already underway. He'd thought about the safety of back home. Tending his goats and plot of land while the other side of the world was burning. He could not have sat back and listened to it from an old radio late at night when his mother was sound asleep.

Someone raised the lid of the piano and started tinkling on the keys until the semblance of a song developed. A man with a warbling voice began singing. Eugene knew the words and sang loudly in a cockney accent, holding the dregs of a pint glass above his head. A family – an elderly man, a middle-aged woman and two teenage girls – laughed at him and began to sing, too. By now, Eugene was drunk and so too was LeJeune. His cheeks were numb and he needed to flex the muscles around his face before he could speak.

'I'm feeling hot,' LeJeune told Eugene. 'Where is the latrine?'

'Out de back,' Eugene shouted before bellowing a full-blown cockney assault on the song, *We'll Meet Again*.

'You want to go up the front and sing,' someone said to Eugene as LeJeune began to wind his way to the back of the pub.

LeJeune snaked the crowd of marauders who were happy to step aside, patting his back and thanking him for his service. In the narrow passage outside the bar, a couple – a fresh-faced soldier and a chubby woman – stood kissing.

'I'm looking for the latrine?' said LeJeune.

Without looking up from what she was doing, the chubby woman wiggled a hand towards the door at the end of the passage. It was already ajar. Outside, in the cool night, Le-Jeune rubbed his eyes and slapped his face. He tried to focus his view, finding himself in a tiny yard where a parked van swallowed the space from the gate to the middle of the yard. To his right, a small shed, only just upright, sat in the shadow of a corner. *The latrine*, he said aloud, his voice sounding oddly very London to his ears. He relieved himself in the close quarters of the shed. He would have liked to have washed his hands and splashed his face, but there was no sink. Only the low toilet with a wooden seat and a long chain from the cistern above his head. He tidied his clothes and straightened his tie as he stepped out.

'Johnny,' a voice said. 'You alright, love. You put away a fair few.'

He squinted to see her, the girl with the yellow hair.

'Yes, I'm fine. You know my name?'

'Well, I asked 'cos I was interested.' She had on a cardigan over her white, short-sleeved blouse. Her skirt was narrow and covered the top of her shins. She rocked back and forth on her low-heeled shoes as if she'd been waiting her turn.

'You need help?' she asked. 'Shall I call your mate out?'

'No, no. I'm okay. I just need air.'

She walked closer to him and took his hand.

'It's fresher when you're away from the toilet. Over here, look.'

They walked a few paces to the other side of the van. Le-Jeune noticed that a tyre on that side was flat. So unlike his heartbeat which raced when the girl rubbed her small hand up and down one side of his chest. He held her hand against his shirt.

'My name is Lizzie. Elizabeth, actually, but people call me Lizzie. Or Liz. If you prefer.'

'Liz, I don't know what … I think I want to kiss you, do you mind?'

She shook her head and stepped back against the brick wall that enclosed the small yard. To his right was a tall, metal dustbin. In front of him was Lizzie whose face tilted up, lips apart as she stared at his. She smelt of sweet soap. Her skin, when he touched her face, was smooth. She put her arms up and around his shoulders and kissed him. He hadn't imagined anything like this happening to him, to find someone so soft who would bend her body into his, connecting every part of her to him, allowing him to have full access to all the skin he cared to touch, to stroke. His heart continued to race, his lungs overstretched and his brain light. He thought he would fly into the air with the excitement of it. Her narrow skirt was around her waist, his trousers far down his legs with his underwear. Hers, he held in his hand as she raised a leg to wrap around his thigh, the two becoming one moving part that panted and jerked, gritting their teeth so that they would not cry out.

When they pulled away, she quickly neatened herself up as he dressed, slowly, his eyes never leaving her. With her thumb, she rubbed at his lips and showed it to him, the pink of her lipstick staining it.

'There,' she said. 'As good as new and no one need ever know.' She giggled. He could see her face was flushed. His felt warm, too.

'If we say nothing, then,' he said, 'could we do it again?'

'Not here. Too risky. I'll pop my address down and you take it with you. Somehow, we'll meet again.'

They both began to laugh because the song *We'll Meet Again* was being sung again at full volume from inside.

'Until then,' said LeJeune.

'Look forward to it.' Lizzie ran inside, blowing him a kiss from the doorway.

Chapter 6

Essie

London 1948

I can hear a strange rumbling sound when I finally open my eyes. I'm confused at first, not sure where I am and not able to understand why my bed feels so different. The mattress is deep and soft, and I have about three blankets covering me. I feel something prodding my thigh and moving across the width of my body. When I pull the blankets off my face, I see Moorhouse jumping off the bed, fluffy tail aloft as he slips out of the open doorway. He almost trips Myrtle who is entering the room wearing her nurse's uniform and carrying tea in the familiar thin cup.

'Morning, morning.' She smiles brightly, sits at the edge of the bed and props the cup onto the side table. 'Sleep well?'

I sit up and yawn. 'Very well. I could sleep some more.'

'Well, you do just that. I have to go to work. I'm on shift until late afternoon. Will you manage by yourself?'

'Yes, I think so.'

'Listen. I went upstairs to speak to Mrs Rogers. She says she still knows people over Stepney way and maybe they know the factory your young man is working in. It's a shame we don't have any more information than that.'

A knotty feeling revisits my stomach. The same one I have when people start to interrogate me about what LeJeune actually said and what I know as fact. The real truth is I know nothing. Next to nothing. LeJeune's mother said that LeJeune last lived in Stepney when he was in London around 1942 or 1943. It's now five years later, and how am I to know if he still has any connection with the place? But Stepney is all I have to go on for now. Maybe if this Mrs Rogers knows Stepney well enough, she might shed light on some small clue. A tiny glimmer at least because mercy knows I've been staggering along an endlessly dim road. She might know of some factories, and maybe, if there aren't too many of them, I could go and ask around.

'So, is Mrs Rogers expecting me?' I ask as I reach for my tea.

'Yes, you remember the little passageway you came into from the main door? Well, just outside my front door is another that leads to the upstairs flat. Just knock hers and leave mine on the latch. Only, don't let the cat out. Mrs Rogers is allergic.'

'And you're going to work now?'

'Yes. St Mary's Hospital. It's all the way over to the East End of London. And, as I said, not too far from Stepney. It's the hospital I began my training in. I feel a sort of loyalty to it, that's why I stayed there even when we lost our home. But, here I am. I can't complain. The Rogers are good neighbours to have.'

I hadn't noticed the number of grey hairs Myrtle had. Her hair is brushed back from her face and bound in a bun at the nape of her neck. She looks at her wristwatch and jumps up from the bed. Over the uniform, she wears a navy cardigan. An elasticated belt pinches around her tiny waist. She wears nylon stockings that are tan in colour and make a mockery of her skin tone which is several shades darker. She has neat little muscles on her calves, and her shoes are laced up, flat-heeled and black.

'You sure you'll be all right while I'm gone?'

I nod and smile, feeling brighter because a visit upstairs could lead me somewhere. I wonder how far Stepney is from Paddington and how long it takes Myrtle to get to her hospital in East London. When I go searching for LeJeune, will I need a bus or a train, or both? This might cost me a lot, this hunt for LeJeune, so I hope I can find him soon before what little spending money I brought from home runs out. I have the fair to return home and a little more besides. I had imagined finding LeJeune a day after arriving, he'd explain everything and that would be that. I'd eventually send Daddy back the money he'd given me.

I lean against the pillow and listen to the creaking and rustling that Myrtle makes around the house while trying to get ready for work. She hums, too, and talks to Moorhouse. Then she calls, 'See you later,' on her way out and the door slams shut behind her. I hear Moorhouse cry out when the door closes, and then the flat is silent and I'm sleepy again.

When I wake, I'm not sure of the time. I open the curtain in the box-shaped bedroom situated between the living room and kitchen and see the view is of the outer wall of the adjacent house. A cemented path must lead to the garden. The room once belonged to Myrtle's son who went to university and is now a teacher in a comprehensive school in the Midlands. She doesn't see him often. Myrtle had a husband, too, once. He died very suddenly after a cold turned into an infection and then into pneumonia. He died in the very hospital that Myrtle has worked in since she arrived here, newly married at age twenty. Her accent is not all that Dominican now. Not like Mama, Daddy and me. I like her voice – it's soft and she is very gentle. She is the first person who, after initially looking at me as if I were being foolish, now appears to agree with my decision to come and look for the man I love. At least Myrtle knows what it's like to have lost a husband.

Lost. It is hard to think of LeJeune as lost. But at least he is not the kind of lost that Myrtle's husband is. At least I'll find LeJeune. Somehow.

I turn to see that the cat is sleeping at the foot of the single bed. He doesn't stir when I leave to go to the bathroom. It's an add-on room, leading from the kitchen, where there is nothing more than a sink, a toilet and a wall cupboard. The small room has no warmth or heating, no window, only an air vent high up on the wall. It's open for ventilation but also lets in a chilly breeze that covers all the hard surfaces in the room, particularly the linoleum floor which has me curling my toes up and wishing I had put my shoes on. I'd close the vent if I could only reach.

I have no idea how long I will be here. How long it will take to find my husband and move in with him. I wash quickly, change and go to the kitchen to find the cat curled on a chair. He springs to his feet, shakes his body and stretches as if to ask what took me so long. I look at my wristwatch and see it's nearly midday. Time for lunch, really. In a few hours, Myrtle will return home, and I wonder if I should make dinner for us. Back home, that's what I would be doing. Wednesday is soup day, Mama's special recipe. She and I are the only ones privy to her recipe. It's adapted from the way it's traditionally made, and everyone talks about Mama's soup. I feel a pang, not only of hunger but the desire to be home, in a familiar setting where I know where to find all the ingredients I need. Looking at the ceiling, I try to picture Mrs Rogers upstairs and hope she is as kind as Myrtle and as willing to help.

After a cup of tea and a cheese sandwich, I find the courage to leave the flat. I shoo Moorhouse back inside Myrtle's flat, despite his protests. He bobs his velvety nose at the closing door, and I have a feeling he could work the door open if he wanted to, but he retreats and I put the latch on. I take a deep breath and knock on the upstairs neighbour's door.

I wait a whole minute before I hear feet on the stairs. When the door opens, I'm surprised to find that Mrs Rogers is white. I'm lost for words at this point because I hadn't imagined Black and white people living under the same roof. She just looks at me with pale-coloured eyes and skin that has yellowish hues, crinkly like old newspaper. I place her at close to eighty years old.

'You must be Essie. Myrtle said you had something to ask me about East London? Come up.'

When she smiles, her teeth have an overbite that you wouldn't detect from the tight way her lips were drawn together as she inspected me. She has on a blue cardigan, much the same as my cousin's. Underneath is a chocolate brown dress that looks square and work-like with no frills or buttons. Just two square pockets on the front. Homemade, perhaps. She shuffles back in pink, fluffy slippers so that I can come in.

'Thank you,' I say, though I'm still a little lost for words and very sure that I have not been polite enough on first meeting with her. 'Good afternoon,' I say as I watch the way her slippers flip off her heels because years of ownership has loosened them considerably.

'Eh? What's that?' She stops near the top step.

'I was just saying good afternoon.'

'Oh. Good afternoon to you, too. When did you get here?' She extends an arm so that I can enter her kitchen, which must be positioned above Myrtle's small kitchen and bathroom. At the table, where she clears away a large mixing bowl that smells sweet, there are two chairs and she nods for me to sit down.

'I've been baking. Forgot to light the oven, so my fairy cakes might come out wonky. My daughter-in-law will come and pick them up for her brood. Probably tell my son she baked them. Dozy mare. Don't know what my Graham ever saw in that one.'

I smile because I don't quite understand her way of speaking and what she means, but I don't want to look as if I don't.

She puts on the kettle and brews some tea while she talks about how she met my cousin, Myrtle.

'She looked after me the best out of all them nurses after my hysterectomy. Polite, courteous, gentle and caring. You couldn't fault the girl no matter where she came from. I mean, some of the other patients didn't want her near them. More fool them I say because she's a lovely girl.'

I can't help notice that she calls Myrtle 'girl'. I could never refer to someone my cousin's age as a girl. It would be disrespectful of me, but maybe at Mrs Rogers' age, she is permitted. I hear a loud cough, husky and congested. Mrs Rogers tuts.

'Stan's off work again today. Nasty chest. But I don't suppose smoking's going to help. The way he chugs away at them. Like a bloody chimney sometimes. Pardon my language.'

Mrs Rogers pours three cups of tea, cuts three slices of a fruit bun and carries a cup of tea and one of the pieces of cake to Stan, who presumably is Mrs Rogers' husband. I hear them exchanging a conversation and overhear her saying, '… the lovely coloured girl from downstairs.' He's concerned that I, as Myrtle's guest, might be noisy because Mrs Rogers has told him I'm a young little thing, wet behind the ears by all accounts. She returns and slumps into the chair opposite mine and slides a plate containing cake towards me.

'So you training to be a nurse, too?' she asks after lighting up a cigarette and coughing to a lesser degree than Stan. Her throat crackles with phlegm.

'Oh no. I have a husband and he will support me.'

'So, you're not staying with Myrtle? I thought she said you were.'

'Oh, I am. I do have a husband. I just don't know where he is.'

She holds her teacup midway between her chest and her lips. She crinkles her brow and returns the cup to its saucer.

'Beg your pardon, love?'

'Well. Yes. It sounds silly, but we got married and he was due to go to England the next day. He set sail all right, but he only wrote me one letter since he arrived in London, and so far he hasn't sent for me. That's why I need your help.' I feel my body shrink into the pink frilly cotton dress that Mama made when I was four and that I wore every Sunday to church.

Mrs Rogers tuts again and raises her eyes briefly to the ceiling.

'Sounds like he's done a moonlight flit.'

'A what?'

'A flit. Run out on you, love. That's what he's done. You're not likely to set eyes on him again and doesn't sound like he wants you to, neither.'

'Yes, I know that's how it looks. It would to anyone who doesn't know him. But I know' – I touch my heart with my fist – 'I know he loves me and he would never do a ... a moonlight flit. He is honourable, honourable enough to write and tell me if he'd changed his mind. So I don't think he did ... change his mind. I think something happened to stop him writing more than that one letter.'

She pulls in her lips to prevent herself from laughing. 'Oh to be young,' she says and takes up the cigarette from the bottle green ashtray in the middle of the table.

'You think I'm being stupid. A silly, trusting fool.' I inhale a deep, shivery breath and blink away the gathering tears. Mrs Rogers blows smoke over her shoulder and stubs out the cigarette, which is only halfway finished.

'Don't mind me,' she says, shaking her head so that her thin, grey curls bubble around her crown. 'I don't mean to mock you. I just know men, you see?'

'And I suppose I don't,' I reply politely. 'Not really. But you see, I know him. And I can feel in my stomach this isn't right. Something isn't right. Not with any of it. I don't want anything to have happened to him. But what if something did? In any case, I want to know.'

'You won't rest until you do, I can see that. Love's young dream.'

I ignore the last sentence as I'm not clear about its meaning. I am young. I had a dream about married life. But it was nothing like this.

I touch the handle of my teacup. I haven't had a sip.

'Cousin Myrtle says you know Stepney?'

'Yes. Stan and I moved round Stepney way when we got married. Limehouse, me. Stan's from Whitechapel. We moved here several years ago for Stan's job. And my Graham lives nearby with his family, so it's nice and handy for seeing the grand-kiddies.'

'So, do you know any factories in Stepney where a man coming from the West Indies might have a job?'

'Well, what's the name of the factory?'

I look down at the table, mapping the flowery pattern on Mrs Rogers' tablecloth.

'Oh. Like that, is it?' she says. 'You can understand why, from where I'm sitting, it looks like he's left you in the lurch.' She sighs. 'Look. I'm not promising anything, but I could ask around the people I know. See what I come up with.'

'Will you?' This is the most encouraging thing I've heard in months. I can just imagine it. Someone will ask someone, then that person will speak to the next and, before I know it, I'll find him. I can feel the skin stretching wide across my cheeks. I pick up my cup and drink from it. The tea is only lukewarm but tastes wonderful enough to me. Now that I have hope.

'Now, don't get yourself all overexcited.' Mrs Rogers has had her lips pulled in tight as she watches my silent celebration. 'So, you don't know the name of the factory. But you know it's in Stepney, right?'

I stop smiling.

'It is in Stepney, isn't it?' She knots her brow.

'It could be.'

'Could be? What kind of … okay, never mind. You write down his full name, age, height and things, and I'll see what I can do.'

'It's very kind of you. And you never know.' I put down my cup. 'Oh, but I don't have a paper and pen.'

Mrs Rogers shuffles back to the living room and begins another conversation with her husband. It's too muffled for me to hear this time, but I hear her husband mention something about the docks. Mrs Rogers returns to the kitchen.

'Stan had an idea.' She places what looks like a child's exercise book and blue pencil in front of me before she sits and relights her cigarette. I can't wait to hear this idea, but the lighter she uses won't spark and she shakes it several times before giving up, coughing and dropping the lighter and cigarette onto the table. 'During the war, there was a lot of damage to the docks and it was a big transport system up to then. They're rebuilding the area. Maybe your young man is working there.'

I take in a sharp breath and beam at my host. 'And he was in the war,' I bluster. 'So, maybe he saw the damage and would love to help.'

'He was a soldier?'

I nod enthusiastically. 'And his mother said the last place she knew of that he stayed in London was Stepney.'

'There you are, then. I suppose it's as good a place to start as any. I'll see who knows any West Indian's and whatnot working on the docks out that way. One's who have just come over.'

'Well, he arrived here in June. We got married in May.'

Mrs Rogers looks sadly at me.

'But we're into September, and all this time he's kept you hanging on?'

'Yes.'

'So it's about time you got some answers.'

I write down all of LeJeune's details, as many as I can, and hand the book to Mrs Rogers. She squints at the page and reads from it.

'Ler – Jern,' she says. 'French?'

'Yes, but we pronounce it LeeJen. A soft *jay*.'

She shrugs. 'I'll do my best to say it. Lee – Jen. LeeJen Francis. Well, I suppose it's easy enough. Leave it with me, love. Soon as I know anything, I'll pop down. Let's hope you get some good news soon, eh?'

On her face, I can't see any sign that she believes I will. But in my heart, I know I will find out something. And anything will bring me closer to him. I know this to be true.

Chapter 7

Essie

London 1948

It's 4 o'clock in the afternoon and there is no sign of Myrtle. The cat and I are good friends now. At least he has stopped turning his nose up at me and coming over only to sniff me and circle my legs every once in a while. He curls up at my side as I sit on the sofa in the square sitting room and look towards the window. The row of houses outside the net curtains are replicas of each other. Two-storey, immoveable beasts that are probably mirror images on the inside, too. Apart from the different coloured front doors, every one has indistinctive curtains, grey like the weather outside. I haven't been out yet – I don't have a key. I have no idea how long I'll be here, but perhaps Myrtle will have one cut for me. I'll need to go out sometime to look for LeJeune the second Mrs Rogers from upstairs has found out something about him. There must be someone who knows him. Knows of him, from Stepney. He'd been stationed in London for years during the war and, of course, travelled to other parts of Europe to fight. I know he went to France, but LeJeune didn't say much more than that. Never mentioned Stepney once. He always spoke of his time in London with a distant look in his eyes. I stared into the shades of grey and green when he talked about food rations, mice, people who didn't want his sort around. But LeJeune had been proud to be a soldier. He'd learnt vehicle mechanics and was disappointed that the only job he could find when he wanted to move back here was in a factory. He is very clever with his hands, so maybe he'll find a mechanics job eventually.

I ponder on the idea of LeJeune being back in the army. Maybe he had signed up again. He'd been thinking about it. I hadn't liked the idea. I had always considered myself lucky that he had returned from the war at all. Not that I knew him before then, but he'd come back to Dominica and we'd met and we'd fallen in love. I think about the knots that had tugged and pulled in my stomach when I first saw him. The other girls had been jealous that he'd chosen me.

Mama wasn't sure about him, though. She first met him at the local dance. LeJeune had asked me to go, and Mama insisted that the whole family should attend. Ginnie protested and stayed home with Daddy. All through the dance, I could feel Mama's eyes on my back, and each time LeJeune pulled me closer to him, I'd pull apart – I didn't want him to feel the heat that rose from my body with such close contact and I didn't want my mother coming over and telling me it was time to go. His hands were strong and cool as they held mine. Mine were sweaty and annoying, and I'd wanted to wipe away the perspiration on the top of my lip so many times that I became distracted and didn't always know what he was saying. The music was loud but his voice was soft. I was connecting to the sound of it rather than the words, low like a bass drum, steady like a heartbeat.

It's so quiet in the flat now, and I haven't seen a single soul pass by the window. I can hear the Rogers' radio through the ceiling. I'd popped my head around the living room door to

say a hello and goodbye to Mr Rogers when I was leaving
their flat. He had a large, round tummy that I could clearly
see under the vest he was wearing. It was clean and white,
but his skin didn't look clean and white under it. He had red
cheeks and purple bags under his eyes. He really did look
sick. He had coughed, nodded and looked me up and down.

In the cold kitchen, I decide a cup of tea might warm me
up. I shiver and look around. I open the fridge and all of the
cupboards because I'm thinking I should make something
for the evening meal. Something to warm our hearts, as
Mama would say, and Myrtle is bound to be hungry by the
time she comes home. Considering how thin she is, I think
Mama would make her special soup to put some meat onto
her bones. Mama's special soup is what I need right now.
I'm homesick already as well as hungry. I squint my eyes to
bring the ingredients to mind.

For the soup I need the following: lamb on the bone, carrots, yams, cabbage, dumplings – which means flour, water
and a little salt. Some onions, garlic, oil, seasoning and of
course the callaloo leaves. I'll also need a big pot, but I
doubt Myrtle will have one as she lives on her own. I start
searching through the fridge first of all, hoping to find meat.
I see a small parcel, something wrapped in white paper, and
sniff it. It's meat but I have no idea what kind. On opening
the paper, I see a few small cuts of mutton. That will have to
do. There are carrots, some cabbage and what I think are
English potatoes on a rack next to the fridge. No onions or
garlic and certainly no callaloo. But at least there is salt and
pepper. It's a start.

I chop the meat first in the largest pot I can find. I brown it
and add the salt and pepper. It won't taste anything like
Mama's soup. If anything, it will be a bit disappointing and

I'll not come close to creating the taste of home I'm missing so much. I look around the kitchen again, right into the back of the cupboard for anything that will add flavour, but all I find is a jar of instant coffee, a box of loose tea, biscuits and cans of soup. The meat doesn't smell so fresh. It cracks and hisses in the pot, and because I need to be sparing with the oil at this stage, I'm afraid the meat might burn rather than brown. It shrivels in size, so I turn down the heat, add more oil and hope for the best. I add water and let the meat cook and then wash, peel and chop the hard vegetables. I'm using English potatoes instead of yam. Mama, who warned me there would be no decent food in London, had pulled a face when she talked about white people food. I chop the potatoes up small and cut the carrots into thick discs. The cat sits up, whiskers twitching as he tries to see up to the surfaces. His eyes are asking who on earth do I think I am, I should have waited for Myrtle. I hope she won't mind me using the last of the meat. Next, I make the dumplings. There is half a bag of flour, and I sprinkle some of it into a bowl, adding the water bit by bit until the consistency is just right for the sort of dumplings Mama would approve. With the hard vegetables added, everything is softening nicely. The dumplings, which I've made about a dozen of, are small circles that will bubble and rise and float among the other ingredients, absorbing what little seasoning I had to work with. It doesn't smell like Mama's recipe, but it looks like a fair representation of it. When it is close to being ready, I add an additional dribble of oil.

'You're putting more oil? Now?'

I turn to see Myrtle in her navy raincoat. She removes her gloves and headscarf and puts them onto a chair before coming to look into the pot.

'Mama says the extra oil right at the end gives the flavour a little something, so I always do it.'

Myrtle inhales.

'I know,' I continue. 'It isn't the smell of back home, but I did my best.'

'I'm sure you did and I'm sure it will taste nice. Let me change. You have no idea what a nice surprise it is to come home and smell food on the stove that I didn't have to cook. You can stay here forever.'

I smile as Myrtle leaves the kitchen, but I tell myself I won't be here forever because eventually I'll have found Le-Jeune.

As we eat, Myrtle tells me all about her day, which patients she has seen, who bled, who needed stitches and who vomited all over the trainee nurse whose first day it was.

'What about if you trained to become a nurse?' she asks me. I want to tell her again that my husband promised to look after me and I wouldn't have to work. I don't bother to tell her that I'd prefer to be a teacher if I were to train at anything.

'Mrs Rogers said she is going to ask around her old neighbours about LeJeune. She says that there are West Indian men working on the docks in Stepney, rebuilding it. He could be one of them.'

'I thought you said he had a factory job.' Myrtle puts down her spoon. I look down at my bowl which is close to being empty. 'But that's fine,' she continues, trying not to notice the hopelessness written on my face. 'That sounds very promising, then. I told you she might be able to help.'

'You did. And now I have something to look forward to.'

'Indeed you do. But Essie, don't build your hopes up too much. You know, if I were you, I would start to make this place home. There are a lot of opportunities for girls like you. Factories, hospitals. How about teaching? What do you think?'

'I think I should not give up hope of finding LeJeune.'

'I didn't mean …'

'It's fine. I understand.' I stand to collect the bowls.

'I didn't mean for you to give up hope. It's just that … in the end, we only have ourselves. When I married Moorhouse, I didn't expect him to die.'

'Moorhouse? But isn't that the cat's name?'

'My husband had it first.'

'You named your cat after him?'

She chuckles. 'Only because his fur is the same colour as Moorhouse's skin. Days after my Moorhouse died, this cat followed me in off the street. I hadn't even realised until something soft brushed my legs and began to purr in the same rumbling way Moorhouse used to snore. He jumped up and sat in Moorhouse's chair, the one he used to sit in to listen to the radio and smoke his pipe. And he's been good company ever since. I know he can't speak, but I talk to him anyway because I think he understands. To tell you the truth, though, I was happy you were coming because now I have someone I can converse with again. But if … and don't be upset when I say this … if we never find this missing husband of yours, you will need a job. If you're staying.'

Myrtle looks at me as if she longs for me to say I will. But what about when her son comes for a visit? What if LeJeune walks straight back into my life tomorrow? I'd feel awful about letting her down.

'As Mama says, time will tell,' I reply. 'I'll make decisions once I know. Something.'

'In any case, I have something you could find useful,' my cousin says, quickly turning the conversation around to hide the look of sadness in her eyes. I'm hoping, of course, that this useful thing brings me closer to solving my mystery, but Myrtle returns to the kitchen carrying a large, brown paper bag.

'You bought me a present?' I reach for the package. It feels soft and light in my arms.

'I thought it could come in handy if you are going to be here a while. Autumn can be bleak here, and if it takes time to find him, you'll start to feel the cold and that thin jacket you came in won't be warm enough.'

I put the package on the table, opening it rapidly to find a bright blue jacket inside that is much thicker than mine and a lot more fashionable, I'd imagine. It isn't new but it's clean and looks about my size.

'Try it.' Myrtle grins at me and I do as she says. Once the jacket is on, she smiles proudly, but when I fasten the buttons, it feels tight under the arms.

'It's perfect,' I say, remembering my manners because Mama has drummed this home to me. *Mind your manners, mind your manners.* It is a lovely colour and it will certainly keep me warm. If I stay.

'It was left behind. There is a cupboard of odds and ends near the caretakers' room, lost property that no one has ever claimed, and I remembered that blue jacket because the colour is so striking. I'm surprised one of the nurses didn't take it already. You look like a film star, Essie.' She looks approvingly at me. 'I would have taken it for myself, but it would have been a bit too young for me. I hope you don't mind it.'

'It's a wonderful present. Thank you.' I wonder about the person who left it behind. A patient who died? Was she a

young girl, like me? A married woman who left children behind? The jacket has a history. A sad one, I can tell, and I
don't want it to jinx me as I look for my husband. I shake off
that idea. 'I'll wear it to Stepney when I go to find LeJeune.
He'll probably like it, too.'

Myrtle doesn't comment, and we settle down for the evening for me to write a letter home to Mama and for Myrtle to
listen to the radio, Moorhouse purring at her feet.

Chapter 8

London

1943

They did meet again. Often. Between LeJeune's duties, Lizzie's shifts and another tour in France, they found ways to meet either at the Dockman's, Lizzie's flat – which she shared with a factory worker named Lorna – or the park near the marshes. The park was always deserted, the swings haunted by children who didn't play there anymore, the heavy chains swaying the wooden plank seats, waiting for the noisy little ghosts to rattle and heave them to and fro once again. There was always a pool of water at the foot of the swings that never seemed to dry even when it hadn't been raining in days. At the park, they sat on a bench splattered with gull faeces, dried long ago because not even the gulls flew around there anymore. Air raids were more regular and the birds seemed to scarper, as Lizzie said, by the afternoon: that's when you knew the enemy were on their way. Flying low. Metal birds replacing the feathered kind. She hated the air raid shelters, though. Her local one was the one beneath Stepney Green tube station, and she'd told LeJeune that she was sure she'd suffocate down there never mind being blown to smithereens. Last time she was there, her friend Lorna had befriended a man who'd lost his arm but swore he'd take her out dancing one night even without it.

'To think, girls like us would never have even considered walking out with a one-armed bloke.' Lizzie smoked a cigarette and rested her head on LeJeune's shoulder as they sat on the bench. Despite her blue jacket being fastened tight, it didn't keep out the late autumn breeze. 'But at times like this, you take what you can get.'

'Is that why you're with me?'

Lizzie sat up, promptly. 'What you saying?' She threw her cigarette onto the path.

'I just mean, with all the able-bodied white men at war, you picked a coloured man because there wasn't much choice?'

'Johnny? How could you say that?' She squinted her eyes at him. He loved the blues of her eyes, always changing because of the light or the impending weather, the flecks of grey. How she coated her long lashes in black and how that made her eyes so much bigger. So alive. Her yellow hair tickled his cheek when they snuggled, and he loved to stroke the smoothness of it and watch how the loose curls around her ears bobbed back into place whenever he did.

'I just wonder why you're with me.'

'Now listen, John. Don't go thinking I'd spread my legs behind a pub for any old bloke just because I implied it might be slim pickings around here. You've seen the number of soldiers who come in the Dockman's – our blokes, coloured blokes, men with a leg missing and not to mention them cheeky Yanks. But out of all those, you were the one that caught my attention. You were the one I wanted.'

'And when the war is over?'

'We don't know when that will be. All I know is we're here now and I want to be with you.'

She lit two cigarettes and gave one to LeJeune, resuming her previous position, neck tilted, her head on his shoulder. They sat silently as they smoked. An old man walked into the park with a bulldog off its leash. It trundled lazily around the paths following its master, stopping to sniff the patchy grass. The man walked past their bench, but the dog stopped to make friends.

'What's your name then, eh?' Lizzie scratched the dogs neck and looked at the tag on its collar. There was no name on it.

'Samson.' The old man returned to their bench, keeping his gaze on LeJeune. He saluted him. LeJeune sat up and saluted back. 'Off duty, son?'

'It would appear so,' said LeJeune, adding 'sir' in case his displeasure of being asked such a banal question echoed in his voice.

'Seen any action, have you, or had your hands full with other things?'

Lizzie angled the dog towards its owner. 'What can you be referring to?' she asked, jutting out her chin. This was something else LeJeune really liked about Lizzie. She wasn't afraid to speak up for herself. He smiled.

'Nothing,' said the man. 'You just want to be careful how you present yourself. That's all.'

'Well, if that's all,' said Lizzie, 'you'd best be on your way.'

The man tutted and whistled for his dog to follow him. Reluctantly, the dog obeyed.

'We need to be more careful,' LeJeune said.

'No. He wants to mind his bloody business. I'm not ashamed of being with you.'

'You sure?'

''Course I'm sure. I love you don't I, you big idiot?'

LeJeune's heart thundered in his chest. The word *love* had been seconds from leaving his lips since the day he'd left The Dockman's Arms, taking memories of his brief moment of intimacy with Lizzie with him. Her scent, her physicality and her desire for him. He hadn't been able to say a proper goodbye to her, tumbling out of the door as he went, supporting a drunken Eugene who had convinced people that he was a famous singer from Jamaica and that he'd cut records back home. The rowdy punters had nicknamed him Nat King Cole and bought him more drinks during the time LeJeune was out the back with Lizzie. He had tried to hold her hand to stop her from leaving so soon after they'd had sex. Her eyes, her hair, the way their kisses had melted into each other had stayed with him all through the night. He'd never had sex before and he hadn't rushed to tell Eugene about it. He'd kept it to himself, the smell of her shampoo, the heat and slide of her body. It was all he lived for. Being with her and making love to her had consumed him. It was a frightening feeling, that urgency within him to abandon everything just to go and sit in her presence, just to see her, just to hear her voice. What was it about this girl? He didn't know. All he knew was that he had wanted to say, 'I love you,' so many times before. He wanted to try to explain his feelings but was too afraid she'd laugh. She was not the sentimental type, Lizzie. She laughed loudly at dirty jokes, swore a lot, got drunk. Never once said it to him. I love you. Never until now.

'Well, don't just gawp at me like I've got two heads.' She chuckled. 'Kiss me or something. Tell me that you love me back.'

LeJeune sat up and leant towards her ear.

'I do. I love you.' He grinned like a child and had to catch himself, rein in some of the emotion that wanted to gush from him both in words and physically.

'Ever been in love before?' she asked him. Lizzie looked serious now, so unlike her.

'Never. Have you?'

'Once,' she whispered and pulled her body to face forwards, leaning her elbows onto her thighs and LeJeune followed suit. 'There was a boy I once knew. Seems like a while ago now. I haven't seen him in a year and a half. Maybe it's almost two.'

'Did he leave you?'

'You could say that. The war started and off he went. Signed up in an instant just because his dad said he should. Prove he was a man not a boy. I begged him not to go. I just had a feeling about it. This war is all wrong and so was him going. I was eighteen, he was nineteen.'

'He was young.'

'I know. Barely out of nappies when he started following a gang of wrong 'uns. The war was a convenient way for his dad to be shot of him. Said it would be the army or prison and only one of those would make a man of you. But before he left, he asked me to marry him.'

LeJeune sat back, bracing himself for when she confessed that she was a married woman.

'But Mum said no. Wait, she said, we had our whole life ahead of us and that there was no need to go rushing into marriage. My mum got married at nineteen and had four children she could barely feed and clothe, and my dad was hopeless. Was like she was all on her own, 'cept for me helping out with the little 'uns. Then up pops Micky and that was me. Love's young dream. But I promised Mum we wouldn't marry until after the war. Then the bloody war dragged on and Micky never came back.'

She sniffed and wiped her nose with a swipe of her hand. She shrugged her shoulders and sighed, turning to LeJeune with a sparkling smile. One of her brightest.

'But then you come along. And how could I resist that big smile and that lovely wavy hair. Proper handsome, I thought when I saw you, and then you were my hero. Saved me from a run-in with them mouthy Yanks.'

LeJeune smiled.

'I saved you? No,' he said. 'You saved me, more like. Since I was a boy, I grew up without a father and I had no one to teach me about life. My mother hardly spoke to me. But I was always searching for something. For what, I didn't know, and whether or not it even existed. I was mad keen to fight in this war.'

'Like Micky.'

'I suppose. But I dreamt of flying a fighter jet.' He chuckled. 'A silly little boy's dream. But I found myself here, and I found you and I don't want to go anywhere.'

'What about back to Dominica when we've won the war?'

'If you come with me.'

'I'd go with you. 'Course I would. If they'd have me. Looking like this.' She flapped at her hair. 'Maybe the sun will turn me black.'

'You just stay as you are. After the war, we could stay here if you prefer. I just want to be with you.'

They kissed each other softly and reclined into the bench, Lizzie's head against LeJeune's shoulder, his arm tightly placed around her so that her body was pressed in close to his. He rested his cheek on her head, closed his eyes and inhaled her. He would take that scent, the warmth of her body and all of the emotions that ran through him on his next tour of duty. He was to leave the next day. This time he would be away a long while; he wasn't sure how long, but he hoped the memories of that day on the park bench would feed him until they met again.

Chapter 9

London 1948

The streets around my cousin's flat have been intriguing but not exceptional. Myrtle has had two days off from the hospital, and she has taken me for mini tours of the area. One time we walked as far as Paddington Station where we stopped at a tea shop on Praed Street. I hadn't noticed the station until we sat down by a large window facing the street. I recognised the enormous building from where I'd emerged and remembered the hordes of people in the station, all oblivious to me. I had stared at them for ages, lost. Watching them walking around, carrying heavy holdalls, briefcases and leather handbags. Busily trying to navigate train times, buying tickets, dodging each other as they moved in and out of the station. I don't know how long I stood there, afraid to ask anyone for directions to the exit – the smartly dressed women, the men in dark suits. They were all filled with purpose and intention. They had an air of belonging to the place, the area, the very brickwork. I didn't have any of that. I watched them in envy because I wished I could look so purposeful, not so little and scared, trembling in a thin jacket and carrying a case that made my arm ache, filled with nothing but clothes lined with memories of home, longing in the creases and neat folds of my blouses and skirts. My shoes for church stuffed with hope that one day I would have a home here with my husband.

LeJeune's face and the memory of it as he stood at the altar is what I picture every time I think of him. It was the happiest day of my life, and it's been hard to feel anything close to happiness since he left. I miss home terribly, and the blue jacket Myrtle gave me does not help. The way it fits, the way it pinches under the arms. It's a constant reminder like a niggling voice in my head that tells me, *Essie, you won't find what you're looking for.* The jacket even has a smell. Myrtle says it's mothballs and she has sprayed it with the bottle of scent from her dressing table, but it still doesn't cover the memory of a person unknown and a life that I will never come to know. Whoever owned the jacket, I hope they are happier than I feel in this moment.

It's now late afternoon and we're walking around the little patch of green not far from Myrtle's. She says children play here, but there are none around as we walk through.

'I expect you will have children one day,' Myrtle says as we leave via a creaking gate whose black paint flakes and is mostly coated in rust.

'I'd like to. Though I've never really thought about it.' I hadn't thought much further than setting up a home with LeJeune in London. But now, as I think about the children we could have, I feel my lungs overfill. Air rushes out of my throat and makes me gasp.

'Are you all right, Essie?'

'Fine, just thinking about what it will be like to raise children here. Without Mama around to help me. And my sister, Ginnie, she'd be the perfect example for any child. She's so smart and brave.'

'I know it's not the same, Essie, I'm not your mother but I'll always be happy to help you.'

We turn into Myrtle's street, and I think I see someone going into the house. They can't be here for Myrtle, so presumably Mrs Rogers has visitors. I've heard nothing from her since she said she'd ask around about LeJeune. I've wanted to knock on her door to make sure she doesn't forget about me, but Myrtle said these things are bound to take time. Not everyone has a telephone, and word of mouth can be slow. Except when it's bad news. Bad news travels fast, my cousin says, and I've taken comfort in that. As long as I haven't heard anything negative, there is still hope.

Myrtle unlocks the front door, and the door leading up to Mrs Rogers' flat is ajar.

'Strange,' says Myrtle as she goes to close it.

'Myrtle?' Mrs Rogers calls from upstairs, and I hear the shuffle of her oversized slippers as she makes her way down. 'I was hoping to see you. Well, I wanted a word with your Essie, actually. Might have a bit of news.'

My chest raises to make space for the thump of my heart, and I can hardly breathe. Mrs Rogers doesn't look as if she's about to deliver bad news, so I turn to Myrtle and grin.

'Come up a second.' Mrs Rogers starts to mount the stairs. 'I've got a name and address for you.'

'I'll take this.' Myrtle helps me off with my jacket, and I trot quickly up the stairs behind Mrs Rogers.

The smell of cigarette smoke is strong and it makes me cough. Mrs Rogers has a lit cigarette propped on the side of the ashtray on the kitchen table, but I notice cigarette smoke is also coming from the living room. Perhaps Mr Rogers is still off sick and smoking with the visitor I noticed going in. I sit at the table because Mrs Rogers beckons for me to. With her cigarette now balancing on her lower lip, she roots around a kitchen drawer for something and the grin fixed on my face since she said she wanted a word with me is beginning to slip. I'm now feeling dread because this is taking too long.

'Ah,' she says at last. 'I put it out the way so I could cook. Didn't want to get gravy on it or something.' She unfolds a sheet of paper that looks as if it came out of the notebook I'd used to write LeJeune's details on. She spreads it out on the table in front of me and keeps trying to flatten it with her palms even though I'm desperate to see what's written on it. When she stops fussing, I see a name and an address. Not LeJeune's name but perhaps the place he is living. It's not a factory or place of work.

'I said I'd do some digging and this is what I come up with.'

I read her scribbles aloud. 'Eugene Price, 27 Harewood Road, Stepney E9.' I look at Mrs Rogers, now sitting opposite and happily puffing on her cigarette. 'Does he know Le-Jeune?'

'Claims to by all accounts. I had a word with an old neighbour, Dottie Bridges. She and I go a long way back. Known her since school, so I knew I could rely on her. Luckily she still lives in Stepney. Married a chap from Lancashire but didn't move up there. Not sure I'd want to move all the way up north, neither.'

I patiently wait for her to continue.

'Took a day or two to catch her in. She's working in a factory and does the odd shift. You got to do what you can to keep the food on the table. Rations are no joke. I'll be glad when this place starts feeling like normal again. Mind you, you'd think I'd be used to rations. We had them all through the bloody war. And I mean that literally. Poor old Dottie lost her boy. Poor cow.'

'And so she knows this man? Eugene Price?'

'In a roundabout way, I suppose you could say. She asked about lodgings where coloured chaps resided, especially working on the docks, and she came up with a name.'

'But who is he? A friend of LeJeune's?'

'That I couldn't tell you. But he fought in the war, same as your young man. Whether they were friends or not, I don't know, but he claims that he knows who you're looking for.'

'So if I go to this address, he'll be able to tell me something?'

'Well, let's blimmin' 'ope so.'

'Thank you, Mrs Rogers. I'll ask my cousin to give me directions.'

'Well, you want to be careful, love. I mean, I don't know this Eugene bloke from Adam. Don't know how genuine this lead actually is. And that's a home address. Meaning, he's at work during the day so you'd probably only find him there of an evening. The East End can be a bit murky, if you get my meaning, 'specially for a young girl on her own. Even if your cousin went with you, you'd need to be on your guard.'

I nod. 'I understand. Maybe I could go there in the day, put a note through the door and ask if he could write me.'

'If you like, but the place will probably be full of lodgers and who knows if he'd get a note. Best off asking Myrtle who she knows that could go with you.'

'I'll ask but it might be that I'll have to do this on my own.'

'Or I could go with you.'

I turn in shock to see a man standing at the door who isn't Mr Rogers. He's wearing a brown suit. He's tall and wiry and he rubs his chin as he eyes me. It's the man I met the evening I arrived at Paddington Station. The one who'd offered to walk with me to find Myrtle's flat. I'd been nervous of him then and I'm equally so now.

'I, I…' I can't form a sentence, and I don't know how to tell him I don't need his help without offending him.

'This great lug is my boy, Graham,' says Mrs Rogers. 'I told you about him. Works in the solicitors. Lives not more than ten minutes or so from here.' She looks up at her son. 'But I'm not sure your missus will take kindly to your escorting a young woman across London at night.'

Graham straightens up from leaning on the door frame. He pulls up another chair, sits and scoots the legs under the table, making them screech.

'Well, Bet should know she married a gentleman and that it's incumbent on me to make sure a poor single girl walking the London streets feels safe. Make sure no harm comes her way.'

'I'm very thankful,' I manage to say. 'But I don't want to trouble you or make life difficult.'

He laughs this away. 'Life is what you make it. If I want to help a damsel in distress, then Bet needs to understand that. And she will. Or perhaps I don't tell her. Will that make you feel more comfortable?'

Nothing about Mrs Rogers' son makes me feel comfortable, and travelling blind, as it were, with this man makes the back of my legs feel weak. But he is my neighbour's son and he is trying to be polite, I think.

'I'll ask Myrtle what she thinks and then …'

'Take it or leave it. Up to you,' says Graham. 'But I can take you tomorrow after work.' Graham lights one of his mother's cigarettes and remembers at the last minute to offer one to her. He then holds the packet in front of me.

'I don't smoke.'

'Didn't think so.' He sits back in his chair. I suppose he doesn't look so intimidating as he did in the dark a few nights ago. He'd sprung out from nowhere after I thought he'd walked off ahead of me. This doesn't make a good case for him. But he works in an office, after all. Wears a suit. And I know Myrtle is on nights from tomorrow for the next few days, so it will be at least a week before she can come with me.

Graham looks at me with raised eyebrows.

'Um, thank you,' I tell him. 'When is a good time for you and should I meet you at Paddington?'

'I'll come for you. Around six. After work. We should catch this Eugene fella at home having his tea.'

He scrapes the chair back and returns without another word to the living room.

'That settles that then, doesn't it?' says Mrs Rogers, standing herself.

I fiddle with the piece of paper with Eugene Price's address and wave it as a thank you at Mrs Rogers. Before I descend the stairs, Graham calls. 'Mind how you go.'

I walk back down with mixed emotions, my heart thundering in both excitement and anticipation. This Eugene will lead me straight to LeJeune's house, and I won't even have to come back to Paddington with Graham.

Chapter 10

Essie

London 1948

Moorhouse sits on his hind legs licking his paw and rubbing it over his eyes. Every now and then, he blinks at me and must wonder why on earth it is I keep walking from one side of the living room to the next. Each time I get to the window, I look through the nets for a shadow, a man in a brown suit approaching the flat, knocking on the door announcing that my saviour has arrived. I've been willing myself to see Graham as my saviour and not a threatening pair of footsteps hurrying behind me on a chilly autumn evening.

I turn to walk the gap between the coffee table and sofa again, this time towards the wall cabinet where Myrtle's small radio is sitting in the middle of a knitted doily as if it were a precious treasure. Maybe it is because, apart from Moorhouse, it must get very lonely for Myrtle on her own. A rap of knuckles like someone is in a mad panic to be let in sends a tingle over my skin. Moorhouse rushes through the gap in the living room door into the small passageway. The next knock sounds a bit more friendly. I pull the net curtain to one side and hold up a hand for Graham to see I'm coming. I look around for the blue jacket. I was wearing it earlier, but with all the pacing up and down, it made my armpits clammy.

As I wriggle into it, my handbag in one hand as well as my headscarf, I try to shoo the cat back inside so that I can lock up behind me. This takes longer than necessary. It's as if Moorhouse wants to be certain I can trust Graham, look him up and down with slanted green eyes, check that his intentions are innocent.

I hear Graham speak just as I open the main door. 'Changed your mind?'

'I'm sorry. The cat,' I say.

'What cat?'

'I couldn't get Myrtle's cat to stay indoors so that I could lock the door.'

'Ma's allergic.'

'I know.'

I follow him, hurriedly, up the road. Graham, taking large strides, is oblivious to my having to do up buttons and tie my headscarf under my chin. Once that's all done, I rush to his side and am out of breath by the time we reach the top of the road.

I'm disappointed that we're having to walk. I thought Graham at least had a car which was why I thought he'd offered to go with me in the first place. We stop not far from Paddington Station at a bus stop where there are four other people – a young couple and two middle-aged men. They keep staring from me to Graham then looking at each other with blank expressions. As emotionless as they appear, I can't help feeling that far more is being spoken beyond their vacant stares. Something about the wait for the bus feels unearthly, and no one says a word apart from Graham who asks if I have the address on me.

'Let's have a look,' he says.

I hand him the piece of paper, and he appears to read it over and over for several minutes as if he is trying to commit it to memory. I already have. I just brought it with me to be absolutely certain we went to the right place. A few more minutes pass, and a big red bus trundles up to the stop and hisses as it comes to a halt. The people ahead of us form an orderly line as they step onto the bus, finding seats and looking over their shoulders at Graham and then me getting onto the bus. The conductor screws his brow as Graham boards and rings the bell only a second after my first foot is on the platform when I follow behind. As the bus stutters to a start, I lose my balance. Graham is already making large strides to two empty seats and flops into the one by the window while I'm trying not to topple over. I feel a hand on my elbow.

'Easy, miss. Don't want you hurting yourself.' The conductor's grip is tight, and I manage to right my balance as I settle in next to Graham. He barely acknowledges me but makes a big fuss about paying for both of our tickets.

After a few stops, I turn to Graham who has been staring intently into the dimly lit evening. On the windows, a light mist of rain coats the glass.

'Is it far?' I ask him.

'I'd say. We need to change buses.'

'Another bus?'

'It's a way to East London, darling. You'll have to be patient. Just sit tight. I'll get you there.'

'If …' I begin. Graham swivels his head back to me as if I'm being annoying. 'If we find LeJeune, I could always stay there. You don't have to take me back and I'll find my way in the morning.'

'At the moment, we are still talking "if" so let's not jump the gun.'

'Okay. I won't.' I have to work out what that phrase means. *Jump the gun.* I've not heard of it before, but presumably he means that I should stop doing what I have been doing since Mrs Rogers gave me the address, dreaming of happy re-unions, reasonable explanations and everything working out for the best. But I can't help myself.

We haven't uttered a word to each other when Graham stands and gestures for me to do the same. I assume it is time to change buses. The bus stop is a lonely one. It's already past seven in the evening, and I suppose most people will be home having dinner with their families. But not me and not Graham.

'Did your wife mind at all that you are out tonight without her?'

'Well, bringing her clear across London isn't her idea of a romantic date. Besides, her mother was round tonight. So she didn't mind so much.' Graham pulls out his cigarette packet and waves it in front of me. I shake my head.

'Oh yes, I forgot.' He lights the cigarette, clicks the lighter closed and turns his back to me while looking in the direction of the anticipated bus.

The road is illuminated by streetlamps, their beams making little impact on the indigo hue of night. There are houses behind us, and everyone has their curtains shut, letting out slivers of light where the curtains don't meet. Across the road, the shops are all shut for the night and stand in shadow. I force my hands into my jacket pockets as far as they can go, but the pockets are shallow and my fingers are beginning to freeze. It's not even winter here, so I don't know how I'll cope when it arrives.

'So, are you a solicitor?' I ask Graham. I speak to his back in an attempt to break the silence and to stop myself from freezing to the spot.

'Not exactly, though I wouldn't mind.' He turns. 'The amount they make. I started off as a general clerk but I got promoted into the accounting office. Pay's all right and it's much less pressure than being an actual solicitor, I suppose.'

'Would you ever train to become one? I think that is a good profession.'

'Nothing wrong with what I do, I'll have you know. I'm the manager in my office, after the accountant of course, so I do have some responsibility.'

'I'm sure you do. You wear a suit and everything.'

He looks down at the same brown suit I first saw him in and the one he wore the day before to his mother's flat.

'Not exactly Saville Row, but it'll do.'

'It's a very nice suit.'

'Bus,' he says and holds out his arm. This time he lets me on ahead of him.

There are fewer people on this bus than the first, and Graham seems more keen to have a conversation.

'Shouldn't be long, now,' he says.

'Good.' I smile up at him.

'So, you're a married woman, then?'

'Yes.' I brighten. 'I got married and the next day my husband was on the boat to England.'

'So at least you have your wedding night to remember.' He grins but my cheeks feel hot. 'What?' he scoffs. 'You didn't even do that?' He chuckles and then stubs out the cigarette on the floor between us. Immediately, he takes out and lights another. He inhales from the cigarette on his every breath as if he needs it to survive.

I stare out of the window, trying to turn as much of my face from Graham as I can. He lets out a scratchy chuckle and then another.

'What is it?' I snap my head back to him.

'Well, being as you and he didn't actually … you know? I don't know if it counts as being married. Legally. I mean, he might not think you are and maybe he … you know?'

'What do I know?'

'Maybe he went off and married someone else. Someone, a bit more … amenable, like.'

'You don't know what you're talking about. And I don't think this is a good topic of conversation.'

'It's perfect. I was wondering, you see, how it comes to be that this geezer just doesn't write to you, doesn't follow through on the vows you made.'

'He is an honourable man. He fought in the war.'

'So did I. I got married in the middle of it and I still got to, you know, have a honeymoon as such.'

'Please, Graham. I really do appreciate you taking me all this way, but could we change the subject?'

He tuts and lessens my discomfort by saying nothing at all for the rest of the journey. We are the last passengers on the bus, and the conductor sits reading a tall newspaper, reaching up and ringing the bell after each stop. No one else gets on and I look out for signs that might say we're in or approaching Stepney.

'This is our stop, I think,' Graham says.

He thinks? I begin to wonder if he's brought me out on a wild goose chase and will leave me far from home as some kind of joke. He's already been entertained by discovering my private business, and I feel at a complete disadvantage. Not only do I have to admit that I would have no idea how to navigate East London without him, I'm embarrassed that he now knows something so intimate about me and I want to curl into a ball and weep.

I walk ahead of him as the bus pulls away and he calls me, pulling my arm to lead me across the road.

'This way. I think I can remember it. Haven't been around here in a while.'

I am on the verge of giving up hope when he looks up at the road name and sighs.

'Ah yes, this is the way.'

He slows his pace now so that we are shoulder to shoulder. He takes out another cigarette, and I am so fed up with his smoking and nasty comments I'd love to scream about it. But I have to be patient. For now. While I need him.

'I didn't mean to annoy you,' he says.

'You didn't,' I lie. But a necessary one so that my temper doesn't show. Our footsteps echo down a long road, and I want to know how much further we have to walk but I don't want to start a conversation with Graham if I can help it.

'Oh, I think I did,' he says with a smile in his voice.

'You did what?' I huff.

'I think I did annoy you.' He says nothing more for a few seconds. 'When I first saw you, I didn't think you were bad-looking. You know, for a coloured girl and all.'

I don't reply.

'I'm not racist or nothing. I've got a couple of Jamaican friends.'

I find this highly unlikely. I suspect what that means is he once spoke to a couple of Jamaicans for no longer than to tell them the time or give directions.

'It's true,' he says, interpreting my silence correctly. 'I have coloured friends. And I don't know what game this so-called husband of yours is playing, but I just wanted to say, like ...' He stops and turns to me, and I can feel the blue jacket tightening and constricting my chest. 'If this geezer of yours doesn't, you know, show himself, I would be happy to ...'

'To what?' I squint my eyes. They are already damp from anger.

'Well, London is a big lonely place for a person who doesn't know their way around. For a girl on her own, like.'

'What are you saying to me, Graham?'

'It's just, I like you sort of and I would step out with you. If you don't find your bloke and you need a bit of company.' He leans in close to say the word 'company' as if we should keep this between ourselves. I'd love nothing more than to swing my handbag around his face. That's how Ginnie would react.

'Graham, you're married,' I remind him.

'Yes ... *but* ... she'll turn a blind eye.'

A tear escapes onto my cheek and I attempt to walk away from him.

'Now, don't be like that.' He catches my arm as I'm about to turn the corner now that we've come to the end of the road. 'I know you're a good girl and we could be ... good ... for each other.'

'Is this the way we need to go?' I point as I stop to look down at his unwelcome grip. He waits several seconds before answering.

'Yes,' he mumbles, releasing me. 'That's right.'

A few doors down, there is a lot of chatter coming from a building, the light from its window caressing the paving stones. A sign swinging above it says *The Dockman's Arms*.

'I need the toilet,' says Graham and darts inside before I can protest.

As I wait for him to finish his business, two men stagger out of the door with large glasses of a black drink in their hand, supporting the other with their shoulders.

'Hello, Miss. You lost or looking for business?'

I shake my head, and one of them walks up to me, so close, the large paunch of his stomach is touching the handbag I hold in front of me like a shield. I can tell when a person has had one drink too many, and my feelings of anger diffuse into feelings of fear. I look past the men, through the window in the door, hoping to see Graham appear, the lesser of two evils in this case.

'I'm waiting on someone.' I should say nothing, really, but I hope they will lose interest and go back inside. *Where is Graham?*

'Could that someone be me.' The chubby one sings this as if it is a well-known song lyric, and the other man laughs.

'Or me. I've a few coins I don't mind sparing. If you know what I mean?'

'All right, gents.' Graham comes out of the pub, and I've never been so happy to see him. The door opens again, and a younger man puts his head out.

'Oi! You just bumped into me, mate.' He growls at Graham who becomes flushed and apologises profusely. Graham now looks like a little child in his father's suit. 'That's not enough.'

The young man marches out of the pub and up to Graham. He is shorter but stocky and wears only a thin, short-sleeved shirt under which large muscles bulge. Along the length of his arms are painted snakes and fire.

'You should offer to buy me another.'

Graham walks up to my side. 'I'm sorry I can't stop. I've an errand to run.'

The two men who came out earlier have stepped away to get a better view and burst into laughter. 'That's what they're calling it these days, are they?'

I'm confused, but the younger man with snakes and fire pasted to his skin glares at me, the whites of his eyes looking bloodshot and two roses bloom on each of his sunken cheekbones.

'We need to go.' Graham yanks me away by the elbow and walks so fast my feet are just skimming the ground and I almost lose grip of my bag. We cross the road and Graham looks back. 'Shit,' he says and breaks into a run, dragging me with him. 'They're after me.'

We turn another corner where there is a tall wooden fence running the length of a row of back gardens. A gap appears to break the fence, and Graham pushes me into a narrow alley.

'Stay put here. I'll try and lose them. Don't make a bloody sound and I'll come back.' He hisses, *Don't move*, into the air and he's gone.

I move further along the alley, following the shadows. The fence on either side of this alley is not as tall as the one along the street. I could be seen. I turn quickly when I hear footsteps, and in a blur I see two men run in the same direction as Graham and they are fast. Probably faster than him. I hear their breath, the pounding of their heels and then they are gone, too. I sink down to my haunches, remain small and out of sight. The two households on either side of the low fence are very much awake. There are lights behind the closed curtains, the occupants are in their kitchens, pots and pans are being packed away, water runs into kettles. All anyone would have to do is open a curtain to look at the night sky and they'd see me crouched down, my bottom practically on the ground, knees up to my chest. I've dropped my handbag; my legs are trembling so much I'll lose my balance.

When I can manage it, I take a deep breath and hope that the homeowners can't hear me or the clatter of my heart throwing itself at my ribcage. I can't hear anyone on the street now, no sprinting or chasing. I get up, inching my back against the fence, sure that I'm causing the fabric of my jacket to snag and fray. But I suppose that's the least of my problems. What if they've hurt Graham? Am I supposed to find him, tend to him, see us safely home? I don't feel capable but I must do something.

I can't understand how or why this chase broke out. It all seemed to happen so quickly. I'd heard the men talking as Graham led me away. I couldn't make out what was being said, but I think that some other men had come out of the pub. Maybe they were as angry as the man whose drink Graham had spilt and they'd formed a hasty and angry decision to pay him back. I'm sure it was only an accident, but if Graham had offered to buy the man a drink in the first place, none of this would have happened.

Because it's quiet, I tiptoe back to the street and take a peek around the fence. The street is empty in both directions. I'm half expecting the men from the pub to come back this way. Seeing me, they might become angry again because I was with Graham, and if they didn't catch him, they might seek revenge on me. I go back down the alley and stand at the spot where I'd been stooping, cowering away like a frightened animal. This is not the way I expected the evening to turn out. I should have already seen this Eugene person, found LeJeune and sent Graham back to his wife. Instead ... this. I look up to the sky. It's the colour of ink and swirls like dark smoke above the alley.

'What the hell you doing down there?'

I jump when I hear the voice. A back door is open, the indoor light showing the silhouette of a person in the doorway. It's a woman's voice but I can't tell anything else about her. There is movement at her side, and a large dog yelps and races towards me. I'm frozen to the spot as it jumps and barks, sounding more and more furious that it can't get to me because of the garden hedges. With a running jump, the dog could clear the hedge, leap at me and pin me to the fence. The woman calls the dog and grabs him by the collar as she peers at me in the dim light.

'You lost or something?' she asks.

'In a way.'

'In a way? What way's that then?'

'In that I don't know where I am and the person who was with me had to run.'

'Are you in some kind of trouble?'

'Oh no.' I lean off the fence and offer my hands in prayer. 'I'm not in trouble, but my friend, he might be. Some men ...' I point back to the street. 'They chased him and he told me to wait here while he tried to lose them.'

The dog has lost interest in me and stops snarling. The woman lets go of the collar so the dog can sniff its way around the garden.

'And what was you and this friend of yours doing to cause people to chase you?'

I shrug my shoulders and feel tears threatening to shed. 'I don't know how this happened. My friend, well, he was helping me find an address around here and he stopped in the pub around the corner, spilt a drink and they got annoyed and chased him.'

'Did he look like you?' she asks and rubs the skin on the back of her hand.

'No. Like you.'

'Lucky, else he'd probably end up in St Mary's.'

I cross my brow.

'The hospital?' She tuts. 'You want to come in and wait?'

I look at the dog who has regained his interest in me.

'Don't mind Buster. Gentle as a baby.'

'My friend said not to move.'

We both turn when the dog barks at a figure making its way along the alley towards us.

'This him? Your friend?'

Graham's nose is bloody and his tie is missing. He blinks and rubs his head.

'What happened?' I ask, shocked not only at his appearance but that he actually came back for me.

'Let's go,' says Graham. 'And fast.'

'Are you sure it's safe?' I ask. The woman draws nearer, squints at Graham and folds her arms.

'You want a wet flannel on that face,' she says to Graham. 'Want to come in? Wait until the coast is clear?'

'No. You're all right,' he says. 'Best we go.'

The woman and I both protest because now that I see him up close, his face looks a lot worse than I thought and he's rubbing his head again.

'A glass of water, perhaps,' says Graham, and we follow the length of the garden hedge where the woman lets us in at the gate by the house.

The kitchen is warm. It smells of tea leaves and meat. It's cluttered and messy, but at least Graham can sit and so can I, welcoming the warmth and being off the street. The woman comes back to the kitchen with a white cloth which she runs under the tap and wipes it over Graham's face from forehead to chin, stopping to soak up blood from his nose. He winces while she repeats this process at least three more times until most of the blood is washed away, though there are still tiny dots of red sprouting from the cut by his eye. Graham's face will be blue with bruises by the morning, if not before.

No one has uttered a word. Even the dog has sloped into a corner where he lies and watches with doleful eyes. The kindly old lady drops the bloody cloth into the kitchen sink and wets a tea towel which she dabs on everything that is bruised or speckled red on Graham's face and hands. He seethes as the cloth makes contact with the open skin. He jerks his head away suddenly and holds up his hands.

'I think I'll be all right now.' He looks at me. 'We'd better go.'

'To find Eugene?' I ask.

'No. Home. It's getting late so there's no time for that.' He stands and towers over the woman who looks up at him and back to me.

'Eugene?' she asks me.

'Yes. He lives in Harewood Road.'

'This is Harewood Road,' she says. 'Only, you were at the back, Stonely Road you came from, back there. You'd only to turn the corner to find it.'

'You know Eugene?' I say eagerly, shifting my glance to Graham and hoping he won't insist we leave quite yet.

'Two doors down, that fella lives. Boards at my neighbour's house. Cheeky chap if you ask me. Always a wink and smile. Cheeky so-and-so.' She chuckles and I look at Graham.

'We're here so we might as well knock the door.' I want to smile, but Graham looks so sorry for himself I don't want to show how excited I am.

'Your neighbour won't mind us knocking this time of night?' Graham asks our host, who so far hasn't introduced herself but happily gave away Eugene's whereabouts without even knowing who we are.

'Well, you're here now. You might as well try.'

I can't thank this woman enough, and I go to shake her hand when she sees us to the door. She looks down at my palm and back at me and smiles. Then she shakes my hand in a limp motion and closes the front door.

Outside number 27 Harewood Road, I pause and stare at Graham. He knocks with intention, and I'm worried he might alarm the inhabitants. No one responds, so I tap more gently on the glass part of the door. A light goes on in the hallway, but the person behind the door does not open it or pull back the curtain covering the square window.

'Who's that?' A woman, sounding much like the Samaritan from two doors down, grunts.

'I'm so sorry to bother you at this time,' I say, 'but I think this is the address for Eugene Price and I'm looking for him.'

'How many of you out there?'

'Just me and a friend who helped me find the way.'

'Who are you and how do you know Eugene Price?'

I step closer to the door. 'I don't know him exactly but he knows someone I know. I hoped he could help me find ... this someone.' This is all too complicated to explain through a door, a pane of glass and a curtain. She unbolts the door and opens it by a fragment. Her straight nose arrives at the crack she's made, and she blinks through the thick lenses of her glasses.

'He lodges here,' she says. 'I lock my doors at nine at night, any lodgers not home by then know not to bother because I put the bolt on. I'm not having them traipsing in and out at all hours.'

'Of course not,' I say. 'But it isn't quite nine yet.'

She blinks at me again and purses her lips.

'So is he home?'

The door opens slightly wider, and I can see her pale yellow dressing gown and the pale pink of her crinkly arms as she crosses them over her middle.

'He ain't.' I look at Graham because I don't know if 'ain't' means yes or no.

'He's not here, Essie,' Graham confirms. 'We've come all this way for nothing.'

'Do you expect him tomorrow?' I turn back to the woman. She looks as though she's sorry for me.

'Got you in trouble, has he?' she asks.

'No,' I say hurriedly when I understand what she means by that. 'We haven't met, but I believe he knows my husband and I need to talk to him. So, if it's all right with you, I'll come back tomorrow? See if he's home?'

'Fair enough,' she says and steps back. She pushes the door closed in my face as I thank her. The clunk of the bolt stamps the end of her willingness to help.

'I'm so sorry I made you come all this way,' I say as Graham and I walk away. He's very quiet now, not moving with any of the confidence he had and says nothing until we leave Harewood Road.

'I've a good mind to get a taxi back to Paddington,' he mumbles. 'Not sure I fancy that same journey back.' He rubs his head and checks his hand.

'I'll pay,' I say.

'Save your money. I'll pay. Like I have with this.' He points at his face, and I see the bruises blooming and his eye sinking into the swelling skin.

'I'm so sorry, Graham. Thank you for protecting me from them, but maybe you could have bought him that drink.'

He stops dead. I can tell it hurts for him to do so, but he leans in close, eyes level with mine.

'Don't be silly, Essie. This isn't over a spilt drink.' He flings a hand in anger. 'It's because I was with you. They thought we were walking out. Or worse, married.'

'What do you mean?' I back away.

'Christ's sake, Essie, are you really that wet behind the ears? Black and white aren't supposed to mix. They had it in for me the moment they spotted you.' He nods the 'you' into my face.

'I didn't know. I know Mama warned me about the prejudice but I wasn't …'

'Believe your mum. It exists. And you better wake up to it, Essie. I know I have. Come on.'

The taxi driver hesitates before allowing us to 'hop in' and off we go, Graham's pride and body bruised and me empty-handed.

I am thankful to Graham for what he has done tonight. So much so, he snaps at me because of the number of times I try to express gratitude. The taxi driver keeps eyeing us from his mirror while I look out of one window and Graham the other. We complete the journey to Myrtle's flat in silence. Graham sits in the taxi, making sure that I get inside safely before it pulls away. I have no idea how he will explain his appearance to his wife, and I hope his mother won't blame me.

Standing in the downstairs passageway, I realise now that I am that naive. I am that gullible that I think being over here and finding LeJeune will be so easy. Nothing comes easily in this life. My dream of rejoining LeJeune slips between my fingers like flour for baking, and I grip my fist to hold onto the last of it. For everything that has happened tonight, for what happened to Graham, I must find LeJeune. This voyage across an immense sea has got to be for something. It has got to be.

Chapter 11

London

1944

LeJeune had had to have stitches at the back of his head, the hair around the wound shaved off and a bandage, always starting off clean and white, bloody and sweaty by the time the nurse came by to check on him. She couldn't come regularly enough, so the sheet covering the metal bed he lay on was always rose red. So much blood, he'd marvelled, and yet he was still alive. He wondered if the nurse had stitched the wound up properly, hadn't missed the gap that was oozing blood. He'd gone to touch it, and the pain was more acute than the blast that knocked him flying for several feet and sent him into a hilly mound. A body was strewn across it, the soldier's face upside down from where he lay, eyes open, but he was dead all right. LeJeune had lost consciousness and remembered blurry images of being carried, a bumpy ride and a place smelling of disinfectant where a buxom woman in a white apron told him he was lucky to still be alive. He barely remembered his name when he was asked. Calling himself by his Christian name, seeing faces crinkle with confusion and then uttering his army name, rank and serial number before passing out again for a day, perhaps longer.

He thought he'd dreamt her, but he could swear that Lizzie had come to visit him, stroking his cheek and saying, 'You'd better bloody wake up. You said you wanted to be with me.'

Days after lying in the hospital bed, he was told by a nurse with a strong French accent that he was being returned home. The commanding officer confirmed this, telling Private Francis that he would take up ground duty in London where he'd be of more use. He'd work alongside the Air Raid Precautions Services. He was still unsteady on his feet, and answering a question took him several seconds to compose in his brain before he could respond.

He'd only prayed that it was Stepney he'd be sent to and breathed a sigh of relief when he entered the familiar barracks close to the docks. There was no sign of Eugene. No one had had word of him, though he'd asked after him several times while in the hospital, having to describe him to the nurses because the name Eugene hadn't come easily to his memory. He asked that if anyone saw Eugene Price that they told him John Francis had returned to London. He had been missing Eugene's banter and chatter and hoped that nothing terrible had happened to his friend.

Standing in the deserted dormitory looking at two empty rows of bunks, he could have done with a friend to exchange stories with. His memory had fully returned, and he'd been reliving the blasts, explosions, noise and chaos of the battlefields. He hoped he could talk to Lizzie soon. Not about those things. Not the bad things but of the dreams that interspersed the dark realities, dreams of one day him and Lizzie settling down and getting married. He'd stay in London if she wanted. He'd go anywhere, really. Just as long as she was there.

When he finally saw Lizzie, he fell into her arms like a child, his face nestled into her hair right there in the middle of The Dockman's Arms. They had never openly flaunted their relationship, releasing the other's hand if someone passed them on the street, stealing kisses in the back row of The Regal, hiding away in Lizzie's flat if they didn't want to be looked at with scorn. As they hugged each other for several seconds, the rowdy chatter in the pub died down, the whole place falling silent the instant the young couple shared a passionate kiss among the occupied tables.

'Nice to see you home, Johnny.' Lizzie's roommate, Lorna, was drinking at the pub with friends. 'This man has been risking his life for us for two years. Show some gratitude you miserable lot.' Lorna had been one of the people that had warned LeJeune that he was playing with fire being with Lizzie. She'd warmed to him all the same.

Lizzie took LeJeune by the hand and led him to the bar before going to resume her place behind it.

'This one's on me,' said an elderly gentleman. Dwarfed in a heavy overcoat, he patted LeJeune on the shoulder. 'You're doing a good job, son. I salute you.'

The couple left the pub before Lizzie's shift was over, Le-Jeune's arm around her waist. The crowd had petered out — there was only so far the pennies would go for pints these days. Lizzie had spent most of the evening leaning over the bar, holding LeJeune's hand and telling him all the things he'd missed. How she'd gone to The Regal ten times to see *Gone With The Wind* because she couldn't help thinking how dashing Johnny was compared to Clark Gable.

'They've taken it off now. Put up some Fred Astaire film instead. Maybe we could go.'

'Maybe,' he'd said.

They didn't mind the light rain on the short walk to Lizzie's flat. They giggled along the way, quickening their pace the closer they got to her front door. They kissed on the front step and all the way up the stairs to the chilly flat that smelt of tea leaves and perfume. They undressed with urgency as quickly as the rain splattered the window, their bodies and bedclothes in a tangle. As the night drew in and with the table lamp extinguished, they allowed exhaustion to lull them into sleep until the early hours of the morning.

LeJeune's sleepy mind dwelt on the warmth of Lizzie's body against his chest, but a noise outside the flat put him on high alert. Were they under attack? Lizzie yawned and looked up at him.

'Morning.'

They both stared quizzically at the bedroom door when the bold sound from outside persisted.

'Lorna told me she'd be staying at her mum's tonight. Said she thought we'd want privacy. Wonder what changed her mind?' Lizzie sat up. 'Should I let her in? Sounds like she's misplaced her key.'

'I'll get dressed.'

'No, you just stay there. I'll let her in and I'll get a brew on. No idea why she's here at this hour.'

Lizzie slipped on a dressing gown, ruffled her hair into order and left the bedroom door ajar as she went to let Lorna in.

LeJeune could hear nothing for a few seconds after the door unlocked. Lorna was as chatty as Lizzie, and LeJeune expected to hear her apologise for coming home after all. Then he heard Lizzie's voice.

'*Micky.*'

'That's right, love. Don't worry, you're not looking at a ghost. It is really me.'

'But how? When? I ...'

'Is that it? Don't I even get a hello?'

LeJeune leant up on his elbow. A man was at the door – Micky, Lizzie's boyfriend who she hadn't seen in years. LeJeune froze. But should he get out of bed and go and see this Micky person for himself? Or maybe he should remain silent, and then Lizzie might get rid of him, tell him to come back later. But he didn't want Micky to come back later. He didn't want him anywhere near Lizzie. He could tell they were hugging and he sat up.

'I went round your mum's first, but she said you were probably working at The Dockman's and that you'd moved out of her place. I went over the pub and saw your mate, Lorna.'

'She told you where to find me?'

'Not easy getting much out of her. She'd had a few.'

'Smells like you have, too.'

He snorted a laugh. *'There was a bit of a lock-in. People celebrating my return. Who was I to refuse a pint or two?'*

'Or the whole barrel.'

'Sorry love.'

Love? LeJeune reached for his shirt on the chair by the bed but brought the chair down with it.

'Who's here?'

He heard footsteps before he could get off the bed fully, his arm suspended in mid-air, holding the shirt, one foot on the floor. He pulled a blanket around his middle and stood up. Micky put the light on.

'What the ...?'

LeJeune shot a look at Lizzie who, for the first time of knowing her, was speechless. Micky turned his eyes slowly from LeJeune and towards Lizzie.

'Well?'

She put her hands on his chest. LeJeune saw Micky flinch and Lizzie wring her hands together.

'You have to understand, Mick. Look at how long it's been since I seen you. Everyone thought you were dead. Nothing. We heard nothing. Not your mum or dad. No one knew where you were. If you knew the number of trips I made up to that army office. Asking after you, time and time again. Presumed dead, that's what they said. Your section took a load of fire, they said. They found the bodies but couldn't account for them all. But they told me and they told your mum that there was no way anyone could have survived. There'd been a fire.'

'It's one thing Mum thought she was seeing a ghost when I walked in, but I thought you would at least have …' Here, he turned his focus on LeJeune. 'Do you mind telling me who the hell you think you are?'

'I …?'

Lizzie turned Micky to face her, held his unshaven cheeks within her hands and LeJeune thought his heart would break in that second.

'If you knew how we cried for you, Micky. Me and your family. In the end we mourned you. Accepted you were gone for good. That you really had died. Did you think, after all this time, that I would just be sitting there when everything and everyone was moving on? I drove my parents insane over you. How my heart broke. I was murder to live with, and that's why Lorna and I got this place. She married a man who signed up, died the month later.'

'So you two were playing merry widow behind my back?'

'It weren't like that. You know I'm not like that. Johnny here is the first and only man I've been with since you.'

'Johnny, is it?' blasted Micky. 'Well, Johnny, put your uniform back on and get the hell out of here.' He brushed past Lizzie to return to the living room. She tried to pull him back but he shrugged her off. She turned to LeJeune now.

'Johnny, I'm sorry.' Her voice was a whisper. 'But it's probably for the best that you go. I need to have words with Mick.'

'And tell him you're with me now?' LeJeune didn't feel the need to lower his voice. Lizzie softly closed the bedroom door.

'It's not that simple though, is it? It was him. It was supposed to be me and him. He was the one I gave my heart to.'

'And what about me? Was it all made up when you said you love me? Lizzie, you said it more than once. Tonight ...'

'Tonight wouldn't have happened if he'd come back earlier.'

'But he didn't and I'm here. It's me and you now. He's the one who should go.'

'It's not so easy. If I have to let him down–'

'*If?*'

'Johnny.' She took several large paces to his side of the bed. 'You have no idea what this is like for me. If you love me, if you really do, then give me a little time to sort this mess out.'

'It's not a mess. It's simple. I love you. You love me. Everything was fine and now it isn't. So there is only one thing for it. He has to go.' He jutted his chin towards the door. 'I should stay and tell him with you.'

Lizzie picked up LeJeune's trousers which had been tossed onto the floor. He looked at them in her delicate hand that gently trembled. He had never known her to act so defeated and to seem so unsure. Hadn't she been sure about her love for him? If so, why tell him she loved him and then take it away so easily? Micky had been there but minutes and she'd allowed this stranger to turn his whole world upside down. He grabbed his trousers, dressing hurriedly while she stood with folded arms, rubbing the side of her head from time to time.

'I'm sorry. Try to understand,' she kept saying, but his anger had flattened his words far down into his throat.

Lizzie allowed tears to slip down her cheek. Were the tears for him or for Micky? How could he be sure of anything? She certainly wasn't. If he left now, wouldn't it be inevitable that Lizzie would choose Micky over him?

'Please, Liz,' he said when he was fully dressed. He stroked her arms and found her body was still shaking. 'Don't make a rash decision. Send word for when I can see you again. I don't know when I'm next on leave. This can't be the last I see of you.'

'I never said that. I just said I needed time. I owe it to him to talk to him.'

'Because he was first?'

'Because I need to understand what happened. What went on all this time.'

'And then …?' He turned his eyes to the unmade bed.

'What do you take me for, Johnny? Can't you see how much this is hurting?'

'Of course. Yes. I'm sorry.'

'No, I'm the one who's sorry. What a holy mess. Just, please, let me send word to you. I'll see you as soon as I can.'

He stopped and touched her cheek, wanting desperately to kiss her, take her back to bed and wake hours later from this nightmare. She touched her hand to his, taking it and leading him to the bedroom door. She opened it and went to say something but decided instead to release his hand and put hers into her dressing gown pockets.

'Finally,' Micky said when he saw them emerge. 'See you around, fella.'

LeJeune said nothing and left the flat swiftly without a look back or closing the door behind him. He heard it click as he descended the stairs and looked up through the spindles of the bannister before shaking his head and leaving the house.

Chapter 12

London 1948

Myrtle is fast asleep when I wake. The kitchen is as chilly as usual, and Moorhouse circles my legs, back arching and his thick tail sweeping my skin as if he is trying to capture me there in the cold and uncertainty. The coffee in my cup has grown cold when I dip my head to sip from it, my eyes still on the moody day presenting itself at the naked window. Myrtle must have forgotten to close the bright orange curtain that usually separates us from a grey morning. Behind the orange, I can pretend there are the colours of home. The familiar shapes and sounds. The boys calling for Ginnie from the gate, Mama asking them if they ever sleep or stay there at her gate until Ginnie wakes. I would be making coffee, strong and black, if I were back there, the way Daddy likes it and the way it livens him up before a hard day working up the road, tending the animals and crops.

Everything was simple then. I was just an ordinary girl with no particular plans or dreams who sat by a river one day with her friends and spotted the tall and handsome man with pale eyes and skin that looked white, only just kissed by the sun. Light skin, light eyes were selling points in a place where the fairer your skin, the more beautiful you were perceived. But I didn't believe this to be true: even if he'd been as dark as the rich earth, I would have loved him.

We'd walked down to the river, my friends and I, after church. We did that once in a while. The sermons were so long and our throats would hurt from singing, but that didn't stop us chattering away endlessly as we caught up with our lives. LeJeune arrived by the river with a man called Samuel who used to do jobs around the village but left to go to war, and when he came back, there was no work for him. I hadn't remembered seeing LeJeune before that day; I'd no idea he'd been a soldier, either.

'Him,' Mirabelle had said, pointing out LeJeune with her bottom lip. 'He used to live in Scott's Head before moving here with his mother. He was fighting in the army like Samuel.'

'So handsome,' said Eloise.

'Who, Samuel?' Someone else had giggled. We all knew Samuel, he was overweight and had breasts like a woman. He was always shabbily dressed and not the type those girls would have even looked at.

When my friends laughed, LeJeune looked over. I swear I could see the river and trees reflecting in his bright eyes as if they were a mirror. He looked at me a long time. Or at least I thought he did, and I remember how hot my neck felt and the warmth in every pit of my body. I looked out for him in church the next Sunday but he wasn't there. I looked for him the following Sunday and the one after that, but he still didn't appear. It was as if I'd dreamt him because he never returned. Weeks later, though, I was still thinking about him, the image of him, summoning a fantasy of what it would be like to talk to him. Long after my girlfriends' chatter turned to other stories and gossip, his face never left me. Not once.

When I bumped into him at market that day, he had been on my mind, then, too. It was as if I'd conjured him up.

My basket, which I was carrying in front of me, jammed into his side, and he spun around. He wasn't smiling; he looked a bit annoyed at first, and I began to apologise for all I was worth. I'd been carrying the fresh bread I'd bought from Mrs Mayor, and the dusting of flour had coated the side of his shirt. I tried to brush it off but it wasn't working. He'd held my hand to stop me, and a wave like lightning transferred itself from his hand to mine.

'It's fine,' he'd said. 'No harm ...' He didn't finish the sentence but began another. Well, a question, really. 'I think we've met, haven't we?'

'Not exactly.' I remember my voice was small and I cleared my throat to see if that would help but I continued to stutter and sound like a young school girl. 'The church, the river, I was with my friends. You were with Samuel. Do you know him?' Such a ridiculous question, but LeJeune hadn't minded at all. No, he stopped to talk to me. I had no idea why he was even in the market until a little while later, after we'd talked about almost everything two strangers could find to talk about.

'I'd really like to see you again,' he'd said. His smile was full and came from his heart. It had touched mine.

'Where you been all this time?' An older woman was at his side, eyeing me up and down as the culprit who had kept this beautiful man from her. Surely not a wife. She was too old.

'Mother,' he'd said, taking the large string shopping bag from her. It was full of ground provisions and looked heavy. Then I spotted her eyes, the same colour as LeJeune's, though I didn't know his name at that moment. 'I'm sorry, I got talking to …' Then he'd paused because he didn't know my name, either.

'I'm Essie. Esperanza,' I'd said. 'It means "hope" in Spanish.' I bobbed a sort of curtsy to his mother, which seemed to amuse him.

'And I'm LeJeune Francis. The one whose shirt you probably ruined.'

We'd both laughed, but Mrs Francis hadn't looked too pleased.

'Let's go,' she'd said in patois and hurried away without saying goodbye.

'Mother can be shy,' he'd said before leaving. 'Esperanza, if I asked to meet you here next market day, would you come?'

I'd nodded the way Ginnie did when asked if she'd like soursop. She'd loved it since she was a baby and Mama used to bribe her with it.

'That would be nice.'

'We can meet at midday. If you don't mind?'

'I don't mind at all. I will be here.'

'Good,' he'd said. 'Excuse me. I should catch her up before she gets angry.'

To me, his mother had looked angry enough. Especially with me by the way she cut her eyes at me.

I'd watched LeJeune's broad neck, the short cut of his hair and his wide shoulders as he'd hurried to catch up with Mrs Francis.

I'd smiled then but I can't find that smile now. I just shiver in the icy kitchen before pouring the rest of the coffee down the sink and relighting the kettle so that I can try again.

I sit on the sofa sipping from my cup, Moorhouse asleep in a fluffy, purring ball beside me, and I contemplate the day and the evening to come when I can return to the East End on my own and try to find Eugene Price.

*

I leave before Myrtle goes off for her night shift. She does up the top button of my blue jacket and lightly kisses my cheek.

'You have your keys and enough money?' she asks. I answer yes for the third time now. 'And you sure you don't want me to come with you?'

'It's still early so at least I can see where I'm going.'

'But will you remember the way to go and come back?'

'I'm sure I will.'

I'm not sure, not really. I have a vague idea but that's all. That and hope. I close the main door of the house, undo the top button of my jacket and walk swiftly up the road. I think I remember the number of the first bus I need to catch, after that I'll have to search my memory of last night's journey. I didn't pay close enough attention to where Graham had led me. And he had been leading me, like a little puppy who needed to learn how to cope, how to manage on the road and not be afraid. I kick myself for not being more alert, and I know this is something I'm going to have to master if this search for LeJeune around London is going to be any more complicated. I straighten my shoulders and try to look as if I know what I'm doing, as if I have a destination and someone is expecting me there. God knows what I will do if I get to his lodgings and Eugene Price has decided to stay out for a second night in a row.

Close to Harewood Road, I cross to the opposite side to the pub from last night, remembering all too late that Graham could have avoided this road altogether because we were actually at the back of Harewood Road. The Dockman's Arms seems busy even at this earlier hour. I can see the shapes of people through the frosted glass and hear the animation from behind it, wondering if the men from last night might, for some remote reason, decide to step outside. I turn my head away and make a convoluted circle of the street so that I won't be approaching the lodgings via the back alleyway.

At last, I arrive and knock timidly on the door. The landlady answers pretty promptly, looks me up and down and disappears again, leaving the door ajar. She stands at the foot of the stairs and calls Eugene in a shrill voice. There is music coming from upstairs, a voice from a record singing in the same screechy pitch of the landlady. She jams her feet into each step and is halfway up the staircase when the music becomes louder and a male voice shouts, 'You say something?'

'You wouldn't know for all the racket you're making. And it's gone six. You need to turn that thing off.'

'Yes Iris. Right away.'

'And don't get cheeky. There's someone here for you.'

'Not the police, I hope.' He laughs in a full and hearty way, but Iris stays silent until he stops.

'You'd better come down sharpish because it's a girl on her own.'

His feet thunder down the stairs. Eugene is a tall and rangy man who is wearing socks and black slacks. He stands in front of me, having pulled the door wide open. His brilliant white vest is tucked neatly into the wide-legged slacks. Iris hovers in the hallway and tries to take another look at me by weaving her head around the large outline of her lodger.

'And you are?' His smile cracks his face which was at first quizzical but now looks thoroughly amused. In fact it's more than that. His face tells me that I have arrived here just for his entertainment. I swallow.

'My name is Essie. Esperanza, actually.'

He looks down at the buttons on my jacket, his eyes halting somewhere around the ones near my navel.

'Have we met?'

'No, but you've met my husband, I believe.'

'Oh-oh. What is it? What did I do?' He begins to laugh again. Iris tuts and goes into a room off the corridor.

I pull my lips into a line and wait for Eugene to stop shrugging his shoulders. He smells a little of rum and a lot of cologne. He has no fat on his body just lean muscle, his biceps, large and shiny with long veins along them. I can see thick black hairs under his arms as he rubs a hand up over his forehead and back along his closely cropped hair. It's jet black with smooth waves running through it. He would be considered good-looking back home, I suppose, but right now, he's stretching my patience and I can't bring myself to look at him.

'Sorry, just my little joke. Would you like to come in?'

'No you don't.' I hear Iris from the room along the way. She pokes her head out. 'You know the rules.'

'Iris, please make an exception. I'll leave my door open. You can't expect me to let this poor young girl stand in the street like this.' He turns to me. 'Where you come here from?'

'Paddington.'

He turns to Iris, shoulders raised. He must be pleading silently with her because she tuts again, relents and waves me in. I'm not sure I even want to come in, but I still haven't questioned this man.

'And keep your door open and keep it short,' says Iris as I follow Eugene up the stairs.

'Yes, my lady,' Eugene says. He turns back to me and winks. On the landing, I wince from the sheer volume of his music which further amuses him as he starts to do a dance. He raises his left arm and puts the right across his stomach and steps back and forth in place, hips swaying. I'm already regretting following him up here. I'm frustrated with myself for not standing my ground, stating what I'd come for and not allowing him and Iris to dictate that I be let in. When will I learn?

'Come, come, come, come, come,' Eugene says as if he's the ticket master of a grand show which is, apparently, about to take place in his room.

'Eugene, we could just stand here on the landing,' I say above the music. 'It will make your landlady feel better. I really just want to know when you last saw my husband.'

'And this mysterious husband you're talking about, does he have a name?' His Jamaican accent is heavily laden with large helpings of working-class Londoners and a small dose of the King of England. I grind my teeth together but manage to smile.

'Of course. I didn't get time to say. But his name is Le-Jeune Francis.'

Eugene stops dead in his tracks. He swallows and holds the rail of the bannister.

'You do know him.' I open my eyes wide. Relief floods my body.

Eugene jerks his head towards his room and enters it. I step gingerly to the threshold. Mercifully, he takes the needle off the record.

'Pull the door,' he says urgently.

'But I thought ...'

He stomps over and does it himself, brushing my shoulder so that I'm now inside the room, and he closes the door, tight.

'So it's you. *You're* the one who was asking after him. And you're the one he was talking about.' He is inches from me, looking down at the tips of my flat shoes and slowly up to the place where my hair shows out of the front of my headscarf. Tightening my fingers around my handbag, I briefly look back to the door.

'He talked about me?' I ask.

'Only every two minutes.'

'Do you know him from the docks? Are you doing building work with him?'

'I've been working on the docks for over a year now. But he never came, not once. Though he was supposed to.'

'I don't understand. He told me his job was in a factory.'

'Maybe that's why he came, but when he got there, they told him there was no job, so that's when I fixed him up with one on the docks.'

I'm thankful for this, but I still don't understand how Eugene came to be his saviour and I also wonder why LeJeune didn't tell me any of this in his letter.

'Well, I'm here because you know him and he has only written to me once since he left for England.'

Eugene raises his eyes, scratches his head and puffs air into my face.

'Well, I don't know what to tell you.'

'Something,' I say. 'At least.' I begin to shake, fearing the worst for the first time. My mind has not let me go to a place in which LeJeune has been in any kind of trouble or danger. I've been telling myself that whatever the reason he isn't writing is not because anything terrible has happened, it's because he can't. Like illness, memory loss, embarrassment or anything. I just didn't want it to be something unbearable. If he'd found someone else – as my friends back home had forever hinted at – changed his mind about me, I could learn to live with that. I'm here because I want to know. I'm not here to find out that he has completely disappeared without a trace. I need that trace, no matter where it leads me. There has to be more that Eugene can say.

He goes and sits on the edge of the bed, and I hear a creak on the landing.

'So, what happened when you last spoke to him?' I implore. 'What exactly did he say and where exactly is he now?' I pace across the small room. There is no carpet, just a round rug that appears as a large semi-circle from under the bed. Opposite the bed is the low table with the record player on it and at least ten records on the floor beneath, balanced against the leg of the table. It's a narrow room with a narrow window opposite the door, a chest of drawers sits under it and a high-backed chair is wedged in the corner by the window. It looks and smells clean, but I have no intention of making myself comfortable when Eugene pats the bed beside him.

'Look.' He sighs, not looking at me directly anymore. 'The last time I saw John, we were having a drink in The Dockman's Arms.'

'Who is John?'

'I mean LeJeune. He goes by John or Johnny here. Has done since the war.'

'You knew him back then?'

'Same regiment. John is easier for the English to get their tongue around. Good man, your John. He went back to … where was it? Dominica, right?'

'Yes.'

'I was sorry to see him go. I stayed here when the war ended. Been working you see?'

'I see. Well, he was longing to come back and he had this job all arranged and a place to live. Did you ever go by his place?'

Eugene shakes his head. 'I saw him by chance. We lost touch even before he went back home. I didn't even know he came back to London. I noticed that there were suddenly a bunch of Just Comes arriving from the West Indies and such. Johnny came over with them, it seems.'

'You mean the people coming to England for the first time?'

'That's it. Just Comes, I call them. The government have a kind of mission or something. Temporary housing for the West Indians coming over to work. It's only temporary mind, a couple weeks, and that's where Johnny was, but he would have had to find some place else to live after that and that could be anywhere.'

My shoulders drop and my stomach feels as if I'm back on the ship over from the island. I know where this is going. Eugene doesn't know where LeJeune has moved to after the temporary housing.

'And do you have any idea where he could be working if he never showed up at the docks? And you were expecting him? He said he would come?'

'Yes. Like I say. I fixed him up and no, he never came. I never saw him after that.'

'And when was this?'

'The summer. I remember they made a big fuss over the ship. The Empire Windrush. It was all over the radio. The newspaper people were there and everything. Cameras. You name it!'

How I wish I could happen across LeJeune by chance. Just walk out into the street and see him right in front of me. I pace in a circle, my brain desperately searching for the right question to ask next. 'And what did you talk about, the two of you, at the pub? Apart from me.'

'Well, only that he had a bit of trouble on the boat with two men from Jamaica. Or was it Trinidad? But trouble all the same.'

'Two men? Who were they? Did he say?'

'I doubt he even knew their names. They came up to him when John was talking to one of their wives.'

I swallow hard, my throat suddenly very tight and dry.

'No, no, no. Don't you worry about John. He wasn't talking in that way. But I think one of the men thought he was. A bit of pushing and pulling, but your John is a smart man and talked his way out of a fight. I believe they were sore with him, though. That's what he said, anyway. Said he needed to watch his back.'

'And that means?'

'You know how men can be. Like to get revenge.'

My hand involuntarily shifts to my lips.

'But hold on, hold on.' He springs up from the bed and goes to put his arms around me. I shrink backwards. He raises both hands and steps away. 'Look, don't you worry about John. He can take care of himself.'

I shake my head slowly. I have no idea how LeJeune would react if faced with a man aiming to take revenge for talking to his wife. It seems ridiculous that they'd still be seeking out LeJeune for something that he obviously smoothed over while on the ship. This Eugene could be blowing everything out of proportion.

'I, I should go.' I head for the door but I've got more questions. I just don't know where to start, but I'm in the middle of a stranger's bedroom; it probably isn't wise for me to stay. I could ask for Eugene's number instead. Call him when I'm feeling more composed and had time to digest what he's told me.

'Going already?' Eugene pulls at my arm. He's smiling, moving closer and I don't like the look in his eye.

'Yes, it's late and I've a long journey home.'

There is a bustle at the door and Iris pushes it open.

'What did I tell you?' Her gaze is angry, eyes like tiny bullets aiming straight for Eugene.

'I was just going to see her out,' he says with a smile so wide it seems to melt Iris who releases her trigger. For all her strictness, she has fallen victim to Eugene's charm. I have not.

'I just want to ask something else,' I say and turn to Eugene. 'You say you knew LeJeune in the army, knew him while he was here. Is there anyone else in London that he might know who could give me any information about where he is now?'

Eugene opens his mouth and closes it at once. He can't look at me, but he looks at Iris as if she can offer an answer to my question.

'Anyone,' I say, but really I'm pleading.

Eugene looks down at his feet. I notice for the first time that his socks don't match, and he suddenly becomes less worldly and less of a threat to me. His fists are balled in his pockets, and I see the tension in his throat as he swallows then shakes his head. Still avoiding to look at me.

'Are you sure?' I ask. 'There is nothing you can say that will shock me. I am just so frightened now. I came all this way. Hopeful. Even if it's just for one time only, I want to see LeJeune.' I want to add that even if it's for the last time to say goodbye, but I clear my throat instead.

'Anything you can tell me, Eugene. Anything.'

'Well, don't keep the girl in suspense. Poor mite.' Iris cocks her hip and rests a hand on it. I suspect she has listened to our entire conversation and wants to know the outcome of this disappearance.

'Is it a woman?' I ask before I can remind myself that I might not like the answer to this question.

Eugene shuffles back to the bed, hesitates and then sits. Iris comes in a little further to the room.

'Back then. In the war years, he had a young lady. But most of us did. The white squaddies and some of the locals didn't like it, but some of those white girls liked us. What can I say? We were far from home. And your man wasn't married then. Me neither. So you get lonely, you know, and things can happen. You're a married woman, I don't have to tell you, and from what you're telling me, you know what lonely is like.'

I close my eyes at this and try to turn my head from him. But I can't hide the frustration, the wrenching feeling in my stomach, the disappointment of this journey across London and the tears that are giving my feelings away. But Iris sees them. She comes over to me, takes my hand and leads me out of the room. On the landing, she lets go of my hand. I hadn't minded the feeling of comfort, if only for a few seconds.

'Your best bet is to forget this bloke,' she says. Her voice is less gruff. 'Sounds to me like you might be better off out of it.'

'But I want to know where he is.'

'And you might not.'

I cross my brow as I stare at her, and Eugene appears from his room.

'She means, it's very strange that you've heard nothing. In my opinion, if a man vanishes into thin air, it's because he wants to. He doesn't want to be found and you ...'

'I what?'

'You should have never come over here because ... like Iris said, you might not want to know what really happened.'

I look from one to the other. Shake my head from side to side and feel my vision clouding, my mind, too. I don't know what to think. I don't think. I run down the stairs and out of the door before they can say anything else that will hurt me more than they have already.

I walk quickly to the bus stop. It had already grown dark when I arrived in Stepney, and the night looks blacker now. In fact this night isn't as it should be, it's blurred and hazy. Perhaps Stepney was this same shade of dim earlier but only now am I unable to see my way as clearly. Snapshots of Le-Jeune in the arms of another woman – and a white woman at that – get in the way. And what if she was a properly mature woman, not just a girl like me? She would have had so much to offer him. He hasn't even slept with me: Mama saw to it that we didn't have a first night together, and so he's gone back to the woman who he knows can offer him what I couldn't. I'm so angry. Angry at Mama, Eugene, LeJeune. Particularly him because he is the only one who can break me like this. And I feel broken. I feel like a child, a lost one, and maybe it's time for me to find my way home. Go back home.

*

In the stillness of my cousin's flat, I stand and shiver for several minutes then move slowly around without turning on lights. A growl from my stomach reminds me I'm hungry. Myrtle was going to eat a sandwich at work and had told me to make one before I left, but I'd been too excited and nervous to think about food earlier. She won't be back from the hospital until the morning. Our timelines won't be synchronised for days because of her shifts. She's been so attentive, caring, and I feel almost too embarrassed to tell her that my search has more or less led me to a dead end. What if LeJeune does not want to be found?

I only just made it home by bus. The conductor had told me, when I'd jumped on the one saying Paddington Station on the front, that this was the last bus for the evening. He had looked me up and down then asked why I'm coming home so late and where did I work.

'Nowhere,' I'd said, and he'd looked at me even more curiously. Days ago I would have kept my eyes down, said nothing more than a hello, please or thank you to him. But I'd engaged in an exchange of words with him. Pleased to be having a pleasant conversation and not one that led to tears as so many of mine have done recently. Everyone looking at me in the same way Eugene had. The way Iris had, too. A gullible fool. I'd tried to tell myself for the whole journey back to Paddington that this couldn't be the end. I couldn't really have wasted my father's money and my time coming here when all the while LeJeune was off with some woman, having the time of his life, no doubt, while I sat and pined for him, more like his widow than his new bride.

In my bed, I wish for a pair of warm arms to wrap around me but instead I lie shivering under the candlewick blankets. I should change into my nightdress, but I'm too numb to do anything. Not even sleep. I hear my door push open and search the darkness for whoever it is. They could just as well have come to take me away if they wanted to. Do anything to me. But the someone is Moorhouse whose eyes reflect like green mirrors in the dark which squint and close once he has leapt onto the foot of my bed. He pulls at the threads of the blanket with his claws, then circles and settles like a huge purring cushion on my feet. He falls asleep in seconds and the morning arrives unexpectedly soon.

Chapter 13

Essie

London 1948

For the next two days, I drift around the house. Like dust, I settle on the furniture, and like dust, a door opening or subtle movement from Moorhouse or my cousin and I'm shifted from one spot to the next. The bedroom to sleep. To the bathroom to sob. To the kitchen to look at the sparing supplies and to dream about my mother standing in her kitchen making a soup that will bring life and love to anyone who tastes of it. How I need that medicine. I have never missed a place or people as I do now.

I told Myrtle all about my encounter with Eugene Price, and we talked together at length about the implications of what he'd said. Should I worry, give up or keep on searching? Eugene and what his landlady, Iris, had said had made me weary, feeling beaten, feeling frail. But in other ways, I had sensed a flow of determination to find answers whether or not I found the right answer, the one I'd come here looking for. Then there was the question of whether I should stay or leave. But there was a problem attached to that, too. That being what money I had left. I really didn't have enough for me to stay for an indeterminate amount of time.

'Don't worry too much about your keep or anything,'
Myrtle says as she adds more mashed potato onto my plate.
'You are so tiny, it's nothing to feed and have you here.'

'But I can't live on your charity indefinitely. I have to do
something to help you.' I slide a small amount of this strange
food into my mouth and marvel at the idea of boiling a
potato, mashing it into a big lump mixed with fat and slop-
ping it onto a plate with a slice of ham and a portion of
canned peas. English food. I hate it, really, and want to make
some of Mama's soup, but there are no ingredients for it in
the kitchen. I stare at my plate, white, pink and green, and
wonder what Mama would make of this meal.

'I can get a job.' I say it before thinking first.

'So you're staying?' Myrtle looks really happy at this snap
decision of mine.

'For a while.'

'If you're staying, why does your face tell me you have
given up looking for LeJeune?'

When my cousin had seen how sure I was about finding
him, how in love I am, I think it brought back memories of
the love she'd felt for her husband. I know she misses him
terribly, I can tell by the way she speaks about him. One
night we were a lovesick pair, exchanging stories about romance, dreaming aloud. Finding LeJeune would make me
happy, but it also meant Myrtle could live out her dream of
having love back in her life through me.

'No, not given up but trying to be realistic,' I say.

'In what way?'

'Well, Eugene Price said there was a woman. A white woman.'

'Really?' Myrtle hangs on the word. So far, I hadn't mentioned this part of my conversation with Eugene to her.

Myrtle puts her cutlery down and both hands under chin while leaning her elbows on the table. I put my cutlery down, too.

'It happened during the war.'

Her expression tells me to continue but I can't.

'Oh, Essie, but that was then,' she says. 'He's since been back to Dominica and met you. Whoever he met, whichever woman, it will only have been a fling. Nothing that happened in that time, the relationships, the kiss at a dance, a drunken moment in a dark alley, none of it was meant to last. I was here, I know. I saw many a broken heart when the white men came back and the Black men went home. Very few of these entanglements came to anything. You don't have to worry, Essie. Whoever she was has moved on with her life. She would have forgotten about any wartime romance and married one of her own.'

'You think that's it? You don't think he came back looking for her?'

'If they had any sense, they would just have said a fond farewell and gone back to normal life. That's how it was back then. The war made people do silly things. Short-lived romances. People getting married at the drop of a hat in case they never saw each other again. For all you know, LeJeune's so-called woman was already married when they met.'

I nod, hoping this was the case. Just a wartime fling.

'It was a novelty you see. White women, Black men. Just a novelty.'

'But when Eugene said about her …'

'He was talking about the past. It's been three years, Essie, since the war ended. LeJeune would never have married you if he knew he was coming back here to rekindle a romance.'

I pick up my knife and fork. I hadn't thought about it from that point of view. A practical and reasonable one. I smile at Myrtle who happily sits and chews her pink meat, scratching the cat's head as he circles the table legs, hoping for a second dinner.

She believes in the romance I have with LeJeune. The one that is all set to be as passionate as the ones the men and women in the war had. They carried on as normal. My normal is to find my husband. I make two decisions. One is to go back to Stepney. The other is to write to Mrs Francis and beg her to tell me if there is anything else she knows about LeJeune's relationship with a woman he may well have fallen in love with in Stepney.

Chapter 14

London

1944

He knew the sound of German aircraft. The noise they made vibrated through his body, even the tiny bones that made up his toes and fingers, every vertebrae awakened by sound, jangling, as if they wanted to make music within his body. LeJeune thought about the British planes, not sounding as heavy as the German ones loaded with bombs, the kind of artillery that would see off a whole town. Stepney was on fire. Glass crunched beneath his feet as he walked the pavements with the wardens and police in search of the dead. Gas pipes and water pipes peaked their metal bodies through the enormous cracks in the street, the gas giving off occasional explosions and water spraying, sporadically, like geysers. The people of Stepney carried on through the chaos. Offices, shops and factories expected their workers to come in the day after an air raid. It didn't matter how late they got to work so long as they got there. The buses struggled to get anyone anywhere on time because of the fractured streets. Somehow trains were running fine. The only people the bosses and employers wouldn't be expecting were the poor souls who had sat innocently in their houses when a bomb landed in their living room or kitchen. A whole corner of a street could be missing by the next day, a pile of rubble, bricks and glass in its place, a family permanently at rest beneath it all.

These were the people LeJeune helped out from under the mounds of debris in the Stepney streets. He had counted several Anderson shelters in back gardens with splinters of metal and glass cut through them and seen people, too many to be counted, being carted off to hospital to have splinters removed from their backs, necks, faces. In every bloody, dirty or broken face, he never once saw Lizzie's. Their paths had not crossed in weeks since Micky's arrival back from the dead. A return to which LeJeune would gladly have welcomed for Micky whenever he thought he'd never see Lizzie again. Be in her arms again. Doubtless he was with Lizzie now, being as she hadn't been in touch, sent word as she'd promised. Instead, he rescued people from the arms of death, pulling them from beneath a window frame or mound of dirt.

Lizzie hadn't returned to the Dockman's. He'd been in and asked about her several times. Just as Eugene had disappeared, so too had Lizzie. An old man drinking alone in the pub had taken him to one side, said he knew where Lizzie and Micky had gone.

'Left London altogether from what I can tell. I guess he's no stranger to disappearing acts, that Mick Walters.'

'What do you mean?' LeJeune had pulled up a chair, watching the man sucking beer into his mouth as if his lips were a hose, making a loud hissing sound that grated on his nerves, but anything he could find out about Lizzie and that Micky character would be helpful. He had to find her.

'Well, they say every last bloke in his regiment either got blown up, shot or captured. But not him. This is only what I've heard, mind, I weren't there or nothing.' He chuckled and scratched the last wisps of white hair on his head.

'Seems your man ran off. Jumping on as many ships or boats as he could to get him further and further away from the fighting as possible. Someone said he lost his head altogether and ended up as far as Australia. Then he went to the army offices and told them he'd lost his memory. Eventually, he winded up back here, honourably discharged for not having his marbles.'

'You mean he's mad?' LeJeune leant back in his chair. 'He could hurt Lizzie. I need to find her.'

'What you need is to leave well alone. Michael Walters always had a reputation around here.' The man looked over his shoulder and tapped his nose. 'Light-fingered, quick with his fists and let his mouth run off with him. And one thing I do know for sure, apart from the he said, she said, if he makes a threat, he jolly well carries it out. So you steer clear, son.'

It was the last thing LeJeune wanted to do. Now more than ever, he needed to find Lizzie. What could she be thinking trading him for a deserter, a madman and a danger in one?

Every time he went to her flat, there was no one home. The house on the corner of her street and the bakery beside it were reduced to boulders of brick and stone, heaps of broken furniture and metal shelving from the bakery lying deserted. But just one week after encountering the old man in the Dockman's, LeJeune found Lizzie. He'd turned a corner one evening only to see her casually walking towards her flat. She had on her bright blue jacket, her blonde curls bubbling on the collar and a navy beret worn at an angle on her head.

'Lizzie!' His voice croaked from his throat in excitement and shock. He ran towards her and thanked God that she stopped and looked happy to see him.

'Bloody hell, Johnny, you gave me the flaming fright of my life. What you doing shouting out to a girl like that?' She spoke as if they'd only seen each other that morning. 'You all right, ducks?'

'Am *I* all right? Are *you* all right?'

'Am I missing something?'

'Lizzie.' He held her arms. 'Where have you been? It's been weeks. I've been going crazy with worry.'

'Worry? What were you worried about? I said we'd talk and here I am.'

'Did you even come looking for me?'

'Someone just dropped me off here. They couldn't get through the streets because of the roads and my road is blocked off from the other end.'

He stared blankly at her.

'I've been in Warwickshire. Relatives. Mum wanted us all out of London. I went with them to give her peace of mind, but we're all packed in like sardines and I have to get back to work.'

'And?'

'And … I missed you?'

LeJeune peeled his cap from his head. Rubbing his brow and turning a half circle from her before swinging back around.

'How can you …? Look, the last time I saw you, you were throwing me out of your house in favour of that man.'

Lizzie looked over her shoulder and then down the other end of the street. She took LeJeune's hand and led him to her flat. Tutting at the demolished properties just a few doors down, she let them both inside. In the kitchen was the evidence of someone having had a cup of tea. The dregs of it sat motionless in a cup and a small crust of bread had curled up lifelessly on a side plate coated by crumbs and hardened cheese. Lorna must have still been in London. If she'd been home on the numerous times LeJeune had knocked the main door, she hadn't opened it. Lizzie put the plate and cup into the sink.

'Tea? I'm gasping,' she said. Still in her jacket and beret, she filled the kettle. LeJeune took a seat, didn't take his eyes from her once. He watched her slowly peel off the bright blue jacket, the dark beret and fix her hair before she sat. The kettle steamed, hissing through the lid. Lizzie kept her head bent forward and sniffed.

'Are you crying?' He leant across the table, fiddling with the peak of his army cap which formed a barrier between their hands. She looked up.

'John. Johnny,' she said. 'I've got myself in a right mess.'

'I don't understand what that means.'

'It means I fell in love with you.' The kettle began to whistle and she leapt to turn off the hob. Sitting again, she pushed the cap aside and reached for LeJeune's hands. 'I couldn't help myself, and I wish it didn't happen but it did.'

He held her fingers firmly between his. 'How can you wish our love away?'

'Because, John. How are we ever going to be together beyond this war? How am I supposed to live my life with a Black man and get away with it? My family, Johnny, my family. You don't know what they're really like. And just look at the way people stare when we're together. They think I'm a big tart. Spreading my legs for a Black …'

'I'm a man. A man with a heart. One that knows that you and I are meant to be. That's why he was gone and I came. I came here for you and I always will be here for you. No matter what anyone says.'

She dragged him across the table to kiss him. A hard, wet kiss that felt like a goodbye and tasted of her salty tears.

'Don't leave me, Lizzie,' he whispered. 'Don't leave.'

They stood, foreheads pressing together until Lizzie led them to the bedroom.

The water in the kettle grew cold; the night crept in through the open window of her bedroom as LeJeune stroked her hair.

'I'm sorry, Johnny.' He thought she'd been sleeping she'd been so still. He could hear her breath, just. Felt the warmth of her.

'Don't tell me goodbye, Lizzie.'

'I have to.' She was crying again, her tears trailing his chest and slipping onto the mattress. 'I went to his place, just over the Stepney Marshes, watching the gold and red on the water by the docks at night, watching Stepney going up in flames and not knowing my right from my left. Everything is different. Everything changed the minute he walked in that door.'

'But us, Liz. What we have is—'

'Special. I know.' She leant up to look at him. Half of her face was in shadow. The half of her he didn't know and couldn't understand. He thought she was all his, but half of her was waiting for Micky. Wanting him back, ready to exchange him for that man. 'But I have to think about my future. They'll put this place back together again, but they can't do that to my heart.' She rolled onto her back, hand in the middle of her chest. 'You'll always be in here.'

'I don't have to go anywhere. I can stay right here and we can do battle with anyone who says we shouldn't be together.'

'I wish it was that simple. I'm not as strong as you, John. I wish to God I was, but I'm not.' Then she sat up. 'And you deserve a girl who can love you with a heart as big as yours.'

'That girl is you.'

'She's not me. I'm a big coward. I can't give you my heart, Johnny, but I do give you my love. To keep. To take with you when you go back.'

He felt every fibre in his body melt into nothing. He was fading into the bed as if he were already just a memory in Lizzie Tarping's mind. An episode in her life she was regretting. Her goodbye had been stamped across their relationship from the day Micky came back and she sent him away. She had never intended to see LeJeune after that. He felt sure of it. And the thought of that cut like the tiny shards of glass that penetrated the shelters and lay on the pavements. How useless in their tiny forms, useless as the dust they would become, as useless as he now was to her. He rolled away, onto his side, and wept.

'Jesus, Johnny. I really am truly sorry.' She got out of bed and went to the bathroom. When his sobs died away, he dried his face, the snot from his nose and got dressed. He found his cap and pressed it onto his head. He placed one hand on the bathroom door, sliding it away as he left the flat.

*

The dogs were barking loudly again. A portent to more bombing, more noise and more evidence that the people who had packed up and gone to relatives and friends in the countryside had more sense than those who stayed. The sound of barks, harsh yet plaintive into the night, was silenced; the streets lay empty now, waiting. People hid in their government issue shelters, some in basements if they had them, and the rest had already traipsed to the underground station. LeJeune shepherded people to Stepney Green underground, knocking on doors to make sure no one came to answer because that would mean they hadn't taken shelter. The sirens deafened him and glass crunched under his feet. The air was already filled with dust in anticipation of the German bombers whose planes began to arrive.

LeJeune looked around him. His duty was done; he needed to make his way to Stepney Green himself, but it was too late. The tirade of artillery crashed through the clouds like streamline metal birds. Angry ones, their wings pulled backwards and their aim steady. The first explosion hit and then the next. The warden he had accompanied during the evacuation was nowhere to be seen. LeJeune had been too busy looking up and watching the sky light up over the marshes. The worst damage had been done there, and the planes were just over the docks, just above his head. Though just seconds from the station, he could see the doors were locked shut and barricades would already have gone up so he ran towards an archway that led to a tunnel. It had been part of the railway system but was disused now. Diving within its damp walls, he curled his body against the brickwork into a tight ball, his hands cradling his head. He closed his eyes and prayed. Before he reached the Amen, a bomb hit. It was close. The explosion cracked his eardrums, the sounds still erupting but becoming muffled. He'd experienced this before. A loud explosion and then the noise of it falling away, a temporary loss of hearing. Only that time he'd lost all sense of direction, he'd passed out, waking and thinking he was dead, waking and wishing that he were.

The hiss of missiles and the crash of their landing ceased. Slowly, he moved his hands away and unfurled his body. He wasn't dead this time, either, but that bomb had been close. On his hands and knees, he scrambled out of the archway and tried to peer back into the tunnel. It had been as he'd found it, filled with old tyres and disused junk from the households that were no longer occupied. A dumping ground. He turned towards the station now to bang on the doors and tell them it was safe to come out. But before arriving, he could see the doors were no longer there, just a black open space with smoke leaving it like fog.

He ran as fast as he could. People would be trapped below. He had to get them out. He could hear screams from inside, people on ground level running towards the station, yelling, then the clang and sirens of the ambulance and fire brigade. Army trucks arrived, and a madness of movement and orders being barked ensued. He helped the emergency services, lifting away rubble, helping those who could still walk find their way out onto the street, carrying those who couldn't.

When the underground platforms were mostly cleared of people, LeJeune saw it, like a flag in the landscape to mark its territory. The jacket, bright and blue despite the fog of black. Lizzie's blue jacket, her body not moving. And neither were his legs. His heart skipped beats as he watched a man pulling at the arm of the jacket. Limp and lifeless it was, and LeJeune swallowed hard, at last finding the strength to go to Lizzie.

'I know her,' he said and dropped to his knees. The man rolled her onto her back.

'Johnny?' she whispered, and then her eyes flickered closed.

Everything grew still until the man who had been helping tapped LeJeune's shoulder.

'Sorry mate. Did you say you knew her?'

LeJeune nodded his head.

'Her name is Lorna Smith. She was a friend of mine.'

LeJeune took charge of the body, raising Lorna's lifeless limbs and seeing how blood oozed from the side of her head, leaving a trail on the platform. When he emerged from the station, the body moved in his arms. He looked down.

'My God, Lorna. You're alive.' He hurried her towards an ambulance where people were having their wounds dressed with plasters and bandages. Lorna was taken from LeJeune's arms and placed onto a stretcher.

'Do you know where Lizzie is?' LeJeune took her hand. 'Was she in there?'

Lorna shook her head slowly.

'Forget her, Johnny. Find your way out of this war and out of this country.'

Her hand slipped from his as she was lifted into the ambulance. The doors closed and the ambulance's siren cut into his thoughts. She had gone away again. Left Lorna her jacket it would seem. Left London. Left everything. Left him.

Chapter 15

Essie

London 1948

Myrtle looks tired again. She works long shifts and sometimes confuses day for night. She's never late for work, though.

'I've worked at that hospital since before the war,' she tells me again when I ask her how she manages the long hours. 'So I'm used to it. It's in my blood I suppose. Twenty-five years in the same profession is a long time.'

'So, by now, you must be in charge of other nurses?'

'I would like to have been ward sister, but several women, younger than me, have come and taken that job and then got promoted and moved on.'

'But you've been there for ever. Surely …?'

'That's not the way things work. Not when you look like me. And I wasn't one of the lucky few who do.' She sniffs. 'It's a long way to travel if I'm honest, but there's just something about the place that keeps pulling me back there.'

'They're lucky to have you.' I place a hand on hers and she smiles.

'Well, come on,' she says. 'If we're going on a search of Stepney for LeJeune or for Eugene, then we need to get a wriggle on.'

Myrtle knows all the London slang. Her accent is so watered down, I wouldn't have known she was Dominican if we'd only just met. She sounds completely English when she speaks to white people like Mrs Rogers upstairs, shop assistants and bus conductors. She calls people 'pet' and 'love' and not '*doudou*' as we'd say back home. LeJeune had sounded so unlike a Dominican. He wasn't a cockney exactly, but the people back home did stare at him when he spoke. But then everyone stares at him. So handsome and tall as he is, his striking eyes.

'Okay,' I say. 'But I'll wash up the breakfast things first.'

We catch the bus near Paddington Station and travel, for the most part, on the same route Myrtle says she takes when she goes to the hospital. It's a more pleasant journey to Stepney by day than at night. I can see what's happening in the London streets as the bus judders along, the engine not sounding as loud in the busy traffic. London is like a maze and a mismatched puzzle. The streets around Paddington and the ones in the West End are not so decrepit as the ones in East London. I can sense the change of atmosphere as we leave the city streets where the buildings are tall and a cluster of cars circles Trafalgar Square. The tall monuments remain nameless but stately all the same.

Despite its rowdiness and obvious signs of being harder hit in the war, East London has a homely feeling and village vibration that reminds me of home. Of course, there are no trees – well, maybe just a few – and the colours are drab and grey, but I get a sense that the people here are full of heart. Perhaps Myrtle feels more at home in this part of London and it might be another reason why she still travels so far for work. There must be some magic here in London, whichever the part, because it drew LeJeune back. I'd like to think that it is the place and not a woman that made him want to return.

We get off the bus not far from Stepney Green Station.

'I want to have a look through the market,' Myrtle says. 'It's been an age since I've been to the Stepney one. With work and everything, I don't get the opportunity. Is it okay?'

'Oh,' I say, and she reads the look of disappointment on my face because I've been looking forward to having another word with Eugene. If he wasn't home, and it's likely that he would be at work at this time of morning, we'd talked about hunting him down at the docks.

'We won't have to stay long,' she assures me.

'Of course,' I say. Myrtle has been so patient with me, I should be just as gracious. She knows I have to keep looking.

We cross a road, and the street ahead is crowded with people. Mothers pushing bulky pushchairs and children holding on to them as the women weave around each other looking at the stalls selling everything from fruit and vegetables to fish and eggs. Men in grey flat caps and miserable faces are milling around close by, carrying shopping bags, lighting up cigarettes, clipping a child around the ear as they dart in and around the hoards of people. Stall-keepers in full-length aprons call out, selling their wares at the tops of their voices.

'I've never seen so many people.'

'Stepney was always overpopulated.' Myrtle has an easy way of avoiding collisions with the busy shoppers and finding gaps that enable her to get closer to the food stalls. 'Overcrowding leads to health problems. The hospital has so many admissions from around this way.'

Over my shoulder, I see a child with a shopping bag, a boy of about twelve looking through a barrel of potatoes and placing some onto a balancing scale.

'So are there fewer people now than before the war?'

'Not really. They're planning on building more houses and flats to bring Stepney back to its former glory. So many lives lost.' Myrtle shakes her head and stops for a moment. 'Close to the end of the war, this place took its hardest hit, whole blocks of flats bombed, whole families gone in the early hours of the morning before they'd even thought about getting up for work or school.'

I freeze and think again how lucky that LeJeune survived.

'Goodness me, Essie, you can't imagine the air raids, homes and shops blown up, burnt. People left London during the Blitz, what a time it was.'

I hug my cousin because I realise I'm not only lucky to have met LeJeune, I'm lucky to have Myrtle, too.

She pats my shoulder and edges towards a vegetable stall. I can see the look of past terrors in her eyes and know that both Myrtle and LeJeune have horrific memories. I understand now why LeJeune said so little about his time in the army.

Myrtle is distracted for a moment, buying vegetables from a man with such a thick moustache it is a wonder he can still breathe or speak.

I look around me, listening to the banter of people who, despite their miserable faces, still have time for conversation. ''ow yer doing, love?' 'Mustn't grumble.'

Turning back in the direction we came and seeing the railway bridge over one end of the market, I catch sight of someone. I squint my eyes, open them again and then wider

still. I let my jaw gape and exhale loudly because I can't believe who I've just seen, his strong, wide back shouldering
his way through a crowd of shoppers who have suddenly
multiplied before my eyes. It is him. I know for sure as I see
the side of his face that it is LeJeune. He must have walked
straight past me. How could I not have noticed? How could
he not have seen me?

'Cousin. I have to go.'

Without any explanation, I begin to run, only to be halted
by people both annoyed and startled who either move out of
my way or cry 'Oi' in shrill voices. But if I don't hurry, I'll
lose him. I start calling out his name, hoping he will hear
above the rumbling sounds of the market, a train that decides
to pull away just as I shout his name again.

I pick up speed, regardless of who I have to shove. If I
don't I'll lose him, and if I lose him now, this might be my
only chance for ever finding him in this crowded place. I
think I see him turn a corner, and I run blindly around it, the
top half of my body crashing into a wooden crate. It's
weighty and stops me dead in my pursuit of my lost husband. A man shouts at me to hold my horses.

'I, I'm sorry.' I gasp, craning my head up the road to see
where LeJeune has gone. I haven't taken any notice of what
I've run into or what damage I might have done.

'You want to look where you're going, love. You can't go
haring around corners blind.'

I look down at a man who is picking up dirty bread rolls.
Still looking for signs of LeJeune, I reluctantly bend a knee
and begin to aim the bread into the man's wooden tray as he
tuts and shakes his head.

'Never mind, just leave it,' he puffs at me. I can see his
ears are red. Some of the rolls have tumbled away, trodden

on by people calling, 'What the flamin' 'eck?' When he finally gives up on collecting the bread, he stands to face me.

'What's your game, anyway? Been nicking stuff? Chasing down a crook?' He wants to be annoyed at me but he's half smiling, which begins to annoy me because I was so close to finding my husband.

'I'm not playing a game, and I don't know what nicking is all about.'

'You know? A bit light-fingered. But no.' He runs a hand over his head, his dark, unruly hair springing back into curls, the sides of his head shaved close to his skin. His eyes are dark, the lashes long and give him a boyish look, though I'd put him in his late twenties. 'You don't look the type,' he continues. 'Listen, you weren't running away from someone, were you kid? Everything all right?'

He starts to look around at the market crowd who is getting on with the business of shopping and barely noticing me and the man or the tray of sodden bread rolls between us.

'No, I was actually chasing after someone I know. Well, at least I thought it was him.' I stare off up the road, but Le-Jeune is long gone. If it was him, then he looked perfectly fine and perfectly capable of writing a letter. He did mention a time he'd woken in a hospital bed with very little recollection of how he got there. It had taken him days to fully recover his memory, and even since he's had blackouts and dizzy spells. It was why he'd seen out the rest of the war either on mechanical repairs or marshalling air raids.

'You all right, though? Do you need help finding him?'

'Right now, I'm wondering if he wants to be found.' I look down and see one of this man's bread rolls is just behind his foot and he'll step back into it if he doesn't look first. 'Can I offer to pay for your bread? The ones you lost.'

He looks at the sorry supply that remains. Perhaps he's a market seller and I've cost him his rent money or something. He is well presented in a neat grey shirt that has the top button done up and a pair of braces holding up his trousers. They look as if they are part of a suit. Maybe he owns a bread factory.

'You're all right, love,' he says. 'I'll just have to go back to my kitchen and start all over again.' He chuckles and takes a slight step back. He notices the bread and kicks it aside. 'I'll leave this one for the birds. In fact, I might go down by the waterside and feed it all to the gulls. They'll be pleased even if my customers have to wait.'

'I feel terrible,' I say. 'I should pay you.' I reach to open my handbag.

'No really, love. It's fine. Or, unless you're an excellent cook who can come to my kitchen and save me from bankruptcy.' Though he still smiles, kicking at the sodden roll, I read something quite sad in his eyes.

'I've never worked in a bakery. I'm not sure if I can.'

'Actually it's a restaurant. Well, it's what I'm hoping it will be. At the moment, it's more of a tea shop.'

I'm fidgety but he carries on all the same, his eyes following mine as I look up the road.

'My parents used to own it. Boarded it up while I served abroad, and I'm trying to bring it back to life.'

'You were in the army?' I snap back to attention. I want to ask if he knew any Black soldiers.

'RAF.'

'Oh.'

'Just oh? Most people thank me for my service.' He fakes a questioning look. 'I'm just messing around. How about you? What did you do? Were you serving, too?'

'Me?' I feel my cheeks are warm again. 'I was at school.'

We both begin to laugh as Myrtle comes running up to me. She bends to rest her hands on her knees, her shopping bag scraping the ground as she catches her breath.

'Another runner?' The man with the bread chuckles again.

'This is my cousin,' I say.

'Where did you go?' Myrtle is still short of breath. 'I was talking to you one minute, and when I turned around you were gone. I called you and started looking. I took off in the wrong direction. I was worried sick.' She straightens and looks at the man, then spots the bread on the ground. 'What on earth happened? You wanted to buy bread?'

'I can't apologise more … to the two of you.' I turn to Myrtle. 'You see, I saw him. LeJeune. He ran around that corner, but before I could catch up, I bumped into this man and knocked the bread out of the tray.'

'So where is LeJeune now?'

'I lost him.'

'Who have you lost?' asks the man who has been standing quietly by.

'Her husband,' says Myrtle. The man flicks a look at me and blushes. 'Maybe you know him as we believe he is around here somewhere.'

'What's his name?' he asks.

Myrtle is about to say LeJeune but I talk over her.

'His name is John Francis. He served in the army. He came back home at the end of the war and then returned here to start a job in a factory. But no one knows where he is. Something happened to him, just weeks after he got here.'

'So I presume you've checked the factory?'

'Well, he didn't go to the factory.' The feeling of sounding and looking pathetic begins to cover me like a blanket, invisible but there every time I tell anyone that my husband has disappeared. 'We think … or I do, that he ended up in Stepney because it's the last place he was during the war. Someone who knows him has already told me that the factory job fell through and he was going to take a job locally, on the docks, only …'

'He didn't show up?'

I nod. 'Exactly.'

'But you think you just saw him?'

'I think so.'

The man steps back and takes a quick glance at my cousin who lowers her eyes. They are both thinking the same thing.

'No offence, love, but did you call after him?' the man asks me. I nod. 'Then, I suppose, he either didn't hear you or you got the wrong fella. And if you're so convinced it was him and he never stopped for you, then maybe …'

'It's okay. You don't need to say it. I know. But I have no idea why I'm telling you all of this … you're busy, and besides, it couldn't have been him, he's not the type who would ignore his wife.'

'No one would ever ignore you,' the man says, then clears his throat. 'Look, if there's anything I can do to help. I could ask people who come in the restaurant about him. Have you gone to the police?'

I'm about to answer but I stop. So far, I thought a search around a city I do not know would be enough for me to find LeJeune. I hadn't even thought about going to the police. What would I say to them? But LeJeune is, after all, a missing person and perhaps someone official needs to investigate.

'I get it,' says the man. 'It would be like admitting something bad had happened. Am I right?'

I nod again. 'But if you could ask people for me, I'd be very grateful.'

'Is there a ransom?'

I turn to Myrtle.

'I'm just messing around, love. I know the score. But you'll have to give me some details about him. I know, I'll put up a sign or a notice or something. Then you can pop in and find out if anyone has told me anything.'

'I don't live around here. It's hard to pop in, but I can certainly take the bus here.'

'You could, but I can give you my number. Then I'll put the feelers out and you can call me each day, or week, and check if anyone reports seeing him.'

'Feelers?' I say. 'Yes, feelers. Thank you so much. You're too kind. But please, tell me how much for the bread.'

'I swear it's not a problem, love.' He puts the tray on the ground and retrieves a piece of paper from a back pocket and a short pencil from the breast pocket of his shirt. 'You take my number. Give me a call with all the details of your husband – full name, regiment – and I'll see what I can do. You don't have a photograph, do you?'

I shake my head and take the piece of paper. It's a receipt from Woolworths. I read his name. Bill Harper.

'Mr Harper, you are very kind. Thank you. I'll call you later or tomorrow, but very soon.'

'Of course, and it's no trouble at all. Happy to help.' He stoops to pick up his bread tray. He nods a farewell to both Myrtle and me and walks over to a stall where an angry young woman is shaking her head at him.

'What the 'ell am I supposed to do with this lot?'

'Cheap at 'alf the price, these,' I hear him say and they begin to laugh.

'Well,' says Myrtle. 'That was a kindly young man.'

'Yes,' I say looking over my shoulder at him. 'We should try and find Eugene now. I need the name of LeJeune's regiment. I have no idea what it was. And can we go via that road where I thought I saw LeJeune going?'

'Of course, Essie. You look so sad but look, someone has offered to help. Ask questions of people around here. Anything could happen from there. Come on, put a smile back on your face. You have such a lovely smile. Have faith in God the Father and he will provide. He sees all, and if you believe in Him and follow His words, you will get your answers. You will see if you don't.'

My cousin hooks my arm and marches me off. We walk down a narrow street where houses are joined in pairs that look to be holding each other up. Down the sides of houses, I see there are lines of washing. Sheets and shirts swaying in the hopes of getting dry on this dank late morning. I stare into as many windows as I can, slowing the pace so that I don't miss a single one. Myrtle is looking, too, clinging as tightly to her faith as she does my arm, holding me up because there is a chance I could collapse like one of the houses, a pile of me on the ground and LeJeune never knowing I came looking for him.

Chapter 16

London

1945

It wasn't until people were dancing in the street that LeJeune believed the war was over. He'd heard Winston Churchill's announcement with his own ears and still remained in a state of disbelief. When a woman, who said her name was Daisy, swung him around at an all-night celebration at The Dockman's Arms, he began to realise he had a choice to make. To stay in London or to go home. He had been searching desperately for Lizzie for months, ever since the bomb blast that tore the shelter doors away while people were cowering below in the tube station. The blue jacket, the female form lying limply, the tunnels filled with sandbags and blankets, the air black with smoke and the lifeless body he'd carried out to the street had swamped his thoughts and made him more determined to discover where Lizzie had gone.

Wearing a jacket of her own and fully recovered since then, Lorna could only whisper, 'She's gone, love. With 'im. You need to forget her.' But he could never forget her. He wanted to at least say goodbye properly, whether or not Micky was standing right beside her. He wanted to be sure Lizzie knew he loved her and that no matter what, he always would and if she should change her mind, he would stand at her side.

'Penny for them, soldier boy.'

A familiar voice close to his ear made LeJeune jump from his imaginings.

'You?' He couldn't believe it was Eugene Price, standing right in front of him, in full uniform, smile as wide as if he'd been the guest of honour for the party at The Dockman's Arms. 'I took you for dead. No one knew where you were.'

The two men embraced, patting each other on the back while the drunken celebrations raged on around them. The crowd was louder than any air raid, wilder than a darkened sky with bombs flying overhead, but there was no fear here. Not even a word or thought for the war, the reason it started or when it even began. There was just relief and thanks and no idea how the results of this war would affect them. They would drink every last drop of beer until the barrels ran dry and drain every last glass of spirits.

'I was a prisoner of war, my friend,' shouted Eugene above the noise. Everyone sang, whether they knew the words of the song being played on the piano or not, half of them certainly not able to hold the tune. 'Ended up in Germany. Lucky I wasn't shot. Mind you, that might have been better than starving to death. I'll never complain about the food they have in Europe compared to Jamaica ever again. Eating is a privilege, believe me.'

'As thin as you are, it's good to see you again.'

'Johnny, my boy. You don't look like a person celebrating the end of the war.'

LeJeune shrugged his shoulders. 'Of course I'm happy, but after all this time, I thought I was going to stay here, settle down. Now it seems like there's no point.'

'Come outside and talk.' Eugene grabbed his friend and tried to bustle his way outside. They were stopped by a couple of women, their voices raised high.

'You not dancing, fellas?'

'Put me on your dance card for later,' Eugene bellowed back. 'I'll show you how it's really done.'

The women giggled and let the men pass.

Led outside and away from the revellers in the pub, Le-Jeune sat shoulder to shoulder with Eugene on a front door-step. The door was wide open and people were talking and laughing loudly from an inner room.

'Is this about the girl?' Eugene asked. LeJeune nodded. 'Don't you see how many of them in there want to dance with you?'

'I don't want to dance with anyone.'

'Where is she, anyway? What happened?'

LeJeune explained the whole story as Eugene smoked a ci-garette. 'I should not have accepted her goodbye. I should have fought for her.'

'It don't sound like you had no choice. Sounds like she made her decision and you have to accept it.'

'And what? Forget her? I wish I could, but I can't.'

'You need to do something to drown your sorrows.'

'I've been drinking all night. Can't even get drunk.'

'I don't mean that. Plenty more fish in the sea, Johnny. A light skin boy like you with those grey eyes, you'll have no trouble picking up another girl.'

'Lizzie wasn't just another girl.'

'Oh, man. You have it bad.'

'I should go. Let you have the pick of the girls without get-ting in your way.' LeJeune grinned, but there was no joy be-hind his smile.

'You going back to the barracks?' Eugene asked, rising to his feet. LeJeune shook his head. 'We have to report for duty in the morning.'

'It is morning. I'll be there. I'll walk for a while and clear my head.'

'Well, if you walk past here and see me still drinking, drag me back to camp with you. Don't go disappearing on me.' He walked backwards towards the pub. LeJeune sat and watched as the big warm arm of the Dockman's hugged Eugene back in through the doorway so that his uniform vanished into its heart.

LeJeune got up. He dusted the back of his trousers and fixed his cap back on. He walked all the way to Lizzie's flat, knowing that she wouldn't be there but thinking that just being close to the place he'd got to know her, had fallen in love with her, would bring him comfort. He knew it was time to let go: she was gone.

The main door of the house was wide open, and a couple – a soldier and his girlfriend – were leaving. The soldier shook both fists in celebration towards LeJeune.

'We dun it, mate,' he exclaimed and turned to put his arm around his girlfriend's shoulder, walking off down the street with her. Wherever she was, he was sure Lizzie would be proud of him.

He hovered in the doorway, looking at the stairs leading to Lizzie's flat. There was a party going on up there. Lorna was entertaining. But what if Lizzie had come back to celebrate with her? The perfect opportunity to say what he wanted to say. Goodbye? Why did you leave me? Plead with her to stay with him?

As if of their own choice, his feet led him to the top landing where the floorboards were bare and a door led off to a cupboard-sized bathroom. Someone was occupying it now, throwing up for all they were worth as the locals would say. He pitied the poor soul who'd overindulged, especially if it was a soldier having to report back to base first thing in the morning.

LeJeune knocked on Lizzie's door and found it gave because someone was about to leave the flat. It was Lorna, a young officer draped around her shoulder like a shawl. LeJeune stood upright and saluted him.

'Flipping 'eck, Johnny. Is that really you?' asked Lorna.

LeJeune nodded.

'No use standing on ceremony with this one. Completely out of it. Going to walk him a few doors down. He's got family waiting.' She shrugged to adjust her inebriated shawl.

'Is … is she in there?'

'Who you looking for, love? Not Liz. I told you she was gone. Only thing she left behind was her blue jacket, and I managed to lose that in the hospital. Bit like Piccadilly Circus in there it was.' She pulled her lips in and smiled. LeJeune detected the look of pity. 'You can go in and see for yourself if you'd like.'

LeJeune shook his head. 'It's all right. I believe you. I mostly hoped you could tell me more.'

'More?'

The officer began to unravel himself. He pulled a face as he tried to focus on LeJeune. 'All the booze will be gone by now.' He slurred his words and sagged back into Lorna.

'I best go, Johnny. I don't want this one being sick down them stairs.'

'Let me help you.' LeJeune took command of the drunken officer, taking one of his arms and putting it over his shoulder and taking most of his weight. They angled the man down the stairs in a swaying motion which seemed to encourage the officer to start singing a song. A sea shanty with rude words that made Lorna giggle.

'Tell me where she is,' said LeJeune. Lorna stopped at the front door.

'Look, she's well and truly gone.'

'But where? Is she in London?'

Lorna, her eyes pinkish from the booze, began to sober, her smile fading as she twisted her mouth sideways, thinking before she spoke.

'All right, Johnny, she's over in Poplar. Staying with Mick's aunt or something. I know its close to a park and near a bus garage, but she never gave me her address. She said it was temporary while they sorted themselves out. For all I know, she could have already moved on by now.'

They shuffled the officer out of the house. He had lost the use of his feet, his full weight on their shoulders as they carried him, shoes scuffing the pavement.

'This is the one. He waltzed into mine on his way home and we couldn't get rid of him. Lucky he told me who his people are.' Lorna banged loudly on the front door. A dog began to bark, lights went on and a man with an enormous stomach wearing a vest and pyjama bottoms opened the door.

'Shut it!' he yelled at the dog. Turning to see who was at his door, he gave LeJeune a look of disgust.

'Could you take your package, mate?' Lorna said and pushed her half of the officer towards the man.

'What you done to him?' the man asked, casting another glance at LeJeune.

'Nothing,' Lorna exclaimed. 'And show a bit of gratitude that we didn't leave him out on the street.'

'Yes, all right, all right.' The man took charge of dragging the officer inside and then slamming the door, calling to someone named Ivy to give him a hand and for the dog to shut that row up.

'Ungrateful git,' Lorna said and slipped her arm through LeJeune's. 'Look, I hope you find her, John. Give her my love if you do, and tell her Stepney ain't the same without her.'

'I'll do that.'

*

He made the decision to stay in London and that above all he wanted Lizzie back. He didn't care what it took. He didn't want a final goodbye, he wanted her, and in his heart he knew she wanted him. They would fight the prejudices together. He'd seen two mixed couples arm in arm in the street. One of them had a child. A cream-coloured baby in a pushchair, and they seemed to be happy. He was going to find his way, find a job and a place to live. He had fought the war, not only for the mother country, but so that he could start a new life. Had he not fallen in love with Lizzie, he wasn't sure he would have gone back to Dominica, anyway.

Stepney itself was an unsightly wreck, and rebuilding it would take more than his lifetime. Other parts of London were not much better, and to him, that meant there'd be jobs even if he couldn't find something working on cars. Finding lodgings might prove to be more challenging. But his life here as a soldier was over, and he had to prove that he could be just as much use as a civilian.

He took a bus to Poplar, rode it all the way to the terminal, the bus garage that he hoped would be the one near Lizzie's new abode. Poplar didn't seem to be so built-up as Stepney and not so busy with people, either. But just as in Stepney,

151

they stared at him as if he were a curiosity, looking at him with disdain and questioning who he thought he was wearing the uniform. He averted the gazes: he knew that staring too long at the wrong person could cost him a thud in the jaw, spit on his shoes or even his face. He walked around looking for a park. At the end of a sun-locked street, he spotted some trees, sparse and short in the middle of a green. Hurrying towards it he saw a see-saw and two swings. As he stood at one end of the grassy square, he tried to count the number of houses that surrounded it and, therefore, the number of times he'd have to knock on a stranger's door asking if they knew Mick Walters or Lizzie Tarping.

After knocking on the seventh door – three of them going unanswered and four people giving him short shrift before slamming the door in his face – a woman pulled open the next door wide. It was as if she'd been expecting someone, her smile broad at first but crumpling into a suspicious grimace when she saw LeJeune.

'Yes?' She pushed the door to a narrow gap, one that showed one half of her body, the short sleeve of a cotton dress, a pink flabby arm, and a gold wristwatch that was pulled too tight.

'Good morning.' LeJeune nodded and took off his cap.

'You haven't come bringing bad news, have you?'

'No, not at all.'

'Good. Then what you come here for?'

'I'm looking for someone. A woman by the name of Lizzie. Lizzie Tarping.'

The woman heaved in a breath and stepped out onto the pavement. 'What you want with her?'

'You know her?'

'Ain't saying I do, ain't saying I don't.'

'So, you must be Micky's aunt.' LeJeune looked to an upper window, expecting to see Lizzie poke her head out, blonde curls surrounding her face, a smile and her cheeky way of asking, *What the flaming 'eck do you want, then*?

'What's he done now?' the woman asked.

'Done? No, he's done nothing. It's just Lizzie is … Lizzie is a friend of mine. We are friends. Very good friends, and I have something I need to say to her.'

The aunt narrowed her eyes.

'Um, so could I see her?'

'She ain't here. Gone the shops for us.'

'And Micky?'

'Not seen that sod in days.'

'Could I wait for her?'

'Not in here you flaming can't. And you'd best be off in case Micky shows up. He won't take kindly to some bloke, soldier or no, wanting a word with his missus.'

'Missus? You mean as in …'

'That's right. Missus as in they're married. A month ago.'

The woman shuffled back inside and closed the door. LeJeune staggered back a couple of paces, his legs feeling lifeless. Married. He hadn't expected that. It was one thing to try to persuade Lizzie to come away with him when she was Micky's girlfriend. But now she was his wife. He walked over to the swings and sat in one of them. He put his cap back on. It sat slanted off his brow, and he didn't care how well presented a serviceman he was or not. He loosened his tie and looked back towards the house. He saw Micky's aunt at a downstairs window, the net curtain pulled wide until she flicked it closed again. He'd wait for Lizzie, all day if he had to, and if Micky showed up, he'd deal with it.

The sun heated his back. It was warm for spring. His body temperature elevating as rays penetrated the thick fabrics. Beads of sweat pricked his skin, but he would not budge until he saw her. An hour later, he caught himself in a light nap and snapped to attention when he spotted a pretty blonde woman carrying a full shopping bag, wearing a dark blue dress. She stooped at the door to put the bag down, squinting across to the green as if she couldn't believe her eyes.

'Johnny? Is that really you?'

He stood, dazed, not knowing what to say. He hadn't rehearsed a speech, believing that the right words would come when he needed them and they'd be enough to convince her of leaving Micky for him. He couldn't offer her a home, he had no solid plans for his future, but he would remain in London for her. That he was sure about.

Leaving the bag by the door, Lizzie walked across the road. Her hair was longer, tied back in a bow, and she had no make-up on, her dark dress loose-fitting.

'What in the name of Christ are you doing here? How'd you find me?'

'Lizzie, I'm sorry to come like this. I know what you said before, that things couldn't work out for us, but we never ever gave it a try. And that's why I'm here. I want us to try. Together.' He pulled off his cap and mopped his upper lip with his cuff. He looked down, embarrassed that he'd fallen asleep and that he might not look the way she liked him to look. Smart and dashing in his uniform.

Lizzie stepped in closer to LeJeune. 'And you weren't listening when I said. What I told you hasn't changed, John. We can't be together because my parents would never allow it.'

'But what do they think of Micky? I know he has a reputation. People say he deserted. I'm not like that. I'll do right by
you.' He flicked a glance towards the dilapidated house.
That was not a place for his Lizzie. He would do better than
that.

'True, they might not think the world of him but they know
he loves me.'

'I love you.'

'It's not the same thing. In their eyes, Micky might be
down here'–she marked a place by her waist with her
hand–'but when they look at you, you'll be all the way down
here'–she dropped her hand further–'if they even look at you
at all.'

'Come with me to Dominica.'

Lizzie burst out laughing. 'Johnny, no. What the hell would
I do out there. I'm a Londoner through and through. I burn
even in this heat.' She gestured to the hazy sky. 'God knows
how I'd fare. That's not for me, John.'

'This is a big world. We could go anywhere. Anywhere
where people won't put me down there. I'm not down there.
I feel as though I am way up there. Sky high. Or at least I
can be.'

'And you're a dreamer. The world isn't fair, John. You
know that better than anyone.' She looked over her shoulder
at the house. 'Look, I shouldn't have put myself in your life.
I don't know what I was thinking. The war does things to a
person, makes them think things are one way when really
they're not.'

'That's just what you want to tell yourself because you're
afraid. Afraid of what people will say if you're with me.' He
held her upper arms. 'I'm not giving up on us.'

A voice called from across the road. 'You all right, Lizzie, love. Outside without a hat. Come indoors.'

'I'll be in in a minute, Aunty. Just give me a second. Take the cod in before it spoils.'

LeJeune released his hold of Lizzie's arms and took a step back. 'Can we just walk and get you out of this sun?' he implored.

'No, John. We can't.'

'I know you love me, Lizzie. Tell me you don't and I'll walk away.'

'I …' Lizzie walked past him over to a tree where she rested a palm on the thin bark and stood shaking her head, her eyes closed. He came and stood in front of her.

'You love me. I know you do. So why do we have to break each other's hearts like this?'

'You don't understand. Look.' She held out her left hand, a thin golden hoop adorning the third finger. 'I married Micky.'

'I know.'

She snapped a look at him. 'Then you'll know I'm a married woman and I shouldn't be talking to you about all this.'

'Married women leave their husbands, Lizzie. Especially if they made a mistake.'

'It weren't a mistake.' She straightened up, crossed her arms and looked at LeJeune with an expression he could neither read nor had seen before. It scared him. 'You think I'm some dumb young girl who doesn't know her mind. It was good while it lasted, John, but the minute Micky knocked on my door, I knew where the mistake was. It was with you. Not him. He's the one I love and that's why I married him. One day you'll get that in your thick head, your stubborn thick skull, and you'll know what I'm saying is true. I don't love you, Johnny. Never have, never will. So.'

The tears brimmed from LeJeune's eyes. She turned her head while he wiped at them, his hands shaking. He sniffed.

'No, Lizzie. Why are you talking like this?'

'I tried to let you down gentle but you won't have it. Now, I'm telling you in plain English. I want you gone. Stop looking for me. I don't want to be found by you, I want to get on with my life.' She rubbed her abdomen as if the thought of him was making her want to vomit and then she ran all the way to the house. Her aunt had left the door ajar. Lizzie slammed it when she entered, and LeJeune let out a sigh, heavy with sadness, anger and disbelief.

Minutes later as he stood beneath the stunted silver birch, he put his cap back on and straightened his tie. His tears had subsided, and he felt ashamed that he had shed them like that in front of Lizzie. That would be the last thing she would remember of him, crying in the street like a child. He would remember her blonde silky ponytail against the dark-coloured dress, Lizzie not turning back once and the soft milky colour of her cheek before it disappeared behind the closing door.

Chapter 17

Essie

London 1948

When I knock on the door, Eugene's landlady tells us that he is upstairs. It seems that Myrtle's inclusion of God the Father into my search for answers has led us to find Eugene at home rather than at work. He is grumpy looking when he comes to the door but perks up when he sees me. He frowns a little when he sees Myrtle but then bows graciously.

'You must be the mother of this beautiful child. I can see a likeness.'

'I'm not the mother, I'm her mother's cousin. My name is Mrs Young, and we've come for some information.'

'I already told Essie what I know. I don't know no more than that.'

Crusts of sleep have collected in the corners of his eyes which he rubs now and lets out a yawn that reeks of stale booze.

'Don't tell me you woke me up to go through the whole thing again.'

'I thought I just saw him,' I say before he can start throwing me off the trail again. 'Someone I thought was LeJeune. I mean John.'

'And?'

'I called after him. He didn't turn around so I knew it wasn't him.'

'Unless he deliberately wanted to avoid you.' Eugene raises his eyebrows as further warning that I should give up my quest.

'It wasn't him. He wouldn't leave me standing in the middle of the market and ignore me like that.'

'The market you say?'

'Yes.'

'If Johnny was that close, there is no way he wouldn't come to look me up. So you're right, it wasn't him. Unless he'd come over for a quick visit to …'

'To do what? See someone other than you?'

He hesitates before shrugging. I close in on him. Eugene has given something away that he hasn't intended to. He begins to backtrack.

'Look, I have no idea who or what business he has round here. Like I say. It can't be him and you shouldn't waste your time.' He steps back into the house and motions as if he is about to close the door.

'We haven't finished,' my cousin says. 'We have other questions about him. But before we get to that, I want you to look me in my eyes and tell me you're not holding something back that could help this child. Answer the question about who else he could be visiting. Can't you see she is desperate? She doesn't want to make trouble. Just find answers. Answers she deserves.'

'Please.' I screw my brow. 'Do you know of any other person who he might visit?'

'Listen, love. I don't know much. Just one thing.' He looks at his bare feet and shuffles both, like a child about to confess to a misdoing. 'Before he married you, there was a particular girl he saw during the war.'

I swallow and I want to ask her name, her age, if LeJeune was in love with her.

'Go on.'

'Everyone had a girl. And it was all a bit of harmless fun. After the war, everyone was supposed to go back to normal. But Johnny, he was on a mission. He wanted to stay for her. But she doesn't live in Stepney anymore, so it can't be her … she moved.'

'Moved where?' Myrtle's voice darkens.

'Poplar,' says Eugene. I immediately turn to Myrtle who shakes her head.

'It's not far,' she says, 'but it's no use if we don't have an address.'

Eugene raises both palms. 'That's all I know. I promise you. Like you say, it wasn't him you saw. I told you about the job and everything. Why he didn't come, why he disappeared, I don't know. I don't know anything more.'

I shake my head and look at my cousin. This is hopeless. I'm going around in circles.

'What was the other thing you wanted to ask me?' Eugene is well and truly fed up and wants nothing more than to close the door on this whole affair.

I push my hand into my pocket and take out the receipt with Bill Harper's telephone number on the back.

'Please could you write down all the details for John – his regiment, any rank or number – whatever you can say that will help people identify him.'

'You mean like the police? Don't go troubling the police about Johnny. I'm telling you. That man doesn't want to be found.'

'Well, let me just find him and then he can tell me himself.'

I push the piece of paper under Eugene's nose. He takes it. 'You have a pen?'

Myrtle produces a ballpoint pen from a pocket in her handbag. Eugene scribbles the details while leaning against the doorpost. He keeps shaking the pen when the ink runs to the bottom, and I feel all patience leaving me. When I try to settle my breath, I give way to a knowledge, rooted far inside me, that it is true. LeJeune has loved another woman. He is twenty-nine, so it's ridiculous to think that there could never have been anyone before me. But what hurts is that after the war he wanted to be with her instead of hurrying home to his own country, his people. Even me, though he wouldn't have known that. She must have rejected him, otherwise he would never have returned to Dominica. We would never have met. The idea makes me shiver.

'Here,' says Eugene, handing back the pen and paper. 'Is there anything more?'

'Nothing,' Myrtle says, beginning to usher me away. 'And thank you for your time.'

'My pleasure,' he says, looking directly at me. He winks. 'And if you never find him, you know where I am.'

I tut and leave with my cousin. Along with the million and one thoughts and questions that jangle my nerves, I'm instantly angered again by Eugene and I don't know how he and LeJeune could ever have been friends.

We make our way to the bus stop, and while Myrtle is wittering in the background of my thoughts about food she'd picked up in the market that you could never buy in England before the war, I'm thinking about taking a trip to Poplar. But where in Poplar would I start looking for answers about this woman whose name I don't even know?

'Wait.' I stop suddenly and make Myrtle jump. She is mid-sentence when she turns to me, checking me over with a swift look as if I've hurt myself or taken ill.

'What is it, child?'

'We have to go back. We didn't ask enough questions.' Before she can utter a word more, I turn and run back to Eugene's house. I find him on the doorstep, still looking only half awake, smoking a cigarette and chatting to another man with red hair that looks painted to his head.

'Back so soon? Want to take me up on my offer?' he asks.

'Is this the missus?' the man with Eugene asks. I shudder at the thought.

'I'm working on it,' says Eugene, and they both start laughing.

'Please,' I say, knowing that neither can hear me. I wait until they can compose themselves. A bout of coughing finally makes Eugene calm down and they both stop giggling.

'I don't want to use up too much of your time, but I meant to ask you before. The woman you said who was connected to John. What was her name?'

Eugene is very serious now and takes a long measured look at the red-haired man who himself is looking downward.

'What is the problem here?' I ask. 'It's a simple question.'

'The answer isn't so simple.'

'Why? Because there was more than one woman?' Tears of anger and frustration catch in my throat, but I hold them back.

'Back then, for him, there was only one.'

This thought chills me to my bones. I've only ever loved one man, and that LeJeune had found his 'only one' before he'd met me makes me want to cry in pain. I hate this. Standing here, begging to know her name. I want to die.

'So tell me.'

'Elizabeth. Lizzie Tarping.'

'Anything else?'

'Look, young Essie …'

'I'm not so young and don't call me that.'

'Miss Essie. You're wasting your time going after her.'

'But not if she has information about John. You said he wanted to see her after the war. So she was special to him.'

'That's true but that was then.'

'And when I saw you last time, you more or less told me he had someone *now*.'

'Yes, but not Lizzie. Maybe someone he met on the ship. Maybe someone he met between me getting him the job on the docks and him showing up the first day. Like I said before. He's found another something or someone and he doesn't want to tell you.'

'And what if that something or someone is Lizzie Tarping?'

'You're not listening. Only a fool would run after someone who doesn't want you.'

A tear lies dangerously in wait of spilling. 'I am not a fool.' I say it so loudly I shock myself.

'So, my dear girl, don't act like one. Go about your business. Go back home, stay here, but stop looking for Johnny. I well and truly believe it is a big, big waste of your time.'

'So you say, and I say again, he is going to have to be the one to tell me. To my face. If nothing else … he owes me that.'

Either I turn away or Myrtle turns me. But we're walking, now, away from Eugene, hopefully for the last time. He is of no more use to me. He has given me more clues but a lot of riddles, too. I now have a name which might help me to unravel this mystery. It's a mission now that I discover LeJeune's whereabouts or his secret hiding place. And what if he did meet someone on the ship to England? The journey lasted days. LeJeune had got himself entangled with a married woman whose husband had started a fight with him. He could either have found a way of seeing her again or there really is someone else. Someone who isn't married. And what of Lizzie Tarping? If I found her, would I get any more answers? My thoughts spiral, and I'm aware that Myrtle is allowing the turmoil within to settle as she walks slowly and silently beside me.

'Cousin, I'm sorry,' I say at last. 'I've got you mixed up in my mess.'

'Oh, Essie, you know I'm happy to help but …'

I stop and turn. 'But what?'

'As much as I dislike the man and as brutal with his words as he was … there was a bit of truth in what he was saying.'

'Myrtle, don't you go giving up on me now.'

'No, no. I'm not giving up. I just don't want you to build yourself up so much that when you find him it might break your heart.'

'You think I'll find him?'

'A man can't just disappear into thin air, can he?'

'Exactly. And I'm stronger than I look and I can accept anything. I just want the truth.'

I jump and turn around when I hear someone running along the road towards us. It's Eugene and he has something in his hand. He's out of breath when he stops.

'Did you come to tell me how silly I am again?' I ask him. 'What a child.'

'Look,' he says and holds a folded newspaper. It's an old edition of *The Evening News*, dated June.

'What is it?' I ask impatiently.

Eugene turns open a page and holds it close enough for me to see. There is a large picture, at the top of the page, of West Indian people walking down the stairs of an enormous ship, which the photograph only shows in part. There are families, young children, single men, all of them immaculate in smart suits, fine dresses and hats. On the dock, a line of West Indian men stand in front of some wooden crates. They are unsmiling, looking seriously into the lens.

'Why are you showing me this?'

'Look!' He shakes both his pointing finger and the newspaper so the whole image is blurred. I grab the paper from him and hold it still. Myrtle looks over my shoulder. Then my focus sharpens and so does the place in the photograph where the tip of Eugene's finger rests. It's LeJeune. He faces the camera but is looking off into the distance. He is wearing the same coat and carrying the same suitcase that he had when I waved him goodbye. I look up at Eugene.

'Why do you have this?'

'I buy this paper most days, and imagine my surprise when I saw my old friend. He was back in England and he hadn't looked me up. But he found his way to the Dockman's, and as luck would have it, I went for a drink that very evening. The rest you know.'

'Well. I still don't know everything. The rest of it. But I'm glad you kept the newspaper.'

'It's not every day you see your friend in the news. And he was my friend. A good friend. He made the war bearable.'

'You talk about him as if he isn't here anymore.'

Eugene shrugs. His whole demeanour has changed, and I don't hate him right in this moment because he has shown me an image that pulls LeJeune right into the present. A feeling that we are standing close together, holding hands, looking into each other's eyes.

'You keep this,' Eugene says.

'Are you sure?'

'I don't need it. All my memories of those days are in here.' He taps his head and then his heart, and for a second, I can understand why LeJeune had him as a friend.

'Thank you.'

Myrtle puts the paper into her shopping bag, and we say a final goodbye to Eugene who is still standing and watching us walk away when I turn back to wave at him.

*

We both feel tired by the time we get home, but in the kitchen, Myrtle finally has a chance to show me what she'd been so excited to find in the market in Stepney. Pumpkin and callaloo leaves. They are recent imports the stall-keeper had told her, and she'd spotted them when I was busy looking around at the faces of people in the market and then, as I'd thought, or hoped, found LeJeune's.

She lays the produce on the table along with more ingredients that had been missing from my attempts to make Mama's soup. And now my mind turns to home. My parents, my sister, the rich earth, the tranquil mornings and the warmth on my face. And now my stomach rumbles for the comfort of Mama's food. I begin to chop, fry, stew and boil. I make Mama's soup. I make so much there is enough to

166

feed the neighbourhood. I would do like Mama and take it around to people if I could. Fill their tummies. Make them feel good.

I close my eyes with every mouthful, tears slipping down my face, and I dream of a day when I can cook this very meal for LeJeune. When he sees me, whatever has kept him away won't matter. We will have a moment of sitting and eating happily together. We'll have several. I repeat these thoughts over and over until my bowl is empty.

Chapter 18

Between Islands

May 1948

Choppy, the seamen called it. Choppy. More like ferocious. Waves lashing the body of the ship, passengers throwing up over the sides of it. LeJeune was used to sea travel. He'd had lots of it during the war years. He'd sailed around Europe, three countries in total, but always thought of England as home. He'd reluctantly sailed away from home to return to Dominica after having stayed in London for almost a year after the war. Once again, England was his destination and he was returning for good as a married man. He couldn't wait until he could send for his wife, Esperanza. Still, he couldn't force the memories of that year in London away.

For most of that year, he'd hoped to one day bump into Lizzie, just at a time when she'd started to regret marrying Micky. He didn't imagine it would take long for her to real-ise her mistake and want him back. But he never saw her, never ran into her again. During the first month or so, he'd spent the odd night out with his army friend, Eugene. That was before Eugene found a young girl who he quite liked, and LeJeune didn't want to get in the way. Eventually, Eu-gene moved in with the girl but they travelled around within the shadows of night in order for him and the young girl, who was English, not to be seen together. Eugene would have welcomed a bare-knuckle brawl with anyone who said he shouldn't be with a white girl. But in time, she felt weighed down by guilt and shame and gave up on the relationship. When LeJeune heard about their break up, instead of going to console Eugene, he began wondering if it was time for him to leave London. Maybe everything Lizzie said about their doomed love affair might hold some truth. He'd found a job in a garage where he could continue tinkering with engines, and he'd started saving money. The job hadn't paid very well, but it took his mind off Lizzie. He kept busy, and the small attic room he was renting in Shoreditch reduced the likelihood of ever bumping into her.

Close to a year after the war ended, LeJeune left in the early hours for work. That morning, a spring morning, his hands were so cold he'd dropped a spanner five times, once just missing his foot. And his mind went to Lizzie. Then it dwelt on the misery of chilly and solemn mornings, the unsavoury bathroom he had to share with three other men and a kitchen whose sink was either blocked or filled with dirty plates. That's when he realised it was time. He wrote to tell his mother he was returning to Dominica. She didn't respond, but he paid his passage and sailed away without even letting Eugene know he was leaving. It had been the loneliest year of his life, and he'd secretly rejoiced when he saw his island again. So hot it looked to be steaming from the small passenger boat, the colours alive and the people so friendly he forgot the trials of the war and the year he'd spent mourning the love that had died between him and Lizzie.

In the middle of the ocean, he sat on a bench, the wind spinning the clouds overhead and the hiss and spray of the waves as loud as the motors in the ship's engine room. Now he was returning home after having spent two years in Dominica, mostly wishing that he hadn't left London. Those two years had made him realise that London was the place he wanted to call home, and his need to return was only upset by his meeting Esperanza. She was a beautiful girl. Thick, black hair to her shoulders, large brown eyes that flashed like the sun and lips he longed to kiss, right from the day she bumped into him in the market. Straight away, he'd wondered how tied she was to the island and whether she'd entertain the idea of leaving her family and sailing with him to England. She was a girl he could marry and spend the rest of his life with if she was willing to follow his dream. He knew she loved him and might go anywhere he wanted to go, and with each meeting, he could feel his heart melting for her in a way he hadn't expected. He'd thought his heart was frozen solid after losing Lizzie so finally. Esperanza broke through the ice with her innocence and her laughter and her chatter like a girl younger than her nineteen years. But she was perfect for him. To everyone else, he came across as icy, but she left him in a molten state with just one of her kisses.

He thought of her smile as the ship arrowed its way onwards through the sea. The other passengers seemed to settle now that they were days into the journey. People smiled and he smiled back, all the while thinking of Esperanza and the thought of sleeping side by side with her the moment she arrived to join him. He would get his head down and work, scrimp and save and make sure Esperanza would be with him as soon as possible.

The sun began to sink now, and people were going below to eat and get out of the wind. The wind calmed him and gave him space to imagine his new life with Esperanza. But his empty stomach was relentless in its pleas for food and moaned loudly for him to go below deck to fill it. Climbing down the narrow metal stairs, he could smell boiled meat and he could hear something, too. A beautiful voice. A girl was singing, and she had managed to quiet the whole of the canteen floor with her magical notes that swirled into a rhythm LeJeune found mesmerising. She was young, he noticed when he glanced over his shoulder, plate outstretched for the canteen assistant to slop boiled meat and potatoes onto it. She reminded him of Esperanza: they were about the same age, but this girl was a lot bolder the way she rocked her hips from side to side, singing to a roomful of strangers. He had a feeling she would not remain a stranger to the passengers for very long, especially if she was going to captivate them with her voice every evening.

'Anything else?' the canteen assistant asked.

'Er, no. No, that's plenty.' The food on the ship had been the worst he'd tasted in his life, but they were days away from landing in England and he had to eat something.

LeJeune found a seat on the edge of a long table of passengers. Most of them were Black, most of them were men. Black families joined The Empire Windrush from the West Indies, mostly from Jamaica. Several Europeans were already on board and others were to be picked up from places of rescue. He thought he recognised Polish being spoken having met some Poles in London after the war. He recognised their pale blue eyes and the look of a person far from home. *Like the rest of us*, he thought. He began to eat, carefully picking around the meat for gristle, which he hated, but was stilled by the singer again. He looked up at her, forgetting his food for a while as he listened to her sing a song whose lyrics mourned of sorrows past and hope for a brighter tomorrow.

'You like calypso?' A voice interrupted his musings of dancing at his wedding with Esperanza.

'Excuse me?' he asked, turning to the woman on his right. She was smiling at him with a wide gap in the middle of her front teeth. She was very attractive and seemed friendly. Her friend leant around her to see him, smiling with cheeks full of food. Both women appeared very interested to engage with him. 'Oh yes. Yes. I suppose I do.'

'That girl,' said the woman with the gap in her teeth, nodding to the singer. 'She comes from Trinidad. She's a big sensation there. Been on the radio and everything. They say she is going to England to become a star.'

'Good for her.' LeJeune put a piece of meat in his mouth, instantly regretting it as it was nothing but stringy fat. The girls beside him giggled when he grimaced.

'Doesn't look like you enjoy the food onboard. Bet you wish you were back home.'

LeJeune nodded.

'Go on, spit it out,' said the girl, handing him a paper napkin. 'I wouldn't blame you.'

As discreetly as he could, LeJeune rid himself of the foul texture and taste. He sipped some water.

'So where you from?' the girl asked him. 'I'm Bettina and this is Mary. We come from Jamaica.'

'Pleased to meet you. I'm John. John Francis. Dominica.'

The girls giggled again.

'We thought so,' sang Bettina. 'Those grey, grey eyes of yours. Must be the French in you. Right? At first we took you for a white man because you're so pale.'

'No. I'm far from white.'

'And far from home. Who you leave behind?'

'Just my mother and my wife. For now.'

'You going to send for her?'

'As soon as I'm settled. I have a job waiting. Just need to find some permanent digs.'

'Digs? What is digs?'

'A place to stay. For me and her.'

Bettina and her friend turned from him and started clapping now that the girl had finished her song. He'd been embarrassed to answer Bettina's questions because the girl sang so wonderfully but also felt rude shushing Bettina who had been the only person kind enough to strike up a proper conversation. He would like to have talked about Esperanza to someone. He missed her and it surprised him how much. She had been the one who had been able to reach into his soul after so much darkness and bring him back to life. Woken him from a grim and endless dream.

'She's wonderful,' said Bettina. 'Now, eat your potatoes. You have to keep up your strength.' The women laughed again, gathered their plates and excused themselves leaving LeJeune picking the eyes out of his boiled potatoes and listening to another song by the young girl. She had wanted to leave the canteen but had been encouraged by rapturous applause and cheers for an encore. He had a feeling it would be a long night for her below deck.

*

He spent most of his time alone or in his shared cabin with two sets of bunk beds. Shuffling along the top deck the day after meeting Bettina and Mary, he saw them huddled together with blankets over their knees on a pair of deck chairs that were always occupied whenever he passed them.

'Afternoon ladies.' Out of politeness, he stopped. They immediately started regaling him with their thoughts on the Catholic sermon that had taken place that morning. They were both Anglican and were discussing the differences.

'Do you go to church, John?'

'Apart from my wedding day, not regularly. And never at all when I was in England.' When he had returned to Dominica, he had visited an old friend and stayed up all night drinking. His friend had persuaded him to go with him to the Catholic church the next morning. It had been his first encounter with Esperanza. How beautiful she'd looked, a vibrant flower by the river, her smile blooming. He hadn't heard a single word his friend had said.

'You already been in England?' shrieked Bettina.

'I fought in the war.'

She shrieked again and pulled LeJeune to his knees so that he was at her eye level and stifled him in a hug.

'How brave you are. I thought you had the look of a soldier.' She held his chin and moved his face from side to side. 'Or were you a sailor? Or perhaps RAF?'

LeJeune grinned as she appraised his face. Chuckling to himself about coming close to fulfilling his intention to fly but being persuaded otherwise. How different his life would have turned out had he stuck to his goal. He had felt uncomfortable about someone else making the decision for him, but he hadn't hated being a soldier. Not for one moment. It had been the first time in his life he'd had a sense of purpose.

Bettina stroked his cheek and sighed.

'You know you are a very handsome man.' She pinched his chin between her thumb and finger. LeJeune began to lose his balance and toppled towards her just as a man with a thick Jamaican accent yelled a string of abuse. He hadn't realised it was directed at him until the same man caught him by his collar, dragged him up to standing, almost choking him in the process. With a bold shrug, LeJeune freed himself. Turning to see who his assailant was, he pushed out at him.

'What the hell do you think you're doing?' LeJeune's cheeks burned.

'Me?' the man yelled. 'Who tell you you can manhandle my wife?'

'I don't even know your wife.'

'Look she there, sitting down. Wasn't that you I saw with your hands all over her?'

'We were just talking. I lost my footing.'

The man squared up to him. 'If I see you anywhere near her again, you and I will have more than words.' He stepped in closer. 'You hear me?'

'Loud and clear.' LeJeune began to step away.

'Yes, it's best you go. I don't wish to see your face on this ship again.'

LeJeune turned his back. Happy to leave them to it, he walked with clenched fists to the starboard side of the ship. There he exhaled and leant his elbows over the rails. The sea overwhelmed the view. Miles and miles of it, and every one taking him further away from Esperanza. He was glad she hadn't had to witness that ugly scene. She might have been afraid. But then Bettina would never have spoken to him at all had Esperanza been there. He felt another tug at his heart as he remembered a time when he missed someone else as much. He had fallen out of love with Lizzie a while ago now. Had he held on to the strength of his feelings, there would have been no room at all for Esperanza. Not for anyone. There was once a time when he could not imagine life without Lizzie, that when they said goodbye he would never find love again. It's not that he'd forgotten Lizzie: there would always be a place in his heart for her. She was, after all, the one who taught him how to love and how to find the good in people. Esperanza was his new teacher, he thought, his second chance, his future.

'It's not going anywhere.' A voice disturbed his train of thought. So fixated on Esperanza, the speed of the wind and the slick of ocean spray on his face, he thought he'd imagined it.

'I'm sorry, I didn't quite …' He turned to find the girl who had been singing below deck standing so close that their arms were almost touching. She had on a short-sleeved dress, and he could see goose pimples covering her skin. Her wavy, jet black hair was sleeked back into a ponytail that the wind whipped away from her shoulders. How she reminded him of Esperanza.

'You're staring so hard at the sea, it's like you want it to vanish or something.'

'Not vanish, just hurry up and get me to England.'

'You have someone special waiting?'

'A job. Hopefully the start of my life.'

'How old are you that your life hasn't started yet?'

'Well, I'm twenty-nine but I've already seen a lot of life. Done a lot of things, things I never imagined I'd ever do. But lately, I feel as if I've come back to life.' He spoke so personally to a near stranger, something the old LeJeune would never have done.

She laughed, putting her hand over her lips the way Esperanza did.

'And how old are you if you don't mind me asking?' LeJeune turned sideways on to her, one elbow still on the rail. She laughed again.

'A gentleman – and I did take you for one – doesn't ask a lady her age. Besides, you don't even know my name and you're asking my age.' She had long white teeth that were straight and pretty and rested on the plum colour of her lips. Her lipstick glimmered and silver-hooped earrings framed her face.

'I know your name. You're Mona Baptiste. They tell me you are a famous singer from Trinidad.'

'You are correct, Mr …?'

'Francis. John Francis.'

They shook hands. The sweet scent of tropical flowers floated from her on the breeze towards him. He looked around, briefly, for a jealous husband. He shouldn't get too friendly. But he could sense that becoming more friendly was what Mona wanted. Her face was happy, in fact everything about her spoke of a carefree lightness which, without realising it, was filtering into him.

'If you must know, I'm twenty. I've been singing for years, but I want more than Trinidad can give me. I'm taking my chances in England. I'm going to cut a record and sing on the stage. One day.'

'You have your whole life mapped out, then?'

'I'm open to surprises, but I know what I want and I know I'll get it, too. The land of opportunities.'

'I thought that was America. Did you not think to try your luck over there?'

'It wouldn't suit me. Besides, someone from home had some contacts and I've been chatting to a few of the musicians onboard. Forming alliances shall we say.'

'There are other musicians here?'

'Goodness me, are you blind? Lord Kitchener, Lord Woodbine are here. Lord Beginner from Trinidad. He and I have been deep in conversation, and I'm singing in a show he already has lined up. You should come to see it.'

'Of course.'

They talked for over an hour, and when she began to shiver, LeJeune took off his jacket and placed it over her shoulders. By then, she knew he was a married man and he knew that she was a single woman.

'Your wife is very lucky that she married a gentleman.'

LeJeune shrugged. He knew that he was lucky to have found his wife.

'We are giving up the sun for our new lives,' Mona said, clinging to the lapels of his jacket as it swamped her shoulders. She was still shivering a little, looking out at the ocean where grey and white clouds floated away on lazy streams of air, the wind speed reduced now. The sun was only just visible, and far in the distance what looked like land came and went like waves on the shoreline. 'Are you sure you can leave the island life for good?'

'I managed it before. And it's not as if England doesn't have sun. It's just …'

'Different?'

He nodded and looked at Mona's face in profile. A long, arrogant nose and childlike dimples about to deepen with a smile. She turned to him.

'Well, I have my warm clothes all ready. I'm ready. Ready to become a star. I really hope you can come to the show. I'll write it all down for you. Date and time and everything.' She returned her gaze to the sea and LeJeune followed suit. He was ready for his new life. He was excited. Just as he began to grin to himself, a strange emotion, one he'd never experienced, shrank his smile and left a film of goose pimples over the entirety of his body. He shivered and shoved his hands into his pockets. The ghostly mirage of land vanished for good, and all he could see was the endless, unrelenting water.

*

Two days later, The Empire Windrush was drawing in closer to the docks at Tilbury. There was a fizz of excitement on every deck: chatter, bustle. People were gathering themselves, bracing themselves to face the next phase of their lives. The passengers – those who had never seen England, and that was the majority – wanted to get the first look. LeJeune saw Bettina and her husband holding hands as they watched the British Isles becoming larger, becoming real. Passengers had been discussing their plans on the journey; LeJeune had overheard the conversations. The jobs they were going to: nursing, teaching, factories. The places they would live: London, Birmingham, Bristol. From what he could tell, like him, a few were also going to temporary accommodation. His was in Clapham, a part of London he didn't know at all.

There was a lot of commotion on the dock. There were photographers and crowds of people just standing and waiting. He hadn't anticipated such a spectacle. The West Indian men and women were in their best clothes, shoes shining, stylish, hope and fear oozing from their pores. Some posed for photographs. *Stand this way. Give us a smile.* They smiled and strutted in their hats, thin ties, Sunday shoes and neatly combed hair. It was a thing to behold, and LeJeune knew these images would be captured forever in news reels, a photograph in his own memory forever. He held onto his suitcase and looked around for an escape out of the mayhem, unable to extricate himself from snapshots that were happening all around him.

'Mona!' 'Mona Baptiste!' 'Miss Baptiste!'

LeJeune looked around for his new friend who breezed past him, tapping his arm as she went to join a line of photographers eager to take her picture. LeJeune stood to one side as cameras were pointed directly at her. She was being pushed and pulled by the press and the photographers, but she seemed not to mind in the least. She had forgotten about him, forgotten to give him the details of her show. She would disappear, become a star, and he would never see her again and never convince anyone that he was once friends with the great Mona Baptiste. Mona was wearing a dark suit. Underneath it was a peach-coloured blouse with a ruffle down the sternum that flapped in the breeze. She wore high heels. She'd never done so on board. She had always been in flat, shiny pumps and a colourful summer button-through dress. Her luscious hair was parted in the middle now and waved into the fashionable style he'd seen movie stars wearing. To see her now, so stylish, he believed the gossip that she had travelled on the ship with a first-class ticket. Of course she had. Mona couldn't stop smiling as someone handed her a saxophone that he didn't imagine she knew how to play because of the curious way she looked at it. The same someone led her by the arm so that she could pose with the saxophone in front of a line of Black soldiers, clearly there for this purpose. A moment captured in time of the singer Mona Baptiste who LeJeune was lucky enough to meet on a long and strained journey across the sea.

Seeing the soldiers smiling happily in two rows, one kneeling, one standing, made his heart swell with pride and longing. They looked sharp in their neat and pressed uniforms. Ties straightened, chins shaved. But he quickly shook the thought of re-joining the army from his head. His future was in London with Esperanza. As the fuss continued around him, he saw Mona, still posing for photographs, pretending to play the saxophone, giggling from time to time as the instrument was almost her size. *She looks so happy*, LeJeune thought and decided to walk away despite not having the means to contact her again. He put a hand in his pocket to check the address of his next destination only to find an extra piece of paper there. The name of a guest house, a time, a date and the name *Mona* with an X beside it. Mona would be a part of his life after all.

Chapter 19

Essie

London 1948

When I got up this morning, I felt disorientated. I'd woken with a sense of confusion, not knowing where I was, whose bed I was in and in whose house. I felt that LeJeune didn't want me here, didn't want me to find him. That I should go back home. I sobbed silently in my bed so that Myrtle wouldn't hear and wiped away the thoughts as I did the tears. I wondered when the last teardrop would fall for him, when the smiles and laughter would begin.

This voyage across the ocean, leaving one island to travel to another so far away, was supposed to turn out differently. By now, I should have been reunited with LeJeune. I'd dreamt that we would hug each other endlessly, me as the saviour who had come to England to rescue him from whatever had befallen him, and him the hero whose journey had taken a detour but was now firmly on track.

It's so difficult to keep the happy ending in mind because if I am to believe Eugene, this was just a wasted trip. My husband doesn't want to be found. But meeting Bill Harper has given me another glimmer of hope. Of course I must increase my search and, very possibly, I must involve the police. I decide to call Mr Harper to let him know the details I

182

have for LeJeune. If he can ask around about him as he'd offered to do, I might be a few steps closer to discovering what on earth has become of my husband.

In the red telephone box at the far end of the street, the phone rings for several minutes as I hold the receiver away from my face. It has a funny smell that I can't get used to, like stale cigarettes, mouldy food and unwashed bodies. Myrtle said I could ask Mrs Rogers to use their phone upstairs, but I didn't want to intrude again as Mrs Rogers has already gone out of her way. That said, I do owe it to the Rogers family to let them know my progress so far. Especially Graham who I haven't seen since the night we were chased. They have done a lot to help me and I'm thankful. Ideally, I'd like to present them with LeJeune on my arm and to let them know that I was never a sorry, young fool in love.

I hear pips on the phone and push a coin into the slot. It enters with a loud clonk and I hear clarity like a big open space on the other end.

'Hello?' I say into its vastness. 'Is that Mr Harper?'

'Hang on,' a voice says, and I hear women's heels and the voice calling for Bill. He comes quickly to the phone.

'Hello?' he says brightly, his kind face coming to mind.

'Oh, hello, Mr Harper. This is Essie. Esperanza Francis who bumped into you in the market and knocked over all your bread rolls.' My throat feels dry, and I'm speaking loudly in case he can't hear me.

'Ah yes,' he says. 'The young girl with the missing husband.'

'Yes, that's right.'

'I take it, then, that you haven't found him. Or, mercifully, you're calling to tell me that you have.'

'I wish I could tell you that, but there's still no sign. I have my husband's regiment details, and now I have a photograph of him. Well, a picture from a newspaper on the day he arrived in England.'

'Well, that's something to go on. Maybe we can get some posters printed up, ask the printers if they can use the newspaper photograph. Well done.'

I sigh a laugh. It doesn't feel very well done but it's a start. Maybe a good one if someone recognises LeJeune.

'You should come over and bring me all you have. I can help you make a mock-up of the poster and we can walk it around the printers to see if they can run something off.'

I hadn't imagined involving a printer. I wonder what the cost will be. I think about my dwindling funds. But then, if this helps me find LeJeune, it will have been worth it.

'I can come tomorrow morning if you tell me how to get to the restaurant. And you have the time, of course.'

'I'll certainly make time for you. I mean it's important, isn't it?'

'You have no idea and thank you, Mr Harper.'

'And none of this Mr Harper malarkey. It's Bill. Just Bill. The restaurant isn't far from where we met. Ask anyone in the market for Harper's and they'll point it out.'

The sound of those pips returns.

'Ten o'clock?' I ask.

'Perfect.'

The phone goes silent after a click, before I get the chance to say goodbye. I don't have any more change for the phone but it's all arranged. I go back to the house to cut out the picture from the newspaper.

*

184

By now, I know my way to Stepney. The woman I ask for directions to Harper's is the one who had chastised Bill for having lost her supply of bread rolls to the dirty Stepney Market ground. She looks at me through squinted eyes.

'What business do you have with Bill? I remember you from the other day.'

'I remember you, too.' I square up to her the way she does me. Although I don't want to be impolite, I don't know who or what she is to Bill and I need her help. I just want people to stop regarding me as a little girl and perhaps I'll start to get somewhere. I look at her with all the defiance of my little sister, Ginnie. It seems to weaken the stall-keeper's resolve.

'You didn't answer the question,' she says.

'If you want to know what my business is with Mr Harper, then you should ask him. It's a private matter and I won't be telling you.'

She folds her arms and pulls a face that tells me she likes my attitude, though I suspect she thinks me a little cheeky. No more than her for asking me in the first place. Mama always tells me to be careful who I tell my business to, and I don't know this woman, though she smiles warmly to me now and points a finger with traces of sugar on it.

'You turn that corner and you're on Dunstable Avenue. It's a big road with lots of tea shops and a cinema on it. Harper's is right next to the cinema.'

'Thank you,' I say with a nod.

'Welcome. I'm sure.' She does a slight curtsy and winks at me before turning to a customer who has just asked if she's 'serving today or what'.

'All right, keep your hair on, love. Not that you've got much left,' she says, and the two burst into gales of laughter as I set off to find Dunstable Avenue.

It's a wide road lined with shops on either side. Hardware shops, hairdressers, a pub, a newsagent. The frontage of each of these looks as if they need a good wash and the front porches a good sweeping. A group of scruffy young children tear past me and almost knock me over. I wonder why they are not at school now that September has arrived. They wear short trousers and short skirts, their socks wrinkled at their ankles and run as wildly as Ginnie and her friends with all the freedom of the world in their grasp.

The day isn't as chilly as the last few, so I'm not buttoned in tight in my blue jacket. I walk casually as if I know the place and I feel that Stepney will become a more familiar area in time. With each step, I know that I'm no longer afraid of my own shadow or like the lost little girl I was when I first arrived. I have a real sense of purpose, and with each step that takes me closer to the cinema and so to Harper's, I feel my confidence grow and I feel positive that this visit to see Bill will be the turning point of my search.

The cinema on the corner is showing *Anna Karenina* starring Vivian Leigh. I think about a time that I can go and watch a film, sitting side by side with LeJeune, holding hands in the dark. I stare at the dusty looking cinema and can't imagine the seats inside being particularly comfortable or clean, judging by the look of the neighbourhood.

'You found it all right, then?'

Bill Harper stands outside his small restaurant, rocking backwards on his heels, wearing a long apron, his sleeves rolled up, hands buried deep in his trouser pockets.

'Oh, Bill,' I say with a start. I had been letting my mind wander while standing directly outside Harper's.

'Come in, come in,' he says in his friendly manner. Now that I see him again, I notice what a handsome man he is. I suppose I had been a little too flustered to notice before. Bill holds open the door, and we walk into a tiny restaurant with about five square tables all covered in plastic tablecloths patterned with pictures of herbs and spices or fruit and vegetables. There is an ashtray on each plus a salt shaker and a bottle of brown sauce. The air is filled with the smell of baked bread.

'Would you like me to take your jacket?'

'Thank you,' I reply and allow Bill to remove it and hang it on a coat stand by the door where there is a redundant red umbrella waiting within a metal bucket for rain. There are no customers. Perhaps they only serve in the evenings.

'It's a nice place you have here,' I say with all sincerity. 'Cosy. Like home.'

'Well, that's what I'd like to think. A bit of home cooking and the odd sandwich, sometimes a roast if I'm being fancy.' He chuckles. 'And if I'm feeling extra fancy, then I throw in some gravy.' He starts to laugh, but who serves hot food without gravy? My mind flashes to Myrtle's kitchen where the remainder of the large amount of soup I made with the pumpkin and callaloo leaves sits in the fridge. Tasty, but not like Mama's, not until I can find the right ingredients.

'Tea?' Bill is asking.

'Please,' I say, and he disappears through a pair of swing doors into the kitchen. I hear him whistling a tune before a radio comes on. He pops his head back out.

'Didn't ask how you like it. Let me guess. White with two?'

I nod and smile instantly at the warmth his own smile generates. He reappears with two mugs of tea and sets them noisily onto the table before pulling up a chair.

'So, if you don't live in Stepney, where do you live?' He sits back in his chair.

'I'm staying with my Mum's cousin in Paddington.'

'Paddington? That's a way to come.'

'Well, my search led me here.'

'Of course. Of course. It's a queer thing this missing husband of yours. I mean, London can be a big place but there's not much chance he's lost.' He blows into his tea, sips and his cheeks redden. I know what he's implying. The same as everyone else. LeJeune isn't lost. He just doesn't want to be found. 'I suppose you're worried sick.'

I nod and put my hands around the mug.

'I brought the newspaper and everything,' I say. 'I don't know how to go about making a poster, and I have no idea how much a poster will cost.'

'Oh no, no, no. I'll sort all that out. The printers, Vinny and his crowd, they owe me a few favours. Pay them a pretty penny to print up my menu for me, so what's a couple of posters extra? I thought the menus might poshen the place up, but in the end, people either take them away, write shopping lists on them or tips for the horse racing and such like.'

'Oh,' I say. 'That's a shame.'

'Not really. I won a couple of bob on the two thirty at Aintree last Saturday.' He laughs heartily, and I chuckle along as if I've understood any of what he's said. 'I decided I'll just chalk everything on a board and put it outside or up there. The way my parents used to.' He points to a blackboard up on the wall above the swing doors. 'And it's not like there's ever much on the menu, anyway.' He laughs again and takes a big sip of tea. 'Right, let's have a look,' he says.

'I beg your pardon.'

'The stuff you have on the missing John Francis.'

'You remember his name.'

'Photographic memory.' He winks. 'Never forget a thing.'

'I thought it meant that you never forget the things you see.' I screw my brow.

'And I didn't forget you now, did I?'

I feel my cheeks grow hot before pulling out the newspaper cutting and the notes with LeJeune's army details. Bill takes the cutting.

'Good-looking chap. No wonder you want to find him.'

I blush again.

'If you don't mind my saying so, he looks very light-skinned, almost white.'

I look over at the picture. 'I suppose, and where I come from that is considered very attractive. More attractive than say ... my complexion.' I rub the skin on the back of my hand.

'I can't understand that. I look at you and see a thing of beauty. A caramel-coloured one. Much better than pasty old me.'

We both grin at that as he puts his hand next to mine to compare our skin tone. But it doesn't go unnoticed that Bill has told me he thinks I'm beautiful. For a second I forget myself. My mission. I move my hand.

'Mad anyway,' he says, quickly removing his hand, too. 'Beauty is in the eye of the beholder and all that.'

He stares down at the information I've provided, then leaves his chair to dart back into the kitchen. In seconds he returns with a large pad of paper and a pencil.

'Now then,' he says. 'Let's come up with what we're saying on this poster. I've got some ideas. Do you mind?'

'No, please. You go ahead. I'm just so happy to have met
you.' He looks up at me. 'You've been so helpful, and I
really should give you some money for this.'

'I promise. I'm happy to help.' He puts his head down to
write on a sheet of lined paper.

'But I can go to the printers myself. You have a business to
run.'

'Don't worry about that. I was only in to bake the bread. I
don't open on a Wednesday for serving. It used to be a half
day. Now we're closed all day. Business has been that slow
since, you know, the war and all.'

I remember LeJeune had spent a whole year in London
after the war finished. I had tried to imagine the ruins after
the Blitz, the people left homeless in an economy that was
struggling to rehouse the ones who'd suffered and feed the
ones who were starving. Did he return to Dominica after de-
ciding it was too miserable a place, or was the reason more
to do with Lizzie Tarping? I want so much to know if she is
anything to do with his decision to return and his disappearance after.

Since knowing her name, I've lain awake thinking about
the two of them together. I can't help it. Then I get cross
with myself and ask why, for goodness' sake, would LeJeune
tell me he loved me, marry me, only to return to her. I have
the letter he sent signed *Love, LeJeune*. I have it with me all
the time. LeJeune has not left me. And I will not leave him. I
will find him.

'I'm sure things will pick up,' I say encouragingly. 'It's in
the name. Great Britain. Things will be great again, and so
will your restaurant.'

'You should run for prime minister. That would make a good slogan for your campaign. I'll get us another cuppa. You can use that imagination of yours to come up with the wording of the poster yourself.'

'I'll help you with the tea.'

I follow Bill through to the kitchen. It is small. Just one counter for preparing food with a cooker, fridges and shelves along the side, lined with ingredients. The large sinks are on the back wall under a small window next to a door, now ajar, that leads to a small yard. I can see paving stones outside. It's so warm and welcoming in here, another reminder of my mother's kitchen, the thought settling as a lump in my throat.

'Not so impressive in here, I grant you,' Bill says as he notices my thoughts have travelled but will have no idea where to.

'It's a good, clean place to work. I imagine you must have a lot of satisfied customers.'

'Not so's you'd notice. Like I say, business is slow. I only hope I can keep it going. Keep it in the family.'

'And you don't have a sister who could help you in here?'

He grins at me. 'Are you saying men can't cook?'

'Not at all, men can cook fine. But I know a lot of them don't want to.' I smile as I think about life back home, women in the kitchen and looking after the children. Men out toiling and bringing in the money.

'I do have a sister. Two in fact. Neither can cook very well and neither is still in London. When Mum was preparing food, when this was a tea shop, I was the one learning how to make all the cakes. That's how I got into baking. Now that we're not a tea shop anymore, I struggle to get a decent menu together. Something with imagination.'

I know that Myrtle cooks the English way: colourless food, processed food and everything so bland. Myrtle loves it when I try to replicate the dishes from home. The problem is the lack of provisions here, especially the ones we grow at home.

'Maybe some recipe books,' I suggest.

Bill points to the row of recipe books on one of the upper shelves.

'What about you?' Bill finally puts the kettle on. 'What do you like to eat?'

I tell him all about how popular my mama's food is in the village and give him a full explanation about the soup. I speak of how much I love to cook, how much I've learnt from Mama and how much I'm missing being in the kitchen back home. He is gripped and seems to make a mental note of everything I say.

'The soup sounds tasty. I wish you could come and cook here.'

'If I was closer I would. Myrtle was able to get some food from home in the market. In fact, I need to buy some more while I'm here.'

'You know, being a dock, we are able to get quite a few things from abroad. I wonder?'

'Wonder what?'

'If I can supply you with as many of the ingredients you need for your soup, could I convince you to make it as a dish for in here one day?'

I blush and my heart beats a little faster. It's not as though I'm opposed to the idea. 'I would be far too nervous to cook a large meal for so many strangers. Especially English ones who don't really know the food.'

'Well, that's how we learn, isn't it?'

I nod and think about the idea. About how off track from finding LeJeune something like that would take me. But once, for a special occasion, it wouldn't be such a bad idea, and with everything Bill is doing to help me to find him, I should do something to show how grateful I am.

I nod again after staring down at my feet for several seconds.

'Is that a yes?' Bill's smile is broad again, and I find myself thinking about what a good-looking man he is. His eyes are brown like cacao and reflect the kindness he has shown. I smile back just as widely.

'Yes, I'll do it. One day. Just once.'

'Once and just see how it goes?'

'Meaning?'

'What I mean is, if everyone loves it, they'll come back for more and I can't cook Mama's soup.' His grin is boyish and manages to both charm and flatter me.

'You will have to taste it for yourself first. Before making a decision and putting it on the menu.'

'Can't wait.' We have both forgotten that we came to the kitchen to make tea. 'Now, let's get this poster sorted. I'm thinking that when John Francis shows up, you might convince him to move back to Stepney and you can carry on cooking here.'

'You are a dreamer,' I say to Bill. *Like LeJeune*, I think to myself.

'Nothing wrong with dreams. They're what real life is based on.'

Much later, when we have the wording of the poster sorted out, Bill says he'll walk it around to the printers for me. He needs to get off and buy supplies, and I'm aware that I've taken up a lot of his time. It has passed quickly, and I've been completely absorbed in Bill's plan to make Harper's as popular in the future as it was when it was a tea shop. We talk about how charming the entire road will be one day, and I wonder all the while where I will be by then, who I will be.

'Right then, Essie, you mind how you go,' he says when he walks me to my bus stop.

'Thank you, Bill. I feel silly saying it again, but there aren't many people who would take pity on a stranger.'

'It's my pleasure, and if you want me to come with you to talk to the police, you've only to ask.'

My bus arrives, and Bill offers to help me step on-board. He stands there until the bus moves off. I turn to wave from the window seat and catch myself. I have forgotten to tell Bill that I have a name of someone in Poplar who may know something about John. As the bus thrums loudly past the station, I wonder how on earth I could have forgotten to ask him about Lizzie Tarping.

Chapter 20

London

1948

After settling in to the temporary room in Clapham in South West London, LeJeune decided he'd find out the best route to Hammersmith in West London to his new place of work. He wanted to let them know that he'd arrived and that he was ready to start work at the agreed date in his letter of employment. He would have to be fitted for some overalls and possibly hard-wearing shoes or boots – maybe he could do that right away. The factory made parts for hospitals and schools. It wasn't car mechanics but at least this was a job that required a keen eye and someone who was good with their hands. He was sure that in a few weeks he'd be set up with permanent lodgings in West London and sending for Esperanza to join him.

It was a long journey by tube and bus to Hammersmith, and LeJeune was in good humour the whole way. He'd already sent a letter home to Esperanza, telling her that he had arrived safely, that he'd write again soon and that he couldn't wait to see her. He hadn't implied an exact length of time because until he was in his new job and had an idea about the cost of renting a flat in West London, he couldn't really be sure how long it would take him to save up. He would be so careful with his money. He had met with Mona already, and with her thirst for thrills and excitement, he had to be sure he didn't end up broke. She would make sure he had a free ticket for her show, but still, he needed to be careful. Be careful with her.

The bus to the factory rattled in a familiar way. There were no blocked roads to negotiate because of bomb damage, but there was a noticeable amount of building works underway; gradually the city was being restored. He couldn't wait for his wife to marvel at how London would grow and improve.

Jumping off the bus, he whistled for most of the ten-minute walk to the factory. There was a car park before the depot doors where a solitary, dirty white van was parked. He passed it as he headed towards an office just beside the vast depot doorway. The office was empty, so he went into the factory. The place was quiet and unusually dark, not a single soul around. He doubled back to try the office door. If it was unlocked, there might be some bell or something that he could sound and grab someone's attention. Before he could turn the handle, someone shouted, 'Oi!'

LeJeune spun on his heel and saw a man of over six foot wearing a dark blue overall, the seams of which strained around the vast orb of his stomach. He had on a hard hat which he removed as he approached, a deep frown in his forehead.

'What you doing in here?'

'Good morning,' LeJeune said, putting out a hand. The man looked down and hesitated before shaking it. 'My name is John Francis. I'm due to start work here.'

'Oh yeah. Who told you that, then?'

'Well, I wrote. Several times, in fact, to a Mr Peverel.'

'He's gone, mate.'

'Gone? As in he died? I'm sorry to hear that.'

'No, he hasn't snuffed it. Retired. Well, redundancy they call it.'

'I see, so who is in charge now?'

'In charge of what exactly?'

LeJeune cleared his throat. 'It seems I should explain. I answered a job vacancy. I came over from the West Indies just five days ago, but before that I was offered the job in the factory.' He patted his jacket pocket. 'Actually, I don't have the letter of appointment on me but I have to sign some papers and a contract as well.'

The man straightened and shook his head. 'How long ago were you offered this job?'

'Two months ago.'

'Blimey,' he said. 'Two months ago everyone was given their marching orders. The works all moved up north, some factory in Manchester. That's what became of that lot. There's no job here for you. I take it they didn't write and tell you not to come.'

LeJeune shook his head. What the hell was he to do now?

'We're here dismantling and clearing the whole thing.'

'And what is happening here after that? Do you know if there will be any jobs going?'

The man shook his head. 'No idea, mate. Sorry.' He walked past LeJeune, out into the car park, leaving him shaking his head and trying to keep tears of anger and frustration at bay. He stood in a state of disbelief long after the man in the overalls had climbed into the white van and driven away. Stubbing the toe of his shoes into the tarmac as he went, LeJeune left the site. He looked over his shoulder one more time as if the man was playing some kind of trick, but it was very clear just how deserted the factory actually

was. He took deep breaths, trying to hold back the anger, trying to think clearly, shrug it off. There were things he could
do. He knew hard work, he knew car mechanics and, if all
else failed, he knew how to be a soldier. He'd enlist again.
Being in service might not necessarily lead to the life he'd
promised Esperanza, but he was sure she'd understand.

He took the bus to the tube station. In the dark tunnel, he
hoped his mood and feelings of anguish would be masked.
He slouched forward in the seat, his mind working like the
mechanics of a clock to come up with a solution to his problem, one that didn't involve re-joining the military. Entering
another tunnel, LeJeune saw the image of a blue jacket lying
lifeless on the platform in a smoky tunnel. He saw civilians
taking cover from the bombs. His mind drifted back to four
years ago when helping survivors was his mission as he was
not in any condition to fight the enemy, only support the
people the enemy sought to destroy. That had been his final
mission, and he'd done it with as much courage and conviction as his heart could muster. Didn't Stepney owe it to him
to help him now in his time of need? It seemed a ridiculous
thing, but he felt himself drawn to that familiar place, hoping
it would bring him succour. The train that rattled and carried
him south was taking him away from Stepney. But something within him was urging him back there.

LeJeune exited the train and tried to find his bearings. He
saw a Black operative of the London Underground, a Gren-
adian man as it turned out after a friendly exchange.

'Stepney?' he said and rubbed his chin. 'Now, let's see.
You need to …'

It was a forty-five minute journey and a long way from
Clapham. There were rules about coming back late to the
temporary accommodation, but he didn't worry about that,

he just needed to be in familiar surroundings. He thanked the man from Grenada and set off.

Emerging now outside Stepney Green train station, Le-Jeune's shoulders relaxed, the knots by his neck easing as he blinked his eyes and looked around. They had repaired the bomb-blasted doors to the station not long after the explosion, but this was the first time he'd walked the platform since he was last there, saving lives. No sign of the debris, Lorna lying on the ground wearing Lizzie's jacket, his mistaking her for Lizzie, taking her for dead. He shivered at the thought, then turned towards Lizzie's old flat. He knew she wouldn't be there but perhaps Lorna would. A familiar face was what he needed, and Lorna had always treated him kindly.

As he knocked on the door, now repainted black, he heard heavy footsteps and a baby crying, the angry sobs becoming more noisy the closer they got to the door. When the door opened, LeJeune was surprised to see Lorna standing there, a baby of about a year old hoisted onto her hip.

'What the flaming …?' Lorna stood with her mouth agape. The baby, who had stopped crying, stared at LeJeune with the same wide, green eyes as Lorna's. 'Private John Francis. Is that really you?'

LeJeune grinned at her and saluted. He never felt more happy to see her friendly smile. Lorna hadn't changed at all, she was still a feisty-looking girl who dyed her hair blonde, almost the same colour as Lizzie's, whose chin jutted in defiance and whose smile was quick to soften her face.

'I'm one and the same.'

'What are you doing here? I thought we'd seen the last of you. Thought you'd had enough of us.' She stepped back inside. 'Come in, come in. Here, grab this one will you, let's go upstairs.'

She handed LeJeune the baby who still looked up at him in wonder, his cheeks round and red and stained with tears. LeJeune followed Lorna upstairs while she exclaimed constantly about how she couldn't believe it was him. In the living room, another child ran towards Lorna and she scooped her up and hooked this one onto her hip.

'You can put that one down.' Lorna pointed to a rug on the floor where wooden blocks littered it and a naked doll looked up at him, one of its arms lying redundant beside it. He sat the baby down who immediately rolled over to grab a brick and start sucking at it.

'These are both yours?' LeJeune asked, casting an eye on the flat. Its appearance had changed far more than Lorna's. New curtains, a circular rug under a different coffee table, the smell of nappies drying by an electric fire instead of tea, perfume and cigarette smoke.

'For my perilous sins, yes they are. Vivien and Burt. Like the actors. I love my Hollywood movies, Johnny. Remember? Nothing ever changes.'

'Except you got married.'

'I know. Met a bloke straight after VE and was in the family way the next day.' She burst out laughing. 'Hey presto, three years later I've got these two. We had a small ceremony. I would have invited you had I known where to find you. Then I heard you'd moved away. Next I knew you were gone. Poof.' She demonstrated with her fingers. 'Can I get you some tea? Something stronger? Johnny, what the flaming 'eck brings you here? Fancy a spot of lunch?' It was music to his ears.

With Burt, who had taken a shine to LeJeune, sitting on his lap, LeJeune shared a pile of cheese and tomato sandwiches and a pot of tea with Lorna. She talked with fond memories of their shared past as if it happened a hundred years ago. To LeJeune, their conversation brought the past closer, as if only a day had passed.

'So, what will you do for a job?' Lorna asked after returning from the bedroom where she'd laid Burt down for a nap.

'I have no idea. I'll have to start to ask around. There must be something. That's why we're coming over. Help rebuild the nation, the motherland.'

'This place has never felt like a mother to me, but good luck, though. You planning on moving back to Stepney?'

'Without a job, I can't make any plans. I've got a week or two before I have to leave the place in Clapham. I'll be happy to. It's a bit of a hovel.'

'You'll find something. I'll put the kettle on.'

LeJeune was pensive, dying to ask the question that had been on the tip of his tongue since entering the flat. He watched Lorna's daughter stumbling in and out of the kitchen, carrying her doll with the one arm. LeJeune had helped her dress the doll in a light blue baby dress; she'd said the doll's name was Elizabeth, like the princess, making him think of Lizzie all the more.

While the kettle boiled, Lorna spread out some ginger nut biscuits and told LeJeune to help himself.

'What's the matter, Johnny? You look like someone's just walked over your grave.'

He shook his head and kept his eyes down.

'It's her isn't it?' Lorna asked. 'You want to ask me about Lizzie.'

He brightened and looked up at her. 'I was curious. I was hoping she is happy. That things worked out with her husband. She might even have a child, too.'

Lorna shook her head and filled the teapot with steaming water. 'I never see her.'

'She still living in Poplar?'

'That I couldn't tell you.' *Couldn't or wouldn't?* LeJeune wondered. It's not as if he were still pursuing Lizzie. Lorna knew he was a married man now. Newly married and looking forward to the day his young bride could join him in London. Perhaps that's why Lorna was reluctant to divulge any information. She didn't want him doing anything silly like showing up and declaring his love for her the way he had before. But years had gone by. He had moved on. He was happy. Something told him, though, that by the way Lorna's cheeks blossomed red, Lizzie must still be in Poplar. He did have her address, and what was the harm in knocking on her door just to ask after her, tell her that he was back?

'You remember the day of the bombings when you were down in the tube station at Stepney Green and the doors got blasted in?' LeJeune said, shaking his head from side to side.

'How could I forget? But poor you, you thought I was a goner and that I was her.'

'That's right. So many memories I have, and that one sticks out among them.'

'It was the blue jacket, wasn't it? She'd spent a fortune on that. Fancied herself as Betty Grable, tried to get the hair just right. But I lost it that day when I got carted off to the hospital. Some thieving nurse will be swanning around in it now.'

'I can still see her in it.'

Lorna said nothing but poured another cup of tea for them, a curtain of silence closing around the kitchen.

Out of nowhere, the baby woke with a loud wail and Lorna jumped from her chair.

'That wasn't very long. I'd better get a bottle warmed.'

'Lorna, you're busy. Maybe I should go.' LeJeune stood.

'You sure you won't stay long enough for your tea?'

'Your husband will be home, I don't want to impose.'

'It's no imposition.'

The baby let out a siren of sound, angry that his cries hadn't already been answered.

'I'll grab Burt and see you out.' Lorna disappeared out of the kitchen, and LeJeune stooped to say his goodbyes to Vivien.

'You look after your Elizabeth, now, won't you?'

The child nodded and handed the doll to him. Lorna returned with a red-faced baby.

'Stick the kettle on again so I can warm some formula, would you John? You seem to have a way with kiddies. I hope you and your new wife have several. Can't wait to meet her.'

He stayed while the bottle was made, until it had cooled down and while Vivien tried to explain how she wanted to be a princess like the real Elizabeth one day. As she carried the feeding child, Lorna insisted on walking LeJeune to the door.

'You make sure you pop in again, and good luck getting settled in, love.'

'Thank you.' LeJeune stroked the top of the baby's head and pecked Lorna on the cheek. 'I'll see you soon.'

He left the house with the intention of heading back to Clapham but found himself wandering around the streets, through Stepney market whose stalls were all closed now and even to the location of his old army barracks. There was a fence all around it, the structures all gone and signs that suggested a block of purpose-built flats would be coming soon. The land stood like a ghost of his past, but his recollections so vivid. His fingers gripped the wired fence, and the sound of gunshot, explosions, men crying on the battlefield engulfed him. Visions of Eugene being nicked by a bullet, the time he'd thought his friend had died made his heart thump out of time. So close. Even he had been close to death, tasted it like metal in his mouth, only to find himself waking up in a strange place with little memory of who he was and how he'd ended up in the French hospital. Lizzie's face had come to him even before he remembered his own name. The strength of the love he'd felt and the picture of her face had come to him like waves on the shore and had let him know that somehow he would survive his injuries, find the person whose face he kept seeing in his dreams. Lizzie. He blinked slowly and turned to make his way back to Stepney Green tube station.

Chapter 21

Essie

London 1948

Because I've left everything to Bill Harper, I have no idea what the posters we designed will look like. Bill estimated they'd take a good week or so to be printed, but he had promised to put them up straight away. One in his restaurant, one on the church noticeboard, another on the community board by the post office and then he'd see how many businesses would agree to put them in windows. Others could be given out by the station and at the market. He wasn't sure how many people stopped and read the noticeboards, but he'd insist his customers take a good look. See if any memories got jogged. He'd not only told me to sit tight and call him in a couple of weeks to see if there was any news but he'd hinted, more than once, that I report this to the police. I am still reluctant. It's like admitting that something terrible has happened. I'd like to think that the worst thing I will find out is that LeJeune doesn't love me anymore. If something more sinister has happened, I am not ready to know.

As each day passes, it's as though more hours have been added to them. Two weeks is a long time to have to wait for some good news, though Myrtle keeps telling me that no news is good news. She has been so caring, but I can't bear it when she says that. All I want is good news. All I want is to see LeJeune again.

I open the net curtain as Myrtle leaves for work and watch her marching off in her navy raincoat, a grey headscarf tied tight under her chin. I listen to the pad of her work shoes and wish that I had somewhere to go, some way of filling my time that will help it pass more quickly. Moorhouse stretches lazily with an arched back, pulls at the threads of the sofa and then curls himself into a ball to fall back to sleep. I've tried staying in bed, hoping to sleep away a few more hours, minutes, seconds, but all that does is make me bad-tempered because the sleep is more reluctant to come than the two-week deadline.

After a week I call Bill.

'Sorry, love, the poster isn't ready so I'm afraid I have no news.'

As I walk away from the telephone box, I hear a noisy car and stop to let it go by before I cross. The car stops in front of me. Graham leans towards the passenger side window. The car is still rolling before it jolts to a standstill.

'Hello, Essie. Had any luck finding your hubby?'

My lips turn downwards and I shake my head.

'You been back to Stepney?'

'I have,' I say, lowering towards the open window. The car reeks of cigarette smoke. 'Someone is going to put posters up for me.'

He nods. 'That sounds like a good idea.'

We don't really know what else to say to each other. Graham has been a great help to me, even when I doubted him and disliked his ways. He has even scared me, but I know now that he means well.

'And have you tried the police?' he says.

I swallow down my fears about doing this and simply shake my head again.

'It wouldn't do any harm, you know? But, I get it. They can't always be trusted to do their job, so you have to rely on other people.'

'Like you,' I say. 'You helped me a lot. You and Mrs Rogers.'

'Well, we could only get you so far.' He leans further out on his elbow. 'If you get no further in your search, don't forget my offer. You know the one.'

'Graham, you know I already have one husband that I can't find. I'm not going to take up with someone else's.' I tut playfully and he chuckles.

'Fair enough, love. Worth a try.'

'But I do have another name for someone who lives in Poplar. Eugene gave it to me. I'm going to go there. Ask around.'

'Oh, Essie. That's dangerous, love. Some right dodgy types around there. You want to be careful who you ask questions of. I mean, I'd offer to come. Drive you, even, but remember what happened last time?' A sorrowful smile tugs on the side of his face.

'Only too well and I wouldn't ask. I can find the way myself. I know the way to Stepney, so I'm sure I can get to Poplar.'

'Shouldn't be too hard for someone like you. Well, best be off. Engine trouble. Already. Only had it a week, so I'm off to the car dealer who sold it to me.' He rolls his eyes. 'Good luck, Essie.'

I wave as he drives away. I can't wait another week before phoning Bill about the posters no more than I can asking him if he knows of Lizzie Tarping. The chances that he does are admittedly slim, but he will know the way to Poplar. I've wasted time already not asking him before now, but my conversation with Graham has spurred me on and I'm compelled to start searching for her right away.

Back at the flat, I write a note for Myrtle to ask that she doesn't panic when she finds me gone. I don't really know how long I'll be, but I gather some change for the bus and head to Harper's.

When I get off the bus near Stepney Green station, I begin to feel more positive about finding Lizzie Tarping and, I must admit, feel happy to be meeting with Bill again. He feels like a lucky charm for me, and if Lizzie was originally from Stepney, then he might know of her, increasing my chances of getting anywhere. If he has no idea who she is, I will be walking blindly around Poplar, asking questions while trying to be as cautious as Graham advised.

By now, I know how to get to the restaurant but I stop in the market to see if there are more callaloo leaves on the stall and any pumpkin so that I can make the soup again.

I stop at a stall and begin inspecting pumpkins for freshness when something soft rolls into my calf. I look down. A small child has toddled up to me, bending low and searching for the thing that bounced off my leg. I stoop to look beneath the market stall and see a partially deflated ball just out of the child's reach, so I retrieve it.

'Here you are,' I say to the little boy who is too busy grabbing the ball to say thank you.

'Manners, Archie.' A woman with yellow hair approaches and smiles at me before taking the little boy's hand. 'Sorry about that, love. I told him to hold it. No kicking in the market. Didn't I, Archie?'

The little boy looks up at his mother but says nothing. He drops the ball again: it's too big to carry under his arm and it rolls a little way on. He bustles through legs to pick it up again.

'You got kids?' The young woman jerks a chin at me, and I shake my head no.

'Then don't.' She pulls a face, and we both get shuffled away from the stall.

'Only joking,' the woman says as she picks up both the little boy and the ball. He must be two or three and disregards me in his attempts to reach for the ball. His mother, though, won't stop staring at me. Up and down her blue eyes trail the length of me. Then she shakes her head. 'Can't believe it,' she says.

'Can't believe what?'

'It's your jacket.'

I look down at it, searching for a stain or a missing button.

'It was a present from my cousin,' I say. 'But it was second-hand. From lost property.'

'I used to have one just like it. Saved up special and got it from a fancy shop in the West End. I bought it in the sale, but it was still expensive for me. Always tight under the arms, though, so I gave it away before I left for pastures new, as it were.'

'Oh?'

'Yeah. Long story, love.'

Her little boy becomes restless and agitated because she won't allow him to take the ball, and he starts complaining he's hungry and when can he see Nana. He's a darling little man. Big cheeks and full, pink lips shaped like a heart. And his eyes. They are the best of all, large, the whites so white that his light grey irises stand out.

'Patience is a virtue, little man. Can't you see I'm talking to the nice lady?'

I smile at this, especially when Archie looks at me for the first time and deep dimples appear in his smiling cheeks.

'Anyway, best be off,' the young woman says. 'Let you get on. Never know, I might run into you again.'

'Oh, I'm a visitor here. Just dropping in on a friend.'

She smiles and tuts. 'Oh well. Nice chat. Bye then.'

She seems like a nice person, friendly. It would be nice to make a new friend. I turn back to the market stall and choose a pumpkin. I buy some more callaloo leaves and discover they have garlic, too. I look around for more ingredients that will make my soup taste more like home. More like Mama's. But what if the secret to it tasting like home is in the cook herself? What if the only way I can stop longing for home is just to go back? Admit defeat. But no, there is no part of me that could stop looking for LeJeune, live a life without him. I had never entertained the thought until this very moment, and it is all because of the girl I've just met. She seems so confident and so self-assured. Could I make my way on my own, I wonder, without LeJeune? Convince myself that he doesn't want to be found.

I finish my purchase and head towards Harper's, still thinking about the girl with yellow hair.

Chapter 22

London

1948

It was difficult to stay away from the East End of London. Clapham was fine, full of people who were much the same as they were in East London, streets that looked the same, buses that also rattled and similar looking postmen who whistled as they cycled in the early hours. But none of this eased his worrisome mind. LeJeune found it increasingly difficult to sleep, something that had never bothered him before, not even when bombs were exploding around him and he lay in a bunker at night. He still managed to capture a few hours of rest, dreamless naps that went some way to calming his nerves, if only temporarily, and eased the aches and pains in his body. But Clapham had none of the appeal of Stepney and seemed to be lacking in jobs, too. He had tried a few garages, but mostly they were small family concerns that were struggling themselves and couldn't hire anyone, not even someone to clean up and run odd jobs. More and more he thought he should re-enlist; more and more he wondered how he was going to tell Esperanza that his dream of making a comfortable life for them in London had been snatched away.

He found himself on the train to Stepney one early evening with the idea of looking for work there, not admitting to himself that he'd find very few places open at that time and that, most of all, he couldn't face another night alone in a box room where a heavyset man in the room next to his snored so loudly at night, it was like being in twin beds.

He headed straight for The Dockman's Arms. It was congested with men and women from the door to the bar laughing and chatting within its freshly painted walls. They'd got rid of the old piano which used to be jammed against the wall. He looked around at the changes, the biggest being no sign of a single person in uniform. Just as he went to make his way to the bar, someone grabbed at his shoulders and spun him around.

'You're a long way from home, my friend!'

LeJeune found himself staring into the open face of Eugene Price who laughed gusts of beer-laced breath into his face before pulling him into a hug. He laughed into his ear as he clung onto LeJeune, rocking from side to side, not affording him time to breathe.

'It's really you, isn't it?' Eugene held LeJeune at arms length. 'Yes, yes, yes. It really is. I saw you in the paper, and I wondered how long it would be before you showed up.'

LeJeune took Eugene's hand and shook it vigorously before patting his shoulder.

'You really are a sight for sore eyes,' LeJeune said. 'And what do you mean you saw me in the newspaper?'

'You didn't see your ugly face in the *Evening News*? I happened to buy it after work on the day you just come on the Windrush. You looked like a film star. But then you always were a handsome fella. You bastard, you.'

'Eugene, you never change.'

'And thank Christ for that. Let me buy you a pint.'

Eugene dragged LeJeune over to the bar. He elbowed his way to the front and annoyed a few of the men who were comfortably acting as props for the beer-stained surface.

'You wanna watch it, mate,' one of the men said.

'Watch what?' Eugene stormed back. 'This is another war hero returned to his mother country. You just watch your-self.'

'Eugene,' LeJeune whispered to his friend. 'You shouldn't rile the natives like that. You know how it can get.'

'What do I care?' Eugene spoke to the room and seemed to silence it. 'I know how to take care of myself, and anyone who wants to test that can go ahead. I know enough East End gangsters to call if anyone wants to chance their luck.'

LeJeune suspected that he was either a good bluffer or that he had befriended real gangsters. In his native Jamaica, his life had been far from clean. LeJeune had always believed that the main reason Eugene enlisted was so that he could carry a gun and not get thrown into jail for it.

Eugene ordered two neat whiskeys and two pints of pale ale which the landlord told him were on the house. Clearly, his friend was still as popular at The Dockman's. He gave the whiskeys to LeJeune to hold and muscled his way through the crowd carrying two pints of beer aloft saying, 'Make way, make way, war hero has returned.'

LeJeune had, by choice, seen very little of Eugene during the year he stayed on in London after the war. He'd kept himself to himself; more importantly, he'd kept his misery to himself. Thought it only fair. He worked and returned to his attic room to read books he'd taken out from the library along with the evening paper he'd pick up outside the tube station. There was no army pension to speak of, and every penny he earned he kept safe, thinking that one day he'd need a sum of money for something. As it turned out, it was to buy himself a ticket back to Dominica and not a diamond ring for Lizzie as he'd dreamt of doing one day. When his dreams faded and London no longer felt like home, he'd hoped that returning to Dominica would be the answer to his discontent and dark nights spent alone. Strange that Dominica called when one of the reasons he'd signed up in the first place was to escape that very island. In particular, his mother whose bitterness at losing LeJeune's father at a young age had tainted their relationship and he'd grown up feeling unloved and unwanted by her. Still, he thought as he took a seat by the door with Eugene, at least he hadn't regretted his decision to finally leave Dominica forever. Meeting Lorna and then Eugene solidified his decision. This was home, despite his not having a job, despite his not knowing how he would feed himself and find a flat without money.

'Cheers,' said Eugene after introducing LeJeune as a war hero to everyone on the surrounding tables. 'Man, I wouldn't have thought I'd walk into my local and find you of all people here. You back for good this time?'

'Yes, I'm back for good. As long as I can find a job.'

LeJeune told him about the factory; he told him all about his new wife, Esperanza, and how small he felt for not fulfilling his promise to her.

'If it's a job you're after, I can fix you up.'

'You know of a place?' LeJeune sat forward in his chair, feeling the effects of whiskey warming his cheeks.

'Not only do I know a place, I practically run it. Well, when the foreman is on his break.' Eugene exhaled a loud laugh. 'I let him boss people around, but really, I'm the brains.'

'Oh, I have no doubt. But seriously, what is the job and where?'

'I been working to restore the dock area. There wasn't money for it until the council managed to get some grants and what have you. The whole area is under reconstruction. Housing, work places, transport. Everything around Stepney will change. There is plenty of work to be had if you have a strong back and you don't mind the outdoors.'

'Come on,' said LeJeune with a shrug. 'How can you ask me that when I fought in a war for three years? Unlike some who claimed they were prisoners of war but really they were sitting in a Lyons tea shop.'

They both began to laugh, tension draining from LeJeune's brow and shoulders.

'So your foreman definitely needs more men?'

'I was only discussing it with him today. He is going to start advertising, and I already said I'd ask around. Oh, there is a job for you, all right. You just make sure you're ready to report at eight o'clock on Monday morning.'

'I will be there. No doubt about it.' LeJeune slapped his hand on the table.

Eugene picked up his beer glass and sipped some more. LeJeune looked at him and extended his hand.

'What's all this?' asked Eugene.

'My thanks to you,' LeJeune said and shook his hand with a tight grip. 'You have saved my life.'

'Think nothing of it. Now, let go of my hand before you dislocate me whole damned shoulder.'

They filled the smokey corner with more laughter. More pint glasses congregated on their table as they talked about their war stories, telling the other as if they had not been there together for most of it, talking about the times they faced alone and, mostly, how lucky they were to be sitting in The Dockman's sharing drinks.

Eugene ordered another round of drinks to accompany their plates of cockles, courtesy of the landlady who had a soft spot for Eugene. The circle of friendship began to blossom from their table and out into the room as people joined their conversation and stories of the war. LeJeune thought that had Eugene not become a soldier, he could easily have found work in the entertainment industry. He had a great way of recounting stories, especially ones that featured LeJeune for which he had no recollection of his involvement in any of them. He would put that down to Eugene as the great entertainer and falsifier of stories or for the time his memory was affected by his head injury. In an hour the rest of the pub were regarding Lejeune as a war hero and, perhaps, a bigger one than Eugene had made himself out to be. LeJeune could feel the level of alcohol rising in his bloodstream as he sat admiring his friend's way with words.

He was quite drunk when he realised that he ought to take note of the address he needed to report to on the Monday morning. In three days he would be a new man. He'd write to Esperanza and tell her that everything was fixed up and that work had started. He wouldn't have to explain about the factory job straight away: what was the point when everything was suddenly looking up for him and a bright future was now his? His and Esperanza's.

*

When LeJeune woke the next morning, he found himself face down on the wooden floorboards in a room that did not smell like the room in Clapham: damp with stubbed out cigarettes. He was in a strange place all right but with no idea how he got there. The last thing he remembered was a woman who smelt of lavender sitting on his knee while wondering who it was Eugene was kissing across the table from him. He remembered entering The Dockman's Arms and running into his old friend and the promise of a job – there had been a lot of laughter and too much booze as his temples could attest to. Everything apart from that was masked by confusion and cigarette smoke. His mouth was dry and his eyelids fixed so tightly to his eyeballs that it took several attempts to peel them open. When he did, he found himself at the foot of a single bed under which was a circular rug, a pair of formal shoes and a pair of black work boots. The floor was swept clean but littered with men's clothes, his and Eugene's. The curtain was open over the window, the window slightly ajar. The sound of a needle running over the last groove of a record popped and scratched continuously. He rolled to his side to try to get up and stop it. His head thudded and his ears rang as he walked on his knees to the record player, lifting off the needle with shaky hands and blurred vision.

'You up already?' Eugene's voice was muffled by the covers. He pulled them off and grinned at LeJeune. 'I had no idea you could drink so much. All my money is gone.' He yawned and chuckled at the same time.

'I'm sorry,' LeJeune said, dropping onto a low-backed easy chair. 'I'll pay you back some time. Take you for a night out when I'm paid.'

'It's okay. I lost my wages gambling. My friends bought the drinks.'

'You have so many friends. But,' said LeJeune, yawning widely, 'it doesn't really surprise me.'

'Well, you certainly surprised me.' Eugene sat up now. 'You and the young lady you were talking to. What were you saying to her about a girl named Mona? You were trying to make this poor girl sing like a woman named Mona and kept saying, "No, no, no, it's not like that," every time the poor mouse opened her mouth.'

LeJeune covered his face with his hands.

'And then you stood up and started to sing for yourself. Telling everyone you love music and you know a calypso queen.' Eugene rolled back and laughed.

LeJeune began to recall his attempt to re-create the engaging renditions of the songs he'd heard Mona Baptiste perform, telling Eugene more about her.

'Come with me to her show next Saturday night. We won't even have to pay. She said to come early to the stage door and she'd arrange it.'

'So you're really friends with a famous singer? I thought it was just the drink talking. But wait. Does your young bride know about your little fling with a singer?'

'It's nothing like that.' LeJeune went on to try to explain about Mona and about the Jamaican woman who took a shine to him on the ship.

'You mind you stay on the right side of jealous husbands.'

'Yes, he wanted to fight with me then and there. They're somewhere in London that couple, and he gave me some harsh warnings, shall we say. I don't want to run into him again. Especially if he was as drunk as you last night.'

'I wasn't the one singing like a cockerel in a crowded pub.'

Three sharp raps on the door stopped their laughter as Eugene's landlady shouted for them to keep the noise down.

Coming in late, drunk and playing music to boot was enough for an eviction and he'd better not have anyone in there.

LeJeune crept out of the house shortly after washing his face and rinsing his mouth. He looked up and down the street trying to get his bearings and made his way, wearily, towards the station where he stopped at a café. He'd thought to trouble Lorna for breakfast but didn't think her husband would appreciate an unshaven stranger turning up at the door.

The man in the café pushed a plate of burnt toast under his nose while LeJeune sipped some strong coffee and stared blankly out of the window. The trains leaving or arriving at Stepney Green tube station clattered and hissed and made his head thump even more. Of course, it was Saturday, the market would become busy, people out shopping. Already, the café was filling up and pots of tea landed like clanging bells on the surrounding tables. Why had he had so much to drink? He yawned, rubbed his eyes and took a bite from a slice of toast. He sat watching a woman with a small child hurrying to the station. They looked as if they were late for something or as if they were eager to hop on the very next train. He looked at the woman again: she had blonde hair, most of which was hidden by a dark, patterned headscarf. She hurried the child along by his tiny hand. He grinned and swung his arm as if he were running a race, toddling along the best he could. The woman picked the boy up and they both giggled. He heard her say, 'Come on, Archie,' as they passed the window.

He had taken the woman for a spitting image of his past love but had instantly dismissed the idea. But it was her. He stopped chewing, mouth falling open, a sensation running like a wave up his spine. *Lizzie has a little boy now.* He sprung up from his seat, swallowed and ran out of the café.

'Oi!' The owner chased him onto the street and caught him by his sleeve.

'I'm coming back,' said LeJeune, wrestling the man off him. He pointed to the station where he saw Lizzie's back retreating, the grinning face of the toddler looking over her shoulder. 'I need to catch them. My money is in my jacket pocket. There on the chair.' He edged away. 'I'm coming back.'

The man released him, and LeJeune raced into the station, but before he could run down the steps to the platform, he was called back again.

'Where d'you think you're going, son? Ticket.'

'I just have to wave someone off, I'll be right back. I promise.' He clasped his hands in prayer and thanked God when the ticket seller nodded for him to carry on. He bolted down the stairs, aware that the train he'd heard arrive seconds before was waiting to go. He heard the doors close and the engines gear up and the roll of wheels as it began to pull away. Nevertheless, he ran along the platform peering into the carriages. He ran the length of the platform and caught the slightest glimpse of Lizzie and her child looking out of the opposite window to him. The train gathered speed and was gone.

Reluctantly, he mounted the stairs, his mind filled with images of Lizzie and the little boy. He gave a short salute to the man in the ticket office, who nodded back. Taking lingering steps back to the café, he kept turning his head over his shoulder as if Lizzie had miraculously got off the train and chased after him. He felt out of breath when he arrived back at the café. Landing heavily into his chair, he proceeded to

crunch his way through burnt toast, flushing it down with
cold coffee.

Chapter 23

Essie

London 1948

With his usual broad smile, Bill marches straight towards me as I enter the restaurant. There are no customers, just a waitress who is setting salt cellars onto the tables. She barely looks at me, just goes about her work, straightening the backs of chairs and sniffing as if she either has a cold or there is a scent she is trying to identify.

'Hello, Essie. Didn't expect to see you here today.'

'Hello, Bill. I'm sorry, I got so impatient after my call. I know you said a couple of weeks.'

'Not to worry.' He guides me to a seat next to the counter and pulls out a chair that has been neatly tucked under a table. I steal a look at the waitress before sitting. She allows herself a momentary glance in my direction and continues on as if she had only blinked.

Bill ducks behind the counter and feels inside a drawer before returning to my table with a large brown envelope.

'They came. Your posters.'

'Really?' I hold my hands to my cheeks.

Bill pulls the posters from the envelope, and I see that the printers have blown up LeJeune's face and placed it near the top just under the word *Missing*, and below it are the words, *Do You Know This Man*? I stare for ages at it thinking how

unlike LeJeune it actually looks. It's a black and white poster
so, of course, no one can tell he has such light-coloured
eyes, that his chin is actually a lot stronger and, of course, it
gives no idea of his very light complexion, all of which
makes him quite striking and memorable. But at least the
poster shows how good-looking he is. I smile back at Bill
because of the effort he's gone to.

'Did you go and chase them up?' I ask him as he sits waiting eagerly to hear what I think.

'Strangely enough, when I got off the phone to you, I
thought to do that but then I see the printer's boy waltz up to
the door with the envelope under his arm. Turns out they had
a press mostly set up from another job. They only had to ad-
apt it a bit.'

'It's a really good poster, Bill. Thank you.'

'You don't have to keep thanking me, Essie. It's my pleasure to help. I was going to put them up just before lunch was
served, and then in you come.'

Just then, a couple arrive at the restaurant and are seated by
the waitress who commences to tell them that there's only
stew today and they can have vegetables or mash on the side
or both.

'Would you like a spot of lunch?' Bill asks. I didn't eat
breakfast because I'd been jittery when I woke this morning,
but it's already midday and I'm starving if I must admit.

'Only if you eat with me,' I say.

'Your wish is my command. Two stews with mash here,'
Bill says as the waitress passes the table. She nods but says
nothing, thin lips drawn in a line. 'I'll stick one up now, and
then I'll distribute the others like I said I would.' He jumps
up to find a roll of tape from the drawer behind the counter
and sticks a poster on the door so that it faces outwards. The

wording at the bottom of the poster gives information about John Francis of Stepney, his former regiment, the date he was last seen in The Dockman's Arms. It asks if anyone has information that will lead to finding him to please contact Bill at Harper's Restaurant and then the telephone number.

Bill chats the whole time through lunch, asking about me, and I answer in short sentences. I'm distracted as I steal frequent glances at the poster on the door. No one notices it, and my positive mood since seeing Bill and his bright smile begins to wane. I haven't been able to mention Lizzie Tarping yet. I'm waiting for an opportunity to ask even more of Bill than I already have. He stops talking about something I'm only half listening to and places a hand on mine. I've barely touched the food.

'Not hungry?'

'Oh yes, I was.'

'But not until you tasted it?' He laughs lightly.

'Oh, not at all.' I think about the bland food I eat at my cousin's. It's not unlike this which is why I try to do most of the cooking. 'It's very nice.'

'Fibber. Come on, I can take it. What did you think?'

I look down at my half-full plate and over to Bill's which, with the aid of a slice of bread and butter, has been wiped clean.

'It's English food and I'm still getting used to it.'

'Something tells me you never really will.'

'Perhaps I will, and perhaps I can learn to do something to make it taste ... well, interesting.'

Bill laughs aloud. 'So I'm a boring cook, am I?'

'You cook what you know and you do cook it well. There's absolutely nothing wrong with it. I suppose we use different herbs and spices.'

'Like the things they've imported from India? There are some spices in the market, but I wouldn't know how to use them.'

'I could show you. I saw similar food to what we eat at home in the market. A lot of what I'd need to make my Mama's recipe. Or as close to it as I could.'

'Your Mama's recipe. Hot and spicy, is it?'

'You make it to taste. Mama never overspices, and no, it isn't particularly hot just … not boring.' I can't help but laugh at this, and I'm thankful that Bill does, too.

'So we have a deal, then.'

I cross my brow and begin to remember that I did tell Bill that I would cook Mama's soup here one day.

'It's okay, Essie, there's no pressure for you to come and cook for my customers. But how about if you teach me your Mama's recipe and I serve it up in here and see how well it goes down?'

'I would love to do that.' I sigh with relief that I don't have to be the one cooking for all of his customers. If they are all as sullen as his waitress, he could have a room full of dissatisfied people in here.

The waitress hovers by the table. 'Have you finished eating, then?' she asks.

'Yes, thanks,' says Bill as she begins to clear the table. She's noisy and has her eyes on me the whole time. 'And could you do us a pot of tea? And a couple of slices of the cake I made this morning.'

'Right you are.'

Bill puts his elbows on the table. 'You're a story, Essie Francis. You really are.'

'How do you mean?'

'I don't know, there's just something about you. Can't put my finger on it, but I know you and I will get on. And I was serious when I said about getting your chap to move over this way. You know, once you've found him and you're all settled.' It's such a positive thing for Bill to say, but I feel sure I can detect a little sorrow in his eyes.

'I must say, Bill, everything you are doing is bringing me closer to finding him but …'

'But what?'

'I was really coming here to ask for even more help.'

'Anything.' Bill moves closer, but the waitress bustles through the service doors carrying a rattling tray with a pot of tea, two servings of fruit cake and two napkins. The tray claps onto the table, the thin tablecloth not able to soak up the sound. *Plonk*, the cups and saucers land, another bang for the teapot. Bill pulls a face and we silently giggle. The waitress freezes for a second while Bill and I straighten our expressions. In his boyish way, Bill is finding it difficult to contain his mirth. When she finally leaves with an empty tray, it is to settle the bill with the two customers who have signalled that they are finished. Bill snorts a little as she goes, and I put a finger over my mouth.

He sets a plate of cake in front of me and rotates the teapot to stir up the tea leaves.

'You were just about to ask me for help,' Bill says and replaces the pot. 'You can ask me anything, Essie.' He takes a long look at me.

'I was actually coming here to ask for directions to somewhere in the hope of finding someone. Someone who might hold the key to what has happened to John and where he might be now.'

'That's wonderful, Essie. Who and where?'

'Her name is Lizzie Tarping and she lives in Poplar.'

'Used to. She was in Poplar but only a month or so ago – she came back. My mum knows her mum. Lizzie Tarping and I went to the same school, but she's married and uses her husband's name now.'

I want to ask Lizzie's married name, but I'm not without trepidation. I have a terrible feeling that Bill might say it's Francis. That LeJeune came back, saw his old flame and decided to marry her instead.

'So if she's in Stepney, do you know where?' I ask.

'I believe I do. She's back with her mum who was knocking around on her own since her old man died and the rest of the brood moved out. I've no idea how come Lizzie came back so sudden, but I was over at Mum's last weekend, and she said that Maud, Lizzie's mum, has her back home. You want the address?'

I nod with little conviction, my mind turning somersaults as I try to make sense of why Lizzie came back to Stepney so suddenly to live with her mum and if it has anything to do with LeJeune.

'What about Lizzie's husband? Did he come back to Stepney with her?'

'Far as I can tell, she left her husband behind in Poplar. God knows what or why, but I haven't seen him around here. Apparently, her mum was only too happy to have her back.'

'And … and what's her husband's name?'

'Oh, some dodgy sort. Micky Walters he's called. Went off to war, then one day he goes missing in action. A year later, they say he's presumed dead. But a year or so on, he shows up and they get married.' Bill stops to chuckle. 'Mum told me all this. When it comes to weaving a yarn, she goes into every detail.'

I picture this Lizzie, heartbroken, pining for her presumed dead soldier. LeJeune must have met her after that. She must have had another love in her heart when she met him and then left LeJeune when this Micky Walters appeared. Lucky for me, but as Eugene suggested, LeJeune had already fallen for her. I clear my throat.

'So, I should write down the address. Do you think they would mind if I knock on the door unannounced?'

'Shouldn't see why not. I could come with you if you like.'

I begin to tremble at the thought of being so close to finding something out about LeJeune but so afraid to discover what that might be.

Bill pours the tea just as a man in a grey suit walks into the restaurant, pausing for a heartbeat to look at the poster before coming straight in to be seated by the sullen waitress.

'Now, you get this down you and sample some of my cake.' Bill watches as I take a sip of tea. I can tell he has something on his mind. 'I was wondering, Essie, if it's okay, before we go to Maud Tarping's house, do you think you could tell me your mama's soup recipe so I can add it to tonight's dinner menu?'

'Tonight?' I almost choke on my tea.

'No time like the present.' Bill winks at me. 'What do you say?'

I put the cup down and swallow hard. 'All right then,' I say. 'I only hope it doesn't turn out to be a disappointment.'

'You just give the recipe as your mum does it, and I'll multiply it as we go.'

'Fine,' I say. 'I will.'

He claps his hands together. 'I'll get a pen and paper,' he says. 'But looking at the time, how about you accompany me to the market so I can get the supplies in straight away?'

I nod yes but really I'm eager to get over to the Tarping's. I sip some more tea and start to eat the cake, but now I know I will be coming face to face with a woman who was LeJeune's lover, knots contort my tummy and I can't finish it.

Chapter 24

London

1948

LeJeune jangled the change in his pocket and pulled it out to see how much he had. Standing outside the café, he looked towards the station. He had only enough money with him to either follow Lizzie to Poplar, as he assumed this was where she was going, or get himself back to Clapham. If he went to seek out Lizzie, he'd have to walk back to his accommodation. He was aware that he was in the clothes he'd worn since the morning before, and with all the drinking and carousing in The Dockman's Arms and the amount of cigarette smoke that he could still smell on his clothes, he thought it best to return to Clapham, shave, bathe and change his clothes. He hadn't seen Lizzie in over three years; he didn't want to show up in such a sorry state.

On the way back to his room, he thought about his dwindling funds and thanked goodness he'd bumped into Eugene. He patted the inner pocket of his jacket where he had the address for the job on the docks. He hoped nothing would go wrong and that Eugene hadn't blown everything out of proportion, meaning there was no job or nothing available yet. He'd know for sure on Monday morning, but something pressing was on his mind.

LeJeune didn't stay long in Clapham before he was on the road again, clean-shaven, a fresh shirt and a couple of pounds in his pocket. He wondered, just briefly, if he should buy a gift for Lizzie's son, as a token of a friendship he hoped they could foster in the future. He was sure Esperanza wouldn't mind. He hoped they would like each other.

He alighted at the bus garage in Poplar. He knew the way to Micky Walters' aunt's house, but it occurred to him that Lizzie and Micky may have moved out now that they had a child. He hadn't thought any of this through: so busy to follow Lizzie's trail, he hadn't thought about what he'd do if she'd changed address, or if she wasn't home. Would he wait for her in the little park the way he had before? The day Lizzie told him it was all over between them. Married with a child now, she might not even come to the door.

As the park came into view, LeJeune saw a handful of children playing on the green. One on the swings and the others playing a game of chase. Over by a bench, he spotted Lizzie and the little boy. She was pushing a ball to him and he was attempting to kick it back, but with the little balance he had, he fell onto his bottom twice and Lizzie clapped her hands and told him to 'get up, there's a brave lad'.

'He looks very brave indeed,' LeJeune said as he approached them. Lizzie swung around and put her hand over her mouth. 'It's okay, you're not seeing a ghost. It really is me. How are you, Lizzie?'

Lizzie looked quickly at her boy to see what he was doing, only to find him sitting on the grass, patting the ball away, then following behind on his hands and knees to roll it further still.

'Don't go far, Archie,' she said and turned to LeJeune. 'I heard you'd gone back home.'

'I did. For a while. And now I'm back for good.'

'For good?' She checked on her son again.

'Yes, I suppose I couldn't keep away.'

'From me?'

'From London. I'm starting a job on the docks in Stepney on Monday. So we might be neighbours. Sort of.'

Lizzie looked at Archie.

'I didn't come here to make you feel uncomfortable. It's just that I saw you today.'

'Today? Where?'

'I was in the café beside the station, and the two of you ran by. Archie, is it? Tiny little legs but he was trying.' LeJeune laughed. 'He's a good boy.'

'Can be.'

'Well, congratulations, by the way. To you and Micky. I take it you and he are still …?'

'Yes, we're still together.'

'You sound like things aren't so good for you.'

'Come to gloat, have you? Tell me I made a mistake?'

'Not at all, Lizzie. It's nothing like that. I just felt I wanted to see you. Had I not seen you earlier, I wouldn't have come here, but you always had this power over me.'

'Johnny, look.' Lizzie put her head down, blinking slowly as she shook it. 'Nothing can happen between us now. You know that, don't you?'

He held his hands up. 'No, no. That's not why I'm here. I only came because … well, in a way I don't know why I came. But it isn't what you think. I'm a married man now.'

'You are?' She looked slightly pained if LeJeune was reading her correctly. She glanced at the child who was standing now and attempting to kick the ball again. A boy of about five came over to play with Archie and began teaching him the secret to kicking a ball and not toppling over.

'Just,' said LeJeune. 'Her name is Esperanza, and I'll be sending for her as soon as I get settled.'

Lizzie crossed her arms. She wore a thin dress on this sun-starved summer afternoon. If anything, it looked as if it might rain.

'Well, congratulations to you, too, then,' said Lizzie. 'Actually, I'd better go. I had him over my mum's last night and he's a bit tired. Time for some tea I think.'

'It's early for tea. Lizzie, please don't rush away. It's nice to see friendly faces from the past. London can be such a lonely place.'

'Tell me about it.'

'You're not lonely, are you?' LeJeune looked over to the aunt's house. 'You have Micky. The boy. Your aunt, too.'

'She went to live in Margate.'

'So you inherited the house.'

'Wasn't hers. It was the council's. We took over the lease.'

'Well then. It sounds like everything's fallen into place for you.' He remembered that Micky hadn't been working when Lizzie married him. He had worried for her then. Although he hadn't much himself, he'd been certain that he could have given Lizzie a better life than the likes of Micky Walters. And now it seemed that she wasn't even happy. She was jumpy, too, not at all as sharp-tongued. Her whole demeanour watered down to a meek version of her usual self. He turned towards Archie who was chuckling about something.

'Looks like he's made some friends.'

'Oh, he does that easily enough. Bit of a charmer. Like his father.' LeJeune noticed her cheeks redden. He had never taken Micky for a charmer. Yet there had to be something about this man. She married him after all.

'I should get him home,' said Lizzie, though she stayed put, making no attempts to rescue Archie from the five-year-old child who had picked Archie up and begun spinning him around. It was another boy of perhaps ten or eleven who chastised the child and told him to flipping well be careful he didn't drop the poor mite. Once Archie was released from being spun around he tumbled onto the grass. Lizzie looked glazed, and so LeJeune took it upon himself to rush over, gather a tearful Archie and carry him over to his mother.

Lizzie held out her arms to take Archie and hook him over her hip, his chubby legs dangling at her sides like pendulums, his cries becoming louder and louder.

'I'll walk you to the house,' LeJeune offered.

He followed Lizzie, concerned that the unrecognisable quietness in her could be a silent cry for his help. Behind them, the children's shrieks of excitement rose. Lizzie stood limply at the door. Archie screamed in his short, yet loud, sentences of how he wanted to go home, so she pushed the door open.

'Is it all right if I come in?' asked LeJeune. 'For a little while.'

'For a minute. Micky will be home soon. I don't want you here when ...'

'Of course. I'll be long gone by then.'

It was four o'clock. The small park was alive with play and shouts and peels of laughter while the surrounding houses looked sombre, frowning on the idea of LeJeune being within their walls.

The door opened straight onto a box-sized living room with a dark wood dining table partially blocking the way to a small kitchen through to which there was a doorway but no door. Within the living room was a sofa covered by a dark red blanket and a scatter cushion in each corner. A wooden rocking chair with brown heavy cotton upholstery jutted into the middle of the room with a side table beside it, the chair's back to the dining table which was bare apart from a bottle of brown sauce and a jar of mustard. At his feet was a toy truck and an assortment of coloured bricks. Archie stopped crying the second Lizzie released him. Straight away, he picked up a brick with each hand and put one between his teeth before throwing it across the floor with a string of saliva following it.

'Not in your mouth. I told you before.' Lizzie rushed to the kitchen and turned on a tap. She came back with a wet cloth and washed Archie's hands and face with it.

'You want toilet?' she asked her son while still kneeling. He shook his head and began building a tower. He looked at LeJeune for the first time and held a brick up to him.

'Thank you,' said LeJeune. He fiddled with the brick and Lizzie turned to him.

'What about you?' she asked.

'No, I don't want toilet.' LeJeune grinned at her.

'No, you daft sod,' she said, sounding more like the Lizzie he remembered. 'I mean like a cup of tea.'

'That would be very nice. Thank you.'

'Well, sit down. Make yourself comfy.'

She disappeared into the kitchen, put on the light and ran water into a kettle. LeJeune sat at the dining table watching Lizzie making tea. The kitchen was neat and tidy. A tea towel hung over the sink. Above it, the window to the garden was open. He could see the neighbour's washing line, work shirts and overalls hanging out to dry. He wondered what it was Micky did for a living but was loathe to ask because he was the last person he wanted to talk to Lizzie about. When she did return, she sat on the edge of her dining chair and her knee shook rapidly as they waited for the tea to brew.

'So. Married,' she said at last. 'Who'd have thought it.'

'What, you didn't take me for the marrying kind?'

'Yes, I suppose. It's just …'

'You didn't think I could let anyone else into my heart.'

'I didn't say that. I'll pour the tea.'

'Thank you.'

He watched her gentle hands, her slim wrists as she poured. He remembered that with those same hands she had dragged a drunken man twice her size out of The Dockman's Arms one night and then slung his coat and hat out after him. She had called him a cheeky git because the man had got too familiar. The crowd cheered when she dusted off her hands. He had so admired her. He would have defended her himself had he known what had happened. There was a time he'd do anything for her.

They drank quietly while Archie played happily on his own. Trying to speak to Lizzie and not rake up the past was difficult. All LeJeune wanted to do was reminisce, but all that would happen, if he tried, is that Lizzie would sling him out and dust off her hands. He knew she was in no mood for any such conversation, and yet, sitting in their shared silence was just as comforting. His mind conjured up visions of him, Lizzie and Esperanza becoming friends, but the looming figure of Mick Walters kept appearing and he knew that it would never be. If they saw each other, it would be to wave and just walk on, smile from across the street if they were with their respective spouses. He never imagined that their relationship would be so reduced. But there it was.

'Another brew?' Lizzie asked after returning from the outside toilet with Archie.

'That would be nice.' He wasn't sure why he'd agreed to have more tea, but he wasn't ready to walk away from Lizzie just yet.

As Archie continued to entertain himself with his toys, Le-Jeune looked around the room, at the family photos on the wall and the ones along the mantelpiece over the fireplace. There were small photographs here. Family members Le-Jeune supposed. He picked up the one of Lizzie with Micky on their wedding day. Though there was no colour in any of the pictures, he could tell Lizzie hadn't worn white. Her light coloured dress reached her calves and there were plastic flowers in the side of her hair. Micky, in a dark suit and a thin tie had greased down his thin hair. They held hands but neither smiled. LeJeune replaced the photo and picked up the one beside it. A baby photograph of Archie taken, most probably, at the age of one. He was stood holding the leg of a chair. Not in this house but perhaps a photography studio like one of the ones in the West End. He was dressed in a sailor suit, and he smiled with tiny white teeth gleaming like perfect little gems within a round and happy face. LeJeune looked down at Archie who had grabbed the leg of his trousers, a hand reaching up to LeJeune.

'I see it, too?' said the boy.

LeJeune was about to stoop to share the picture when he looked back and thought he saw something familiar about the photograph of Archie. Was it the smile? The abandon of any cares or worries? Here was a happy one-year-old who knew nothing about danger, heartbreak, or the kindness or otherwise of people. A little innocent about to embark on the journey of exploration, of loves won and lost. What an adventure he would have. But there was something else. In the split second between Archie asking again to see it, too, and Lizzie putting a tray on the table, he knew exactly what he recognised in the photograph. The boy's eyes. They were *his* eyes. Archie's face had looked so much like Lizzie's up until that very moment.

LeJeune knelt and gave Archie the photograph.

'Me,' said Archie and took it to show his mother.

'That's right,' said Lizzie. 'That's my little Archie. My angel.' She began to cuddle him. LeJeune observed them for a moment.

'Lizzie?' he whispered. 'How old is Archie?'

'Why would you ask me that?'

'I just want to know. The truth.'

'I'm sure I don't know what you mean, John.'

Just then, Archie broke free of Lizzie and ran to LeJeune with the picture saying, 'Me, me, me.'

When LeJeune stooped to the height of the boy again, he knew that this was his child. He could feel it deep in his heart, and nothing Lizzie could say would convince him otherwise. LeJeune's complexion had been far fairer as a child than it was now. People had taken him for white. His own father had taken him for another man's. LeJeune's mother was very high-coloured but never so much as her son. She had hated the skin that had been passed down from a French grandfather because of the rift it had caused in her marriage when LeJeune was born. The genetics of his French ancestors had reached his son. Here he was looking at the face of a white boy, but all he felt in his heart was love. His child was stroking his face and angling it towards the photograph.

'Me. It's me,' he said to LeJeune.

'Yes, son,' said LeJeune. 'It is you. It was you all along.'

Archie wriggled away from Lejeune, leaving the photo in his hands, more interested now in his toy truck and making the sound of an engine. LeJeune rose slowly, replaced the photograph to its position and turned to Lizzie. Her eyes were watery and she couldn't face him. Her demeanour had diminished once again, and all LeJeune could do was shake his head. He would have cried, rushed to her and held her, but the front door was flung open and there stood Micky Walters.

'Daddy!' Archie rushed to him. Micky, carrying a bag of fish and chips, did not respond to the child.

Chapter 25

Essie

London 1948

The market is less busy. I suppose, just like back home, people shop early to get the freshest and the best on offer. It means we can take our time and look carefully at the produce from overseas and I can select for Bill all the ingredients that are the same or close to Mama's recipe. Bill picks up spices and sniffs them and asks if we can add this or that. He makes me laugh because he is like a child standing in front of a feast of sweet bread and cakes. Like my sister, Ginnie, and her friends when Mama does any baking. Somehow, they would know she had something nice in the oven and they'd leave the river or the woods behind the houses and rush straight to Mama's kitchen with the expression of a person who had had no food for a month. Mama would save their little lives, and I loved to watch them eat because some of the things they lapped up I had made, the way Mama showed me. I now have to prove I have all of Mama's knowledge in the kitchen and somehow cope without her actually standing over me. I need to make her proud and not let Bill down.

His enthusiasm grows with every step we take back to the restaurant. His waitress looks at us as if we've lost our heads when Bill walks in laughing about a very unfunny thing he has said and I'm laughing like a school girl because I just enjoy Bill's innocence when he believes that it's his joke that made me laugh.

'I was about to close up,' the waitress says. 'You never told me when you'd be back.' She throws her apron onto a table.

'Sorry, love,' says Bill. 'I didn't think we'd take this long. I'll lock up if you want to go now.'

'And do you want me on a shift tonight?' she asks Bill while looking at me.

'Oh yes. We'll have a new recipe on the menu.'

'Why?' she asks. Still her eyes are on me.

Bill turns to me. 'Because it's time for a refreshing change.'

'Nothing wrong with stew,' she mutters.

'Well, we're changing things up.'

'Are we now?'

'Didn't you say you wanted to get off?' Bill puts the box of groceries down and walks to the door. He holds it open for his waitress.

'Well, I'll need me bag fetching.' She slips through the service door while Bill tries not to laugh. I wonder who this girl is to him. Just an employee? A friend? She seems to think she's in charge.

As she leaves, she nods to Bill and says she'll see him at five thirty sharp, as if she's the boss and he's the employee. Bill nods back and locks the door.

'Right, we'd better get out the back there and start putting this together for later.'

The kitchen is as I remember it. Not very big but ample. Much bigger than Mama's kitchen, but she is always able to produce a banquet from it. It's nice and clean, though. Bill's waitress has done a good job of getting everything in order.

But then there were only three customers in during the time I was eating earlier and it makes me wonder if anyone will show up in the evening to eat the soup. I can't stay long enough to find out. Myrtle will wonder where I am, and I've yet to go to Lizzie's house before I set off home.

Bill starts to take all of the provisions out of the box. He goes to wash his hands, and I follow suit. He places the strap of an apron over his head and ties it at the back while I dry my hands. He takes a second apron and slowly places the strap over my head like a medal. It looks as though he wants to tie my apron strings, but I pull away and do it myself.

'Right then, where do we start?' he asks.

'You're the boss,' I say and shrug my shoulders.

'No, no, no,' he says. 'Not today. Today you're the boss and you're teaching me.'

'Well, in that case. Take out your pen and paper and let's get to work.'

With a heart as loud as claps of thunder, I begin to relay all of my mother's instructions about her soup to Bill while also trying to quell the anxiety of my meeting with the woman my husband has a history with. One I will never know all the details of because I know that neither she nor LeJeune will ever tell me the truth. I cover the riot taking place in my heart by talking over it, telling Bill to write this down, note this measurement and the timings of this and that. All the while, a tiny fragment falls from my heart as I struggle with the idea that Lizzie Tarping has left her husband and is about to take up a life with mine as I stand on the outside of their world. A world where Lizzie has been more of a wife to my husband than I have. The idea that I am not really a married woman, as Graham suggested, returns to haunt me. Bill's warmth and kindness are the only things keeping me from screaming and running from it all. Right now, I don't want to know where LeJeune is as equally as I desperately do. What is wrong with me? I inhale and blow hard through my lips.

'So,' I say, 'we begin by cutting the meat into small pieces, then season it and let the flavours seep inside. At home, we would have goat but mutton works just as well.' Though I never thought I could cook for a room full of people, the way Mama does, between me and Bill, we're about to make it happen.

We set the meat aside and begin to peel the vegetables. English potatoes, because that's all there are, plus pumpkin and carrots.

I show Bill the way Mama browns the meat, first frying onion and garlic into the large stewing pan, adding the meat after a minute or two along with a couple of spices and herbs from the market that came from India. The stall-keeper, originally from Mumbai, had fought in the war. His English was stilted and he spoke rapidly, telling us stories of how he'd come to England to set up an export business with the intention of bringing food from his old home to his new one. I had thought him bold: it was an enormous venture. He'd shaken his head as if it were nothing and happily added a few extras for me to take back to Paddington when he discovered I was only visiting the area. Bill paid for it all, my food and the food for the restaurant. We took our time, sniffing and selecting a combination of herbs and spices that he thought would be palatable for his customers. He knew pepper, of course, but there was turmeric and bay leaves that he'd never used before and spices I had never heard of.

We chop callaloo leaves and fresh spring onions. I keep wishing Bill could taste Mama's soup because I can only get so close to the original recipe with what we have.

'That's okay,' he says. 'We'll call it Essie's soup.' I like the idea a lot.

We gradually add more water to the pot and in go the hard vegetables. Shortly after, we add the greens and Bill keeps on stirring.

'What next, chef?' he asks.

'Now the dumplings.'

We form small, soft dumplings that we lay on a plate, ready to add later, before the vegetables soften and after the meat has.

'You'll have to warm the soup up again later, when your customers arrive, and when you do, you need to add about two thimbles of oil and stir it in. Mama always does this. It's her secret to a tastier soup.'

We have been tasting along the way, and Bill is so excited for tonight that he can't stop grinning.

'Can't you be here when we open?' he asks. I've lost count of how many times he has tried to make me stay, saying he'll call the hospital to let Myrtle know I've been delayed and then he'll drive me home in his delivery van.

'You'll be tired. It's a long way,' I say, but I really don't want to be here when people are eating. If they hate it, I don't know what I will do. 'And now I should go and see Lizzie Tarping.'

Bill turns off the large pot with all the ingredients added and everything cooked to perfection. We discard our aprons and wash our hands at the same time in the large sink. He gives me the tea towel but dries my hands for me.

He looks at me for a long time before he begins to stumble over his words, and I can't really understand the meaning of them. He can see I'm confused.

'What I mean is, I'm glad you could stay longer, to help me cook and not just write out a recipe.' He stops, my hands still wrapped in the towel which I push towards him.

'Don't forget why I'm here, Bill.'

'I know, I know. But don't get me wrong, I want to help you find your husband. Of course I do ...' his cheeks redden.

'Then let's get going to Lizzie's house. Before I lose my nerve.'

Bill puts down the towel and we leave the kitchen. I welcome the feel of the autumn breeze on my skin. It had grown hot from the steam in the kitchen.

*

We walk all the way to Maud Tarping's house. It's no different from any other around here. It sits in the middle of a long, straight road where children run in zigzags, chasing each other and screaming. They dress in thin shirts and summer dresses with socks that sag and shoes that need repair.

The drab brickwork of the houses seems to link them all as one, as though you could enter by one door and find several inner doorways that could lead from one house to the next. But an Englishman's home is his castle, and these people protect theirs fiercely. Not once have I knocked on a door and had the door thrown open in welcome. Everyone is guarded, everyone seems secretive, yet everyone seems to know what is happening in the house next door.

We stop at Maud Tarping's house whose door is painted the colour of a buttercup. A woman scrubs the front step of the one adjacent, and she stops to look at us.

'You're not those church people, are you? Come to sell Bibles.'

Bill laughs and says no.

'Just as well, you'll get short shrift from Mrs T.' She stands and rubs her red hands on her apron. 'Is that you, Bill Harper?'

'One and the same,' he replies.

'And how's your old mum? She doing all right, is she?' She takes a quick look at me and winks at Bill. 'She never said you'd married a coloured girl.' She pulls a face of approval. 'And a lovely one at that, you lucky fella.'

'Oh, Essie's a friend of mine.'

'Oh.' The neighbour puts her hands on her hips. 'I saw her wedding finger and thought … Still, you make a handsome couple the pair of you.' She picks up her bucket, steps into her house and washes the water off the step. 'That'll do it.'

The foamy water blossoms onto the paving stones, rippling towards Bill's shoes.

'Should I knock or do you want to?' he asks me.

I take a deep breath and tap a buttercup panel on the door and wait. We hear a tiny squeal of a child from inside and someone saying, 'No you don't.' Is that Maud or Lizzie? The door opens but isn't pulled wide, and a woman in her seventies looks through the gap.

'Yes?'

'Hello, Mrs Tarping,' Bill says cheerily. 'How you doing today? How's the leg? Mum said you were suffering a bit.'

She pulls the door open.

'It's me knee, Bill. Practically cripples me if truth be told. Been rubbing all kinds on it. Nothing seems to do the trick. They say it's arthritis and I just got to live with it. I ask you. Arthritis? God spare me.' She draws closer, both feet on the front step, and I see she notices her neighbour has been at work. 'Can't stand the smell of bleach. Anyway. How's your mum?'

'Oh, fine.' Bill looks at me and so does Maud. 'Let me introduce you to Essie.'

'You got married, Bill?'

Both Bill and I say no at the same time, and he tells Maud that we are just friends. She looks as though she finds it hard to believe that's all we are.

'Well then, what's this friend of yours got for me?'

'I don't have anything, but a question.' I stick out my hand, and she shakes it as though she has no strength in her own. 'I was actually looking for your daughter, Lizzie. I think she might be able to help me.'

'My Liz you say? How can she help you? Don't owe you money, do she?'

'No, nothing like that. It's just that I believe she knows the person I'm looking for. Who has gone missing.'

Maud looks over her shoulder, and I see the woman with golden hair that I met in the market. She walks up the corridor with her little boy on her hip, the one with the big eyes.

'You're Lizzie?' I splutter. 'I met you today. At the market.'

'Yes, I recognise you. And the jacket.' She looks anxiously between me and Bill. 'What is it you want with me?'

'Only to ask you about a man you knew back when the war was on.'

'Seems like so long ago, and I also know a lot of people. Who you after?'

'John Francis.'

I see the colour drain from her already pale cheeks, and then a line of pink seeps up from her collar to the limit of her hairline. She looks almost scary with the pink and yellow at odds with each other.

'So you do know him, then?' Curiosity consumes me now as the anxiety subsides. Did they love each other? Does he still love her? Would LeJeune have preferred her over me? Did she break his heart when she married someone else, and is he so broken-hearted he can't go on with the rest of his life? 'Where is John Francis?' The words gush like a fountain from my lips. 'I mean, do you know?'

Her face becomes hard, and her mother stands right on her shoulder, arms folded.

'Why would I know where he is? It's months since I seen him.'

'So you've seen him since he came back to London?'

'He might have popped round when I was in Poplar. To say hello, like. That's it and then he was off.'

Bill steps forward.

'It's important, Lizzie. You might be the last one to have seen him.'

'Well, hello to you, too, Detective Inspector Harper.'

'Sorry, Lizzie. Hello. How are you?'

'I was all right until all this. I don't know where John Francis is any more than you do.' She looks me up and down. 'And how do you know Johnny, anyway? Why you looking for him?'

'My name is Esperanza. Francis. I'm Johnny's wife.'

Her face falls for a moment. She looks at me as if she's seeing me in a different light. Taking a long and lingering perusal of my entire body.

'So, you're the one,' she says. Her little boy is playing with the soft waves of her hair. At the market, her hair was all tied back. It's pretty. Not the same colour as the buttercup door but as rich. Did LeJeune love her hair?

'I'm the one what?' I ask and jut my chin out the same way hers does.

'He told me he got married and that he was sending for you.'

'Well, he didn't get to. Something or someone stopped him.'

'Why would you say that?'

'Well, because he promised me.'

'He could have changed his mind, you know? They do that.'

'Not him.'

She shakes her head from side to side. 'No, not Johnny. You're right about that.'

I look at Bill as if to say, 'see, I told you he is honourable. He wouldn't have abandoned me'.

'So, can you tell Essie anything that can help her locate him?' Bill asks. 'Anything at all that will help her.'

'Other than his mate Eugene Price, I don't know who else he knows.'

'I've met Eugene. He led me to you.'

'Well, it's nothing to do with me where he's gone,' she says and begins to shuffle back inside, her mother moving backwards, too.

'Please,' I say to her. 'Anything you know. What time of day it was when you saw him. How he seemed to you. Where was he going after you saw him? Did he say?'

'I suspect home, but I don't know where or how he was getting there. It was night time, see. Look, love, I don't know what to say to you except I couldn't get rid of him.'

'In what way?'

'Well, he wanted to talk about old times. He talked about you. Said he only wanted to be friends with me and not like we were before.'

'So you had a relationship with him?' I look at the child who is staring right at me as if he could answer for Lizzie, but he wraps his chubby arms around her neck and plants a wet kiss on her cheek.

'Take Archie in for me would you, Mum?'

She passes little Archie to Maud and smooths down his dark brown hair.

'He's a lovely little boy,' I say as I watch his playful form retreat from sight.

'Can be a sod, though. Like I said in the market.'

'And you were saying … about your relationship?'

'No I weren't. You brought that up. And anyway, what happened between me and him, it's buried in the past. Just like the war.'

'The war might be in the past, but my marriage isn't. I need to find out where John is. What happened to him. My marriage is here and now, and I want it back.' Tears choke my words down. I swallow hard and turn away from Lizzie, a thumb by my lips to prevent a sob. Bill strokes my shoulder and moves closer to Lizzie.

'The poor girl is broken-hearted, Liz. Is there anything you can do to help?'

'Like I say, Bill. He left the house when Micky come home with our tea.'

'Your tea? But I thought you said he left yours in the night. What time do you have tea?'

'I don't know. Same as everybody else. Evening. Night. What difference does it make.'

'It could make a world of difference to the police,' Bill declares.

'You been to the police?' Lizzie asks. Again her colour drains and her chin softens.

'Not yet,' I say. 'But we will have to now. You were my last hope.'

'Anyone will tell you, love, I'm not the person to pin your hopes on.'

'Would John tell me that?' I ask.

Lizzie goes back inside and says a muffled goodbye and something about the boy's tea. The buttercup separates us, and my shoulders fall forward. Bill's arms open and I fall into them, overcome with sadness. It's more than sadness. It's hopelessness. It's exhaustion. I cry into Bill's chest like a forgotten child.

'Let me take you home,' Bill whispers.

'Home? I don't even know where that is.'

With an arm around my shoulder, Bill leads me back up the road.

'We tried,' he says over and over as he rubs my arm. I like the feeling of it, but it is little comfort if I'm honest.

At the corner of the road I stop.

'We're not far from the bus stop,' I say. 'I can get home from here.'

'What, on your own?'

'I came all the way from Dominica on my own.' I try to smile. 'You can't come with me. You have the restaurant to open.'

He nods, solemnly. 'Give me a call in the morning, and I'll tell you how the soup went down.'

'Well, I hope. At least I'm good at something. Even if it isn't finding my husband.'

'You will find him, Ess. You just need patience. And you will need the help of the police.'

'I think you're right. I do.'

'And I'll come with you. Why don't you come back in the morning? You'll need the local police to investigate this.'

'I can ask my aunt. Although she is working all week.'

'I'm happy to come with you. Honestly Essie. And I'm not being funny or anything. I want to help.'

'Unlike Lizzie Tarping.'

'What do you mean?'

I look deep into his eyes, questioning his innocence.

'Bill, Lizzie Tarping was lying to me.'

Chapter 26

Essie

London 1948

I wonder if perhaps I should move to Stepney. I seem to be spending most of my time here. For weeks I have been handing out my Missing Person posters with Bill and then helping him in the restaurant, cooking and learning how to waitress. When the kitchen is clean and the restaurant is locked up tight, Bill drives me home. I am trying to come to terms with a future in which LeJeune may never come back, but somehow, being in Stepney – the place where I know he once spent his time, where he drank at The Dockman's, befriended Eugene and, very possibly, fell in love with Lizzie – eases the longing. When I'm cooking or taking an order or delivering sweet rolls to Olive, the girl on the market stall, I always wonder: How much did he love her more than me?

I've seen Lizzie walk through the market with her son. She tries to ignore me, her cheeks flaming like fire, but I stare at her, hard, willing her to tell me the truth. The other day, her little Archie pointed at me and smiled. He recognises me as a fixture here, and no one can tell me that he isn't LeJeune's son: I know he is.

'A penny for them.' Bill makes me jump as I stand by the sink, washing potatoes. 'Didn't mean to startle you, but you've got visitors.'

I wonder who it is until I'm about to open the service doors and through the glass panels I see two police officers hovering by the main door. One of them I recognise as the sergeant who took my statement and filed the missing person report. I swear he would never have bothered for a Black man until Bill put in that John Francis was a soldier and fought for this country.

My arms feel quite limp as I go to push open the door, and it won't give. The officers look through the small window at me, and it's Bill who finally opens the door and waves me through. There are no customers in the restaurant as the lunches have been served. I'm wiping my hands as I slowly walk in and they begin to advance. I can't tell from their expressions what they have to tell me, but I do sense that it isn't good news.

'Mrs Francis,' the sergeant says, and it prompts a sound from me. One that means good afternoon, but it's hard to round out the syllables that go to make up those words.

'Would you gentlemen like to sit down,' Bill asks and points to the nearest table.

'You're all right,' the constable says. 'We won't be long.' His sergeant glares at him and pulls up a chair.

'Take a seat, Mrs Francis,' the sergeant says, kindly. 'I think I might have some news.'

This time it's my legs that can't support me, and Bill helps me into the chair and pulls one closer to me for him to sit on.

'Have you ...?' I ask.

'Well, you see, a body has turned up,' says the sergeant. My hand finds my lips, but I can't speak. I shake my head slowly and feel fear building inside me. 'It's a man bearing John Francis's description and was found close to the arches near the east bank of the docks. Not far from the station.'

I nod in recognition of the area. It's also close to the market, the place I visit each day and the place that in the early hours is ghostly when all the shops are shut and Bill is driving me home. What would LeJeune be doing out on his own in the night when Stepney looks so lonely. Desolate. It couldn't be him.

'We'd need you to come to the morgue at St Mary's to identify the body.'

'That's where my cousin works,' I say, though it's totally irrelevant. The officers look at each other.

'When does she have to go?' asks Bill.

'Right away if you wouldn't mind, Mrs Francis. So that we can round things off,' says the sergeant.

Round things off? They believe it's LeJeune. The constable is rocking in his shoes, eager to leave.

'We've a car outside.'

I always wondered how I would feel to be called Mrs LeJeune Francis. That was back in May when I was about to get married, full of anticipation and happiness all jumbled into a swirl of excitement that made me feel billious, made me feel light-headed. I'm not that person now, and I don't feel like Mrs Francis. Just scared Essie, who doesn't know if she can go through with this.

Bill locks up. He puts my jacket over my shoulders as well as an arm when we walk to the car. People stare, stopping in the middle of what they're doing: walking along the street, about to enter a shop, chatting to a friend. The door slams and they watch us drive away.

It's the first time I've been inside the hospital where Myrtle works. It's big and it echoes and is full of people. They look busy. Nurses seemingly gliding quickly over the tiled floor. Doctors strolling in white coats and reading notes. Patients, visitors. I can't really be sure which is which. A geriatric man, who looks close to death, is wheeled past me in a heavy, clunky wheelchair that everyone in the corridor has to stand aside for.

Four pairs of feet echo down the concrete stairs to the morgue, voices muted. My mind is in a dreamlike state as if I'm only observing myself on these stairs being led downwards by men in black suits, one with a helmet under his arm, the other in a circular cap. Why did they send two, and thank goodness Bill is here to guide me along.

We walk through a set of double doors, and the sergeant speaks to a man in a short white coat who is sat in a side office. The man has thinning hair and dark-rimmed glasses. I can see the veins through his skin, and when he looks at me, he draws in his lips before leading us along a cold corridor and into a room that is colder still. I push my arms through the sleeves of my jacket.

'We only need one person to identify the body,' the mortuary technician says, but I take Bill's hand. The men all stare at each other, but no one insists I go in alone. 'So, are you ready?'

I nod, and without hesitation, the technician lifts a heavy cream sheet from the body that has been waiting patiently to be claimed by someone.

I look down and see a man with chestnut skin who looks as if he is in a peaceful sleep but one so deep it would take a lot to wake him. A dead sleep, Mama would call it. I don't know who this man is, but I hope they find the right person to come and identify him. Arrange his funeral, give him a good send-off and mourn him properly. I, on the other hand, can only pray for his safe passage onwards.

'Is this your husband, Mrs Francis?' I have no idea why he should ask this because I have been shaking my head from the time the sheet was pulled back. I make the sign of the cross and look up.

'No, that is not my husband. It's not LeJeune. I mean John.' It had been complicated to supply LeJeune's details when they couldn't pronounce his name or spell it. I reported him missing by his alias. John. The name everyone in his other life knows him as.

'And you're quite sure about that?'

'Very,' I say. 'Thank you.'

The sheet goes back over this man's body, and we leave the cold room only to begin our silent retreat back to the ground floor where the halls are full of bustle and noise and no one seems to care about the man in his dead sleep below.

'You couldn't drop us back, could you?' Bill asks. 'It's on your way, I believe.'

'Very well,' the sergeant says. 'And please know, Mrs Francis, that we are doing all we can to find your husband based on what we had to go on.'

I couldn't have told them any more than I knew. I know they had questioned both Eugene and Lizzie, but I didn't tell them that I had my suspicions, that Lizzie knew more than she was letting on. I didn't want to cause trouble for her. She has Archie, and where would LeJeune's son be if his mother was a suspect of some misdeed? They had already shown contempt for the fact she'd had a Black boyfriend. So I had hoped Lizzie, out of the goodness of her heart, would tell me something, but it's been three weeks and she hasn't uttered a word. She has barely looked at me. So now, I will pay her another visit.

Chapter 27

1948

Lizzie thought back to the day when Archie was born. He was pink and blotchy. His eyes were screwed closed, his tiny fists shaking at an imaginary contender. He'd opened his mouth in the shape of an O, and when Lizzie thought he was going to let out a scream of joy or anger to have been released into a world where chaos had been normality and where angry voices could be heard almost day and night, all he did was yawn. His little head burrowed towards her breast, and he pulled and pulled on her nipple but found there was no milk. Still, he didn't cry but he gradually opened an eye before blinking them both open. Lizzie brushed a hand over his perfect head where a fine hint of brown hair lay flat. She had said a prayer of thanks to God, a figure hardly acknowledged most days, that her son was white. Micky hadn't seen him yet. They had cleaned up the baby, but she wasn't decent enough for visitors yet, the nurse had told her. She had torn and bled and had needed stitches. She hardly noticed them happening because she was caught up in a tangle of love and other emotions. Relief. Thankfulness. Joy. Contentedness. But mostly love. She named him Archie, put on his little knitted outfit and left the hospital with him in her arms, Micky's aunt beside her. Micky was in the pub, wetting the baby's head. He hadn't suspected for those nine months that his wife was not so much afraid of giving birth but of who she would give birth to.

And in all the noise and madness that surrounded little Archie when he got home, he hardly cried like some babies. He only made a sound when he needed to. Be it hunger, frustration, to share joy or if he had hurt himself. But when his father came home that particular night and didn't look happy to see him, Archie wasn't the only one who fell silent.

The room was like a rock, ready to crack with the crushing anger that pulsed from Micky's veins. So many things angered Micky, and coming home to find a man whom he knew his wife had once loved was, in that moment, the highest trigger on his list.

'Now, before you go getting upset'–Lizzie stepped forward–'he was just going.' She went to take the chips from his hand, but Micky pushed her back, squashing the greasy package into her chest. They slipped down her body as she tried to grab hold of them and only managed to secure them when they were at her knees, and by then, the chip paper was beginning to open.

'If you're going, then go.' Micky's loud voice caused a large bubble of a tear in Archie's eye, and the little boy pulled his lips inside his mouth.

'I'm going,' said LeJeune. 'But not until I clear up one thing.'

'Johnny, no.' Lizzie put the split packet of chips onto the table. A dark stain appeared on her dress but she hadn't noticed. She reached a hand towards LeJeune's arm, but he pulled it away.

'What's going on?' Micky said. His eyes became dark slits. 'What have you been talking about behind my back?'

'Nothing has been said as yet,' said LeJeune. 'But something will have to. Before I leave, there are things we need to talk about. Discuss.'

'I don't have nothing to discuss with you, mate.' Micky took a few paces so that he was in the middle of the room. All eyes were on him. He pointed a thumb at the door.

'Didn't you ever wonder?' asked LeJeune.

'Wonder what?' Micky growled. Lizzie positioned herself between the two men.

'I'm asking you nicely, Johnny,' she said, 'to just leave quietly. Like Micky says. There's nothing to discuss. You've popped in to say hello for old times' sake, like you said, and now I have to ask you to go.' The little boy toddled to his mother's side and gripped the edges of her skirt. 'It's our teatime and Archie will be starving.'

'And that's what I need to talk about.' LeJeune looked past Lizzie and directly into Micky's eyes. The irises were dark brown discs, the whites showing signs of tiredness.

'You're annoying me now. Can you just go?' Micky did not look at the guest. Only down at the carpet as he pointed again at the door.

'I need Lizzie to admit something to us,' said LeJeune. 'Her calculations about the boy's date of birth and who she believes is the real father. I know where I was the night he was conceived, and when I look into that child's eyes, it's my family I see reflected back. Not a trace of Walters. Nothing of you.'

Micky's height grew to the size of a mountain dragging its foundations from out of the earth to soar higher, increasing in volume so that it cast a shadow on any object below it. Without sound, the mountain raged from within as if molten lava was about to explode from the summit and destroy everything beneath it. His large hands clasped the collar of LeJeune's jacket, taking with them the fronts of his shirt, wrenching it loose. LeJeune struggled to settle his feet on the surface of the carpet, coughing as Micky dragged him towards the door. Before he could open it, LeJeune wriggled loose, gasping. 'Get your hands off me. You're making the boy cry.'

'He's my boy, and I can say or do as I please in my own home.'

'And you want him to cry?' LeJeune rubbed his throat. 'Because I don't. All I want is to do right by him. Support him any way I can.'

'You're better off out of his life, Johnny. Truth be told.' Lizzie's voice was tight, almost a whisper, a warning.

Micky pulled her to face him. 'So you're saying it's true? The boy's his?'

'I'm not saying anything. I don't know whose he is.'

'You little tramp.' Micky rounded on her, but Lizzie quickly dodged away and picked Archie up. LeJeune formed a defensive barrier between Micky and Lizzie who held tight to Archie. Her husband was dangerous, and she didn't want any more upset for the child who had buried his face into her neck.

'What are you thinking?' LeJeune addressed Micky in a calm voice. 'Please don't do what I think you're about to do. You are twice her size. And not in front of my boy.'

Micky's eyes darkened further, a mist rising from his neckline to the top of his head.

'In my house, I say how it goes. So for the last time. Get the hell out of here. Don't make me help you out. Not in front of anyone.'

Lizzie pleaded with her eyes for John to back down. His had only questions for her: How could you have chosen him over me? She knew Johnny would have given her the world.

'I'm staying outside so I know you'll keep your promise.' LeJeune opened the front door, Micky on his shoulder.

'What promise?' Micky seethed.

'That you won't harm them.'

Lizzie saw the venom in Micky's eyes when he turned from slamming the door shut behind LeJeune who knocked the door immediately after. Lizzie was quick to leave the house after placing the boy beside his toys.

'Johnny. What are you trying to do?'

'Did you leave my boy alone with that monster?'

'I'm not carrying the poor mite outside. Micky won't harm a hair on his head.'

'Even when he knows he's mine?'

'He never would under any circumstances. He's big and stupid but he does have a heart.'

'He must have had something for you to choose him.'

'There you go again. Choice, choice, choice. I didn't have a choice. You knew that. I told you, my life would've been hell if I'd stayed with you. My brothers. My family. It would never have worked.'

'Stepney isn't the only place in the world. We could have gone away together. Any place you could have imagined.'

Lizzie shook her head. 'He told me to make sure you weren't waiting around. If he comes out and sees you, I don't know what will happen.'

'I'm not afraid.' LeJeune turned his eyes to the lonely green. 'I want there to be a way,' LeJeune said, grabbing hold of Lizzie's hand. She snatched it back. Micky might lose patience and come out at any moment.

'A way for what?' Lizzie was exasperated with him, but he didn't seem to care.

'A way for me to see Archie. For him to know me. To know that someone else loves him. When I'm working, I should give you money. It's only right.'

'And when your missus comes over, you think she'll put up with that?' She shook her head. 'I can't see a way, John. Not now and not ever. A lot of fathers aren't in their children's lives. Can't you be more like that? Or, or love him from afar.' She softened her voice. 'I give that boy everything he needs. I'll love him for the pair of us, only don't cause a rumpus, John. I couldn't stand it, and Mick might be quiet now but he's pulled out a bottle of booze from the side, and once he's topped up on that, all hell will break loose if you don't clear off.'

'Has he ever hit you? Or Archie?'

'Never, and he never would. He keeps his fighting outside the house, but this, this could turn ugly. Please go home, John. For everyone's sake.'

Slowly, he shook his head. 'I can't go. I'm going to sit on that bench back there. When he's had so much to drink that he's fallen asleep, come and talk to me.'

Lizzie watched him walk away, wringing her hands before she gave up and went inside.

*

The empty park bench looked chilly. The swing still against the dusk sky like a photograph. He pictured his son growing up in this square, laughing, running, kicking his ball clear across one side of the green to the other. He thought of how Lizzie's tummy would have swelled each month and him pressing his hand to her stomach until he could feel his son kick inside. That child should know the love of a father. A real father. Not a man like Micky. The area surrounding his heart grew and grew and he wanted to cry out, but the people in the square would not have tolerated it. Lizzie would die of shame.

He went to sit on the bench. He would wait all night and all the next day if he had to. He couldn't imagine sitting on a train to Clapham knowing that he was saying goodbye to his son for good. This was not right. He closed his eyes. It might be a long while but he was positive Lizzie would come.

He dreamt that someone was shaking his arm and whispering his name. He opened his eyes to find Lizzie standing above him, gripping the long housecoat she was wearing. She smelt of the night cream she always used to wear, her hair rolled up at the edges with soft rollers.

'What the hell are you still doing here?' She sat beside him.

'And why the hell did you come?' He grinned and turned to face her. 'Have you worked out a way for me to see my boy?'

'No. I just wanted to see if you were stupid enough to sit out here in the cold all night.'

'It isn't stupidity. It's love.'

'How can you love him? You only just met him?'

'Isn't that when you started to love him?'

'I loved him from the second I knew I was expecting a baby.'

'I didn't get that chance.'

'Look, what did you want from me? I lived nine months in love with a baby whose father I wasn't sure about while married to a man who would have started world war three if it came out brown. It was the hardest time of my life, and I kept wishing that I could just keep it inside my body and never let him be born. I was that scared.'

'So you thought he was Micky's on the day he was born, but at some point you knew the truth, right?'

'I knew as soon as I looked at him. I mean properly and not just his skin. I knew who he was. All I could hope was that he didn't get darker because like it or not, he was growing up with a white mum and dad and living in a street full of white people. He looked enough like me to get away with it.'

'It isn't all right to make that boy pass as white, Lizzie. If nothing else, he should know his history.'

'And what history is that, then? That me and his father had sex out of wedlock and then he left London after the war and I had no idea that I'd ever see him again.'

'I was in London for almost a year, Lizzie. You had every opportunity to look for me and tell me the truth. I stayed away to respect your wishes once before. But not this time. Not when I have something of mine right here in London that is my flesh and blood. I will not stay away. Oh my God.' LeJeune saw a figure rushing towards them out of the shadows, carrying something unknown in one hand.

'What?' Lizzie spun around. 'Jesus Christ.' She and Le-Jeune both stood as Micky's hulking body arrived a breath away from them.

'You have got to be fucking joking.' He growled like an animal circling its prey. He wasn't waiting for an answer, he was poised to strike. Lizzie put her hands on his chest, but he tossed her aside and she fell to the ground.

'What are you doing?' LeJeune yelled and knelt beside her.

'I'm fine. Go, Johnny. Go now!' Her eyes opened wide as she looked at something above her. Before LeJeune could

turn to see what it was, he heard a loud crack, like the sound
of his father's cutlass cracking open the tough outer shell of
a coconut. The morning, the surprise sighting of Lizzie, the
day filled with hope, the night of desperation and pleas
ended at once in silence.

Chapter 28

London 1948

Lizzie steps back into the dark corridor of her mother's house. 'I know why you're here,' she says as she leaves the door open for me to follow her in. She is wearing a pair of slacks that reach her ankles. They look old and must have belonged to someone else, a brother perhaps, left in a cupboard and forgotten. Her blouse is pink, the sleeves rolled up as if she were hard at work, a dark blue headscarf scooping her golden hair off her face and today she isn't wearing make-up. She usually has on black eyeliner and mascara as well as coral-coloured lipstick. She is still as pretty without it, but today there are smudges of purple under her eyes as though she hasn't slept well. Archie is past the stage of keeping a mother awake at night; perhaps her conscience has been troubling her, knowing that she's lied about LeJeune and has been keeping something back from me.

'Can I take your coat? Is it new?'

'I'll keep it on, thank you.'

'A cup of tea, then. Mum has taken Archie over to her friend's house. She's got a nice big garden and a little dog that Archie seems to love. I took the opportunity to wash the windows and bleach the kitchen floor. Mum can't do much these days, and this house is falling apart.' All the while she is speaking, she is going through the action of filling an old kettle and looking for a teapot and cups. She has her back to me, and I can see a loose strand of her hair has escaped the headscarf she has tied in a bow around the front of her head.

'Take a seat, why don't you?' Lizzie scoops loose tea leaves into a china teapot – the tea set must have been in the family a long time. She fills the pot with steaming water and puts a quilted cosy over it as I reluctantly take a seat at the kitchen table.

'Anything to eat?' Lizzie asks.

'No thank you, I–'

'Have you moved in with Bill or something?' She turns suddenly, carrying over a full teapot, her finger hooking the handles of two tea cups.

'No. Why?'

'It's just that I heard you were the new cook and I know how he feels about you.'

'How he feels about me?'

'Goodness, girl, don't tell me you don't know that man is in love with you?' Lizzie returns to the sideboard for saucers, settling our cups into them before taking a seat.

I can feel my neck and cheeks growing warm. 'Bill isn't in love with me. Of course he isn't. He's just been a good friend who has helped me and I help him in his restaurant. I help him serve soup to the men queuing outside the Employment Exchange. It's a worthy cause.'

'Oh and I applaud you both. Quite a reputation you have for helping the unfortunates. But you know men very rarely help women unless they think there's something in it for them.'

'But I'm a married woman.'

Her cheeks redden. 'Well, you probably don't seem it to the likes of Bill Harper.'

'Bill has been a gentleman the whole time I've known him.'

'I'm not saying he ain't a gentleman, I'm saying he's a man.'

'You told me that John came to visit you when he knew you were married.'

She bobs her head down and then reaches for the teapot. Her cheeks are flushed again, and she uses both hands to hold the teapot steady. The sound of tea filling the cups seems endless, and I wish I'd insisted she hadn't bothered. Taking tea with someone is a polite and friendly gesture. We're not friends, and all I need right now are answers to my questions.

'Milk?' she asks and darts to the fridge for a chunky bottle half filled with creamy milk. 'Sugar's on the table.'

I look at the tea cups and watch her add milk to mine, though I haven't asked her to.

'Before he knew you, Johnny fell in love with me,' she says.

'And did you love him?' I ask.

'From the first day I saw him. Did you ever see him in his uniform?'

I'm sorry to admit I have not. I hadn't even seen a photograph.

'Well, he was this tall, dashing fella who told off a couple of Yanks who were trying to chat me up and that. I weren't having any of it, and Johnny put them straight in no uncertain terms.'

'You mean he fought them?'

'Blimey, no. Not our Johnny. He was a master of words. Said very few, but when he did, people listened. I put it down to those intense eyes of his. So unusual for a coloured bloke to have, I couldn't even decide what colour they were. His skin was so creamy that I wasn't sure he was coloured at first. It was dark when I saw him, outside The Dockman's with his army mates.'

'Did he always drink there?' I remember the night Graham entered the place, the hostile people that came outside, leering at me and then giving chase to Graham.

'His barracks weren't far, and when the troops were in town, they'd all come in. I used to work there once upon a time. But I haven't been back since.'

I think it is just as well because I don't suppose it's a safe place for a good-looking young woman like Lizzie. Not on her own.

'How was it?' I ask her. 'Drinking in The Dockman's with a coloured man?'

'Oh blimey. I don't know. It was all right, I suppose. Back then when anything goes. As far as coloureds fighting our war for us went, that was all well and good. But there are people around here who don't care for them moving in next door, if you get my meaning. Most of my family think like that.'

'Did LeJeune … I mean Johnny … meet your family?'

'Not likely.' She sips tea as her eyes stare at a vision of the past. One I would dearly love to see, but I don't know how I would feel to see my husband in the arms of another woman when he hadn't even been in mine.

'Lizzie,' I say, touching the handle of my cup. 'I had a feeling, the last time we met, that maybe there were things you weren't able to tell me about Johnny when Bill and your mother were there. Even with Archie being around.'

'Don't be silly, what has little Archie got to do with any of this?'

'I think you know. And you must know that I saw it, in Archie's eyes. He's John's boy, isn't he?'

She puts down her cup, rattling it into the saucer until it settles in place.

'It's okay. I'm not angry,' I say. 'I know these things happen. I wasn't sure about Archie until the day we knocked at your door. When he looked up at me, I knew at once. Does John know?'

Lizzie stands now and goes to the cupboard to pull out a bottle of whiskey. She sits and waves it in my direction, but I refuse a drink. Lizzie drains her teacup and pours some whiskey into it.

'I've been having a little too much of this lately, but I just can't handle the … well, the things in my life.'

'Please tell me, Lizzie. What's going on and why you are hiding the truth from me? Is there another woman? Eugene said there might have been someone on the ship. Or is this all about you? Does Johnny want to be with you instead of me? Is that why you left your husband? You can tell me. Tell me everything because I can't go on like this. I need to know.' My hand stings because at some stage in my monologue, I slapped my hand onto the table. It made Lizzie flinch; it made her pour herself another drink. She drinks from it now, the rim of the teacup fixed to her lips, and she won't look at me.

'What do I have to do to make you understand what this is doing to me? I move around in this strange town, smiling and apologising, cooking for the people at the restaurant, taking food to the Employment Exchange. But my heart, my mind, is always in one place, on one thing. My husband. Where is he?'

'Micky took him to the hospital, Essie,' she exclaims. 'All right? Now there it is.'

'I don't understand,' I say. 'For all these months, he's been in the hospital. Which one? My cousin works in a hospital near here, she would have known.' Why on earth hadn't I tried the hospitals? I've wasted weeks, like a fool, not searching the obvious places, not the hospitals and, at first, not going to the police, either. Instead, I chased after people who knew him, who had either lied to me or couldn't help me.

Lizzie leans forward and takes my hand. She begins to rub it, then rubs my arm and reaches for my shoulder, squeezing it. Then she pulls me to her and hugs me tight. She is crying, shaking, and I can't raise my arms to hug her back. I am motionless.

Tears stream from my eyes and down my cheeks. I don't weep aloud or let out jagged sobs like Lizzie, I just blink the tears away. Lizzie leans back and looks at me.

'Look at us. What a pair we make.'

The two women who love LeJeune, crying for him as if this were his funeral. I look at the whiskey bottle.

'You want a drink?' she asks, but I shake my head. She gets up and fetches me a tumbler from the cupboard anyway and half fills it.

'That's too much,' I say.

'You might need a drink when you hear what I have to tell you. And you'll understand why it's all I've done since it happened.' She pushes the glass to me.

'I'm listening.'

She nods and sips her whiskey. 'He came to see me, like I said. He found out about Archie and he wanted to be in his life. Provide for him in some way. I said to him no he couldn't and that it was a bad idea. He should walk away and wait for you to come. But he wouldn't have it, even when my Micky came home and found him there. I practically had to force Johnny out the door because I didn't want a row around Archie. He was scared enough as it was. Mostly by Micky because he was like a big ape, an ogre or something. Archie was tearful, so was I, and neither of those men were backing down. Micky wanting him to clear out and Johnny wanting to stay.'

'But he left, didn't he?'

'In the end. Only he didn't leave the area. Sat across the road, waiting for me to come and tell him it was okay to still see Archie.'

'Even with Micky in the way?'

'This is what I told Johnny, that it was impossible. But he wouldn't leave that bench, not for all the tea in China. So I waited, too. Until Micky was drunk and fast asleep, and I sneaked out the house to see if it was true, see if Johnny really was still sitting there. And he was. Then out of nowhere, that monster comes across the green, pulls me away from Johnny and I fall on the grass, and when Johnny came to pick me up – and that's just what he would do – Micky lashed out.'

'So they were in a fight?'

'No, love, there was no fight. Poor Johnny never had a chance. He was carrying this lump of wood, Micky was. He had a stack by the door that he kept meaning to whittle down and make skittles for Archie. They'd been there a year and he never got to them. What possessed him to carry one over that night, I don't know. But it was one blow, Essie. Just the one. Must have caught him wrong, and he fell on top of me, like a sack of coal. I screamed and Micky told me to belt up. He rolled Johnny over and Johnny wasn't moving. I said I was going for an ambulance. The blood, you see, it was coming out the back of his head. And he just looked … he looked like he was asleep. I shook him and shook him, but he wouldn't wake up.

'I looked up at Micky, told him to get an ambulance, but he wouldn't move. He dragged me to my feet, told me to get in the house and he'd take Johnny to the hospital himself. His mate is around the corner, has a van.'

'So they took him to the hospital, and then what happened?'

'Oh, Essie.' Lizzie starts to weep again, her face contorted and red. She flings her upper body to the table and cradles her head in her arms. I watch her body convulse, and I don't know what to say to her. If LeJeune has been lying in a hospital all this time, then it's a very serious injury. A head wound, he could have lost his memory, so if he was in Myrtle's hospital, no one would know his name. He might be in a coma. I have to get to him.

I put my hand on her back, feel her bony frame and I'm suddenly overcome with sadness for this woman. Behind the brashness is a soft-hearted woman who is just as upset as I am that this has happened to LeJeune. But the idea that she has had more of a relationship with my husband, a child with him, fills me with both jealousy and pity for her. I hate this feeling, but I have to know all of it. And I need her to tell me where exactly he is now.

'Lizzie, I know you love him but it isn't enough what you've said so far. You've had months knowing the truth.

I've had months of not knowing. Just tell me where he is. For one thing, I have to go and tell the police to call off the search–' I haven't completed my sentence when Lizzie springs up on hearing me say 'police'.

'You mustn't, you can't go to the Old Bill. He'll know I said something.'

'Who, John?'

'Not him, Micky. Why do you think I left him? I couldn't put up with the lies no more, the not knowing. In the end, Johnny is Archie's father and maybe I should have just agreed to it. Told Johnny yes he could see his son and sent him away before Micky came home. I could have worked something out between us and none of this would have happened.'

'But what about the rest of it? Look, Micky took him to the hospital. You said. They took him in the van. Is he still there? How seriously was he injured?'

'I went to see Johnny at the hospital. A few days later. Took Archie with me. But Johnny weren't there.'

'He had been discharged?'

'He'd never been admitted.'

'Now you're making less sense than before.'

She reaches for more whiskey, but I push both her cup and the bottle away.

'Tell me. Tell me everything and don't miss anything out.'

'All right, love. Give me a second.' She pulls a handkerchief from the pocket of her slacks, wipes it over her eyes and blows her nose. She holds the handkerchief in her hand, twiddling the edges. 'See, I went up the hospital. But like I say, he weren't there. No one had heard of him.'

'So, Micky and his friend didn't take him in the end. Because he must have come round.'

She shakes her head. 'I thought that at first, but I tracked down the place in Clapham where he was staying. It wasn't that hard.' She sighs heavily and looks towards the kitchen sink.

'Lizzie?'

'Johnny wasn't at the temporary place when I went looking. They told me he hadn't been back since Saturday. The day he set off to come to my house. His things were untouched – money, papers, clothes, the lot. I marched back home and confronted Micky with it, and that's when he finally confessed. He said that when they drove him to the hospital, there was no need taking him inside because … because there was nothing they could do for him …'

'So …' My lip begins to tremble; a shaft of cold air surrounds me.

'I asked him what they done with him if they never took him in, and that bastard, that monster, he told me that they … they just left him there, at the hospital doors, and then they scarpered. Took off without a word to anyone. Not the hospital staff. No one.'

I feel as if the life has drained from my body, the blood cold in my veins. I can't move, neither can my heart. Though I can't feel the air making a passage to and from my lungs, it must be happening, otherwise I wouldn't be hearing this, witnessing what they did, finding out, finally, why a letter from LeJeune would never come and that I would never find him. I have been waiting, denying all the negative thoughts every time they entered my head. I wouldn't think them and so they could not happen, could not be true. For goodness' sake, I could not have found love and lost it in an instant. I just couldn't.

'And so where?' I ask Lizzie who looks at me with blood-shot eyes. 'Where is his body now? Did he ever have a burial? Anything?'

She shrugs. She knows nothing more, and she obviously hasn't been to the hospital to find out.

'I have to go.' I get to my feet and hastily rub my eyes dry.

'Where are you going?' Lizzie grabs my hand. So familiar, as if we're in this together. We're not. This is the journey of me and LeJeune, and I don't need to tell her anything.

'I need to find out what came next,' I say. 'I need to bury my husband. Pray for him. Mourn him properly. St Mary's, right?'

She nods rapidly. 'I want to come with you. Will you give me a second to get dressed?'

'You deserted him, Lizzie. What, you have a conscience now, do you?'

'I always cared about him. About what happened to him. I care now. Why do you think I left Micky? I couldn't live with a man like that. Have him raise my son. No, I was best off out of there.'

'Oh yes, how nice it is to choose to change your life. How convenient that you have somewhere to run to now you know you married a murderer.'

She grips both of my wrists. 'Don't say that. Micky ain't no murderer. He'd had a bit to drink. And he was in shock finding out Archie weren't his.'

'But that isn't a reason to kill someone.'

'It wasn't his intention. It was an unlucky swipe. Lashing out in anger. Probably more at me. Don't you think I've wished it had been me Micky hit, instead of Johnny?'

'So you wanted to die?'

'No, I didn't want to die, I didn't want any of this. It just happened. It happened so fast there was nothing I could have done. I thought Micky was asleep, I thought I could reason with Johnny.'

I shake her hands from my wrists. 'But you didn't think to go to the police and report that a man had died. You didn't think to find out if anyone actually found my husband's body. You didn't think to tell me any of this the day I came here begging to know where he was.'

Lizzie's head drops and I swear to Almighty God that if she cries again …

'Let me dress,' she says. 'I'll come with you to the hospital and to the police. Will you wait?'

I nod, cross my arms and stand aside for her to leave the kitchen.

I wait in that position, staring at the teapot, the cups and saucers, the milk bottle, the bottle of whiskey. I could pick it up and drink it all. Be like Lizzie, try to mask the pain with alcohol. But all I'll do is make myself sick. It won't solve anything, it won't help me, it won't bring LeJeune back. My legs lose their ability to hold my weight, and I sink to the ground as if a plug has been pulled from my body and the energy has been allowed to drain. I'm on the kitchen floor, on my knees, bent forward, hands over my face, I can't control the tears or the trembling. I can't stop the harsh wailing sound that leaves my throat or the dryness of it as I choke on the tears. By the time I've begun to convulse, that's when Lizzie comes back to the kitchen in a dark brown dress and kneels beside me, holding me, rubbing my back, saying, 'That's it girl, let it all out.'

And when it's clear that I cannot stop crying, she kisses my cheek, rocks me in her arms and whispers, 'I'm sorry, I'm sorry, I'm sorry.'

Chapter 29

Essie

London 1948

I remember this hospital well: the smell, the bustle, the chatter, the chilly tranquillity of the morgue. I'd like to go there now, all the way to the basement, and sit with my back against the cool tiles of the wall and close my eyes. The last time I was here it was to identify a body. I recall the fear I'd had and the sense of relief to discover that it wasn't my Le-Jeune lying dead on a stark metal bed covered by a thick off-white sheet that perhaps a million bodies had lain beneath. I want so much for that feeling of relief to arrive now. To know that this has been an enormous mistake of Lizzie's. Micky had been so drunk he only assumed LeJeune was dead, that LeJeune had somehow woken up, a kindly nurse like Myrtle might have seen him at the door, rushed him inside and tended to his wound. And what if he had no recollection of his name and was wandering London now, not knowing who he is?

'We need to find my cousin.' I turn to Lizzie who is frantically looking at the names of all the departments.

'Why?' asks Lizzie.

What I really want to do is ask Myrtle if she or any of her nurse friends remembers a man being left for dead but had survived a blow to the head. But I don't say this to Lizzie.

'Because she has worked here for years and she'll know if … what became of him.'

'Where will we find her?'

'She's been in paediatrics for the past few weeks. Wherever that is.' I look around the entrance hall.

'I'll ask. You wait for me here.'

My legs are so leaden I'm glad not to have to move them for a while. Lizzie returns quickly, armed with directions and bursting to impart them, while I feel slow and lifeless, my thoughts mixed and making no sense to me.

'We need to go to the third floor of All Saint's block. We follow this corridor.'

Lizzie pulls me by the arm, and I follow like a lost soul. People, the walls, its tiles, the echoing floor move past me like a dream or that place between being asleep and awake. I blink several times as we approach double doors where colourful cutout drawings of butterflies and ladybirds are taped. Lizzie pushes them open, and a nurse with a crisp uniform rushes to us and says that visiting is not for another hour, some of the smaller children are napping.

'We're looking for my friend's cousin,' Lizzie says and nudges my arm. 'What's her name, love?'

'Myrtle Young,' I say with a voice that isn't mine.

'She expecting you?' The nurse bristles and pinches her lips.

'*Essie*?' Myrtle rushes to me and walks me out into the hallway. 'What on earth has happened? Why are you here?' She looks from me to Lizzie, but I want Lizzie to speak on my behalf.

'You see, it's Johnny. I told Essie about an accident he had and that a couple of fellas dropped him at the hospital door and no one has seen or heard from him since.'

'Oh, Essie.' Myrtle leads me to a row of chairs beneath a window that is open and blows autumn wind into the collar of my coat. It makes me wake just that little bit more from this strange dream. 'You mean LeJeune was hurt? He came to the hospital?'

'No,' I say. 'LeJeune was left for dead. But I want you to find out for sure. Find out if on …' I turn to Lizzie. 'What was the date and time?'

'July third.' I stare at her. 'It was a Saturday, but it would have been the early hours of the Sunday morning when he was left.' Her head sinks.

'I need you to check with everyone if they saw him,' I say to Myrtle. 'What did they do, and is he really dead or can I keep on looking?'

Myrtle holds my hands and looks at Lizzie. I untangle my hands from hers.

'I want to know now.'

'Of course. Let me tell the sister where I'm going.'

'And where are we going?' My voice sounds like a child's.

'To records. They'll know who came and went and if he was here, we'll find out.'

When Myrtle leaves, Lizzie nudges me again.

'But Essie, when I came they said there wasn't a Johnny Francis.'

'How would they know his name if he was … if he wasn't …?'

'I know.'

'And it still could mean that he woke up and left the hospital.'

Lizzie lowers her eyes as she listens to the pathetic glimmer of hope in my voice. Myrtle returns, putting on her navy blue cardigan and folding her arms around her body.

'Follow me,' she says. Lizzie and I trot behind her.

On the top floor of another building, she leaves the two of us sitting on the other side of a grey door while she goes inside to try to find out the truth. All the time, I'm praying and I sense that Lizzie is, too. Maybe she's hopeful that her Micky doesn't turn out to be a murderer while I'm praying that LeJeune can tell us for himself what happened after he was left here for dead.

A full and long twenty minutes later, the door opens. Myrtle emerges with a short woman whose greying hair flicks up at her collar. She is wearing a dark grey suit with a light blue blouse. There is a brooch on the lapel of her jacket with emerald stones, and I stare at it while she stands before me. Lizzie pulls me to my feet.

'I believe you have come to claim a body.'

The instant she says 'body', I sink back to the chair, and Lizzie and Myrtle are at either side of me. The woman kneels; her eyes are a gentle blue and there are lines and brown spots on both of her cheeks. She rests a hand on my knee. How dare she be so familiar? The three of them suffocate me.

'I had a thorough check of the books. We record all the unusual comings and goings. Day-to-day things go into the ward sister's report book. But the gentleman in question wouldn't have gone to a ward.' She clears her throat. 'On the night in question, there was only one unusual incident to report. A light-skinned coloured man in dark slacks and brown jacket was found at the door.'

I look to Lizzie who nods to confirm what he'd been wearing.

'We always check for any identification so that we can no-tify the next of kin. But there wasn't anything. Just some money. I could tell you the amount.'

I shake my head. Close my eyes.

'Then we check for identifying marks on the body. We found a previous head injury, about the same place as the fatal one. Plus a black mole on the right shoulder.' Again, I look at Lizzie who nods. She sniffs and leans back.

'They look for eye colour. They were recorded as grey, though the whites were … well, as you'd expect from a head trauma. It was reported as the only injury. We wait for as long as we can before burying the bodies, but ten days is the most we can keep them, you see.'

'Then what?' I ask in a scratchy voice.

'The unclaimed deceased are buried at Our Lady of Mercy in Westminster. In an unmarked grave. But there is a plot number, and I could let you have that if you wanted.'

'Of course we do,' Myrtle says, and the woman is quick to excuse herself.

Myrtle hugs me, and I allow myself to be pulled in her dir-ection. I cannot cry now. Not in this moment. I can't do any-thing but watch the woman hand a slip of paper to Myrtle.

*

Lizzie deposits me at Harper's. Myrtle wanted to leave the hospital early, but I insisted I'd be all right and she said she would pick me up from the restaurant after her shift. As I open the restaurant door, I pull down the poster with Le-Jeune's face on it and screw the corner of it in my fist. Over my shoulder, I see Lizzie's red face as she turns to leave. She will return to an empty house to mourn her Johnny.

284

Bill walks straight towards me. He envelopes me in an embrace, and all I can do is fall against him. His body is strong but soft enough for comfort, and I don't want him to let me go even while his sullen waitress floats around us, trying to set up for the evening without asking what is going on.

'We're going to be out this evening,' Bill tells her.

'Bill?' she says.

'I'm taking Essie to mine. You and Barbara will have to cope on your own.'

'Bill,' I whisper. 'Myrtle has to come to get me.'

'And tell Essie's cousin, soon as she gets here, where Essie is, would you?'

He leads me out of the door, and I lean against him on the short walk to his flat. He sets about adding kindling to the fire but I stop him. Though I know I'm mourning the passing of my husband, I would much rather his arms were around me.

'Stop,' I say. 'Just hold me.'

He takes both of my hands and leads me to his bedroom. It's dim in the room and he pulls back the cover.

'You should get in. It'll get cold if you just sit still.' We stand beside the bed, and Bill looks deep into my eyes. He stares this intensely at me a lot and turns away when I look back. Mostly I pretend not to notice, but I know what Lizzie said is true, that Bill is in love with me – even Myrtle has hinted as much. But how could I have responded to this quiet emotion within him? Mine were everywhere, and now they are in one place. Deep inside my broken heart. My worst fears come true. Up to the very point of the woman in the records office handing Myrtle the plot number of where LeJeune is buried, I still hoped that I would see him again. It just wasn't supposed to be like this, and I wasn't supposed to have feelings about any other man than LeJeune. What I have before and what I still feel for LeJeune has not disappeared. Far from it.

Bill prises the poster from between my fingers, takes off my coat and shoes, and lays me down on the bed. 'I'm coming back.'

I hear him lighting the fire; the warmth will seep through into the bedroom eventually. I close my eyes and wait for him to return. When he does, it is to snuggle in closely and pull my head onto his chest.

'Why haven't you asked me what happened?' I say in the darkness.

'Because I knew. I had a feeling, Ess. When you were gone all afternoon and when I see you walk up to the door with Lizzie Tarping, I could see it written on both your faces. I don't know the details, but I know he won't be back.'

At those words, a flood of overwhelm arrives to choke me. I cry into Bill's shoulder, and I only know I must have cried myself to sleep when he's not with me and I can hear voices at the front door.

'I think it's best we let her sleep. You're welcome to stay if you want.'

'No,' I hear my cousin say. 'You can look after her tonight. You make sure you keep our Essie safe. I leave her in your hands, and I'll be back in the morning.'

'Thanks for trusting me, Myrtle. You mind how you go.'

The front door closes and Bill returns to the room. I want his body against mine so badly I begin to ache again. He slips into the bed beside me without a word, and I allow his calming proximity to take control of everything.

*

It's only Archie who can illicit a smile from me. Here in the restaurant with the tables dressed in clean, white cloths and pushed to the outer edges of the room, I see nothing but gloom. The kind of gloom that reminds me of how months ago, when this journey began, I came to find my husband. I wonder now, while people shake their heads with pity, what to call myself. Am I a widow? My marriage to LeJeune was never consummated. Was Lizzie his real bride? The one he first fell in love with; the one who has his child.

What happened over the last few days happened without any thought or control on my behalf. Decisions were made for me. A trip to Our Lady of Mercy was arranged, a wake at Harper's, a gravestone saying *beloved husband*, flowers bought and a grieving widow being shifted from pillar to post without one word to say for herself.

Archie holds up a sagging stuffed rabbit for me to take. He is a child of few words and little noise, just like his father, but his expressions are full of depth and a knowledge he was probably born with. I feel as if I could come to love this child. I already feel so much affection for him. If he grows up to have the good qualities his father had, the ones I came to know, then I am bound to love him. But then I look at Lizzie as she stands on the other side of Harper's, sipping a glass of neat gin, wearing a black dress, her yellow hair piled in a conservative bun. I wonder if he will grow up to be a liar and someone who will lead a person to fall in love with them and then abandon them for practical reasons. But I'm keeping Lizzie's secret. If I go to the police about Micky, she will be implicated and where will that leave little Archie? He returns for his toy rabbit but hovers in front of me, so I pick him up and sit him on my lap. The only thing there is left of

LeJeune, a man he will never know and whose mother will continue to lie about his origin. Passing for white. I pity the boy as I rest my head against his smooth brown hair, and he leans into me so that I can only hug him closer.

'Would you like another drink?' Bill stands before me now and pinches Archie's cheek. 'This little one looks tired.'

It has been a long day. At Our Lady of Mercy, a priest from the local church agreed to come and say a few words at Myrtle's insistence. They were beautiful words nonetheless. Kind words for a man he never knew and one I thought I had. If only LeJeune could just have waited for me, forgot about Lizzie.

Now as I stand with Bill, contemplating the next stages of my life, I have to decide whether I stay in this big city or return to the bosom of my tiny island, the arms of my family. Bill places a hand in the curve of my back, and Eugene recounts yet another war story about him and Johnny. As for me, I already know what I will do next.

Thank you for choosing
Wherever You Will Go

I really hope you enjoyed it. Your thoughts mean the world to me, and I'd love to hear what you think. If you have a moment, please consider leaving a review—it makes such a difference in helping new readers discover the book.

You can share your review on Amazon or your preferred retailer.

I also love connecting with readers on social media, so please do follow my journey and say hello on Instagram and TikTok. @franclarkauthor

Thanks so much for your support!

Fran x

This book is Book 1 of the Hope Series

Book 2, ***However Far We Fall,*** is out **June 2026**. For updates follow or join my mailing list!

Connect: Hop onto my ***website*** for links & info!
franclarkauthor.co.uk

And: Join my ***mailing list*** for a Free Read! And be ahead of
all my offers, news and updates!

Also by Fran Clark

Lovers

The Island Secrets series:

Holding Paradise

A Prayer For Junie

The Long Way Home

When Skies Are Grey

About the author

Fran Clark is an author of emotive women's fiction, whose stories are deeply rooted in the connection between London and the Caribbean. Born to Dominican parents and raised in West London, her work explores themes of identity, resilience, and the strength of women—often inspired by the vibrant storytelling of her mother.

Her first novel, *Holding Paradise*, was published in 2014 and later reimagined as the first in the *Island Secrets Series*. Fran holds an MA in Creative Writing from Brunel University and lives in the English countryside, where she teaches vocals and leads a local choir.

She also writes contemporary fiction under the pen name Rosa Temple.